HALF-MAST FOR THE
DEEMSTER

ALSO BY GEORGE BELLAIRS

HALF-MAST FOR THE DEEMSTER

AN INSPECTOR LITTLEJOHN MYSTERY

GEORGE BELLAIRS

OPEN ROAD

INTEGRATED MEDIA

NEW YORK

Copyright © 1953 by George Bellairs

ISBN: 978-1-5040-9253-1

This edition published in 2024 by Open Road Integrated Media, Inc.
180 Maiden Lane
New York, NY 10038
www.openroadmedia.com

HALF-MAST FOR THE DEEMSTER

1

HALF-MAST

"Any sign of land yet?"

The little man in a cloth cap and an overcoat several sizes too large for him, regarded Littlejohn with pathetic dog-like eyes. His complexion was pale green and he had only roused himself from his stupor in the hope of receiving some good news.

"I can't see anything..."

Littlejohn wasn't feeling very good himself. He had done a fair amount of sea travelling in his time; several trips to the Continent for holidays or to see officials at the Sûreté in Paris. Once he'd been over to New York to consult the F.B.I... But never anything like this! People said that on certain days you could see the Isle of Man from the mainland; now it seemed at the other end of the earth. This little man with his coat sleeves over his knuckles, made retching noises, hurried to the rail of the ship, was met by a large wave, and retreated soaked to the skin. He didn't seem to mind...

"If I ever reach land, I'll never go to sea again..."

Archdeacon Caesar Kinrade, Vicar of Grenaby, in the Isle of Man, was the cause of it all.

"A friend of mine would like to have a talk with you," he had written. "And besides, if you don't pay me the promised visit before long, I will be too old to show you my beloved Isle. I am, as you know, eighty-three next birthday."

Mrs. Littlejohn wasn't with him. Her sister, who had a Canon of the Church for a husband, and eight children, was moving again, this time to Comstock-in-the-Fen, and there was a vicarage with eleven bedrooms. With her ninth on the way and domestic help hard to get, the Canon's wife had sent the usual S.O.S. to Hampstead...

It was the middle of September and the weather on the mainland had been fine and bright. It had continued so across the Channel just long enough for an excellent lunch to be served and thereupon the *Mona* had started to roll, then to pitch, and then both. Some of the passengers began to disappear down below; those who had been singing to the accompaniment of Sid Simmons and his Ten Hot Dogs, picked-up and broadcast over the ship's loud-speakers, had grown silent. Some lay on the floor and groaned; others were strewn all over the place. The timbers rolled under Littlejohn's feet; a blast of hot roast beef and cabbage rose from the dining-room and swept the deck. Littlejohn struggled to the top deck and looked out at the heaving water and the leaden sky.

"You ought to cross by boat," his wife had said. "It'll blow the cobwebs away..."

As he stood miserably peering ahead, the prospect slowly began to change. It was like the transformation scene at a pantomime, where the electricians by juggling with the lighting suddenly convert the devil's kitchen into the home of the fairy queen. The *Mona* was tossing in tortured gloom, but ahead the sun was shining on calm water, the sky was turning to blue, and, like a backcloth slowly illuminated by unseen floodlights, the Isle of Man with gentle green hills sweeping down to the sea, was stretched out before them.

The man in the big overcoat was at his elbow. He tapped

Littlejohn's arm gaily. His complexion had changed to a rosy pink and the brandy he had absorbed rose abundantly on his breath.

"What did I tell you?" he said, as though he'd been a prophet of salvation all the way. "What did I tell you? There she is..."

He flapped his sleeve at the Island, like a conjurer who has performed a difficult trick. Having thus justified himself, he made off to the bar to celebrate. People were surging on deck smiling and congratulating one another as though the end of the world had somehow been deferred. As if to cheer them up still more, the *Mona* slid into calm water and blew a wild blast on her siren to those ashore, like a badly frightened cock which crows when danger is past. The echo from Douglas Head threw back the sound.

The man in the overcoat was back.

"What about a li'l drink?" he said to Littlejohn.

The holiday season was drawing to an end, but there was a good crowd waiting on the pier for the arrival of the boat, which glided comfortably into harbour and which, by an admirable piece of practised seamanship, the captain brought gently along-side in a matter of minutes. Someone waved to Littlejohn as he tried to catch the eye of a porter and get rid of his luggage.

The Rev. Caesar Kinrade, Archdeacon of Man, was standing sturdily among a crowd of his friends, his shovel hat riding above the gallant white froth of his whiskers, his blue eyes sparkling. He wore his archidiaconal gaiters, too, but not like an immaculate prince of the Church; they looked utilitarian, like those of his forebears who, riding from parish to parish in the course of duty, found them more convenient on horseback than a cassock. The group round the parson all scrutinized Littlejohn with genial curiosity. The old man, with the native delight in tale-telling, had been treating them to the saga of how Littlejohn and he had between them solved the case of the man in dark glasses, and thus laid the foundation of a firm friendship.

Lying in ambush in the quayside car-park were Teddy Looney

and his chariot. The old touring car, looking like a cross between a charabanc and a hearse, had been spring-cleaned and the brass bonnet shone in the sun. Looney grinned and bared a gap in his teeth. He was pleased to see Littlejohn again and glad that the prompt arrival of the boat would get him safely home for milking time.

"Good day, Parson..."

"Now, Reverend! Good to put a sight on ye..."

"Nice day, Master Kinrade. And how's yourself...?"

It was like a royal procession to Teddy's rattletrap. Everybody knew Parson Kinrade and everybody was glad to see him around.

The porter with Littlejohn's bags wouldn't be paid when he found the Inspector was a friend of the Archdeacon, and Littlejohn had to thrust five shillings in the man's pocket to ease his own conscience. The pair of them were almost hoisted into Teddy's tumbril by friendly hands and with a jerk the vehicle made a start. They ran alongside the old quay, bristling with the masts of tiny craft of all descriptions, dirty coasters busy unloading, trim yachts, timber boats from the Continent...

"Hullo, there, Parson..."

The good vicar of Grenaby shook his head at Littlejohn.

"I'll have to stop coming down to Douglas. They all get so excited to see me, and I get too excited, too, at seeing them. I'll be giving myself a stroke or something..."

The old car tossed round the bridge at the end of the quay and took to the country. Beneath the agitation of Teddy's conveyance, Littlejohn could still feel the roll of the deck he had endured for, it seemed, untold hours.

"Take the old road, Teddy..."

The car rattled through Port Soderick village, raced down Crogga Hill, turned on two wheels at the bottom, and snorted up the other side. They reached the top with difficulty and there stopped, for the contraption seemed to have caught fire. Dirty smoke oozed from under the bonnet, which Teddy opened to disclose a lot of dirty rags, smouldering with choking fumes.

"Forgot to take out me cleanin' cloths," he said, scattering them over the stone wall which skirted the road.

The parson, who hitherto had seemed half asleep, happy to let Littlejohn enjoy the scenery on the way in peace, suddenly roused himself.

"Let us out of this, Looney. We'll stretch our legs and if you can get going again, you can catch us up. Come on, Littlejohn, stir your stumps. I've something to show you..."

They strolled to an eminence in the road and the old man pointed in the direction of the sea.

"There! Did you ever see the likes of that?"

Difficult to believe the ocean had ever been rough, for now it stretched like a sheet of green glass as far as you could see. Between the road and the sea, undulating fields, divided by sod hedges, with gorse flaming on top of them and with clean white farmsteads dotted about them. Beyond, a long spit of land, like a granite spur, jutted out, with a ruined chapel and a fort at one side and a lighthouse on the other, and in the middle of the base of this triangle of rock, the towers of King William's College, in the old island capital of Castletown, rose strong and grey.

Parson Kinrade fished in the tails of his coat and brought out an old pipe, which he filled from a pewter tobacco-box, after telling Littlejohn to help himself. They leaned their elbows on the wall and smoked, and Looney who had drawn up beside them, knew better than disturb them.

"We've to call at Castletown," said the Archdeacon at length. "The court's sitting there to-day and I've promised we'll pick up the Deemster when it's finished... Know what a Deemster is?"

"A judge here, isn't he?"

"More than that, Littlejohn. A very ancient office... very ancient and stands in eminence next to that of the Governor of the Isle himself. In this small place, the Deemster's all His

Majesty's mainland judges rolled into one. Civil, Criminal, County Court, Quarter Sessions... All rolled into one. Judge of Appeal, too, against the decisions of his colleague, the other Deemster, when he sits with a judge from over the water to help him..."

"A busy man!"

"That's right. And before the laws were written or decisions recorded, he'd to remember the law... Breast Law it was then, as if cherished in his heart... They only take civil cases in Castletown now. First-Deemster Quantrell's sitting to-day. I'm calling to bring him with us for dinner at Grenaby. He wants to meet you. He's in trouble. Somebody's tried twice to murder him."

The parson dropped his last sentence like a bombshell and then was silent. It seemed impossible to think of murder in such a place. The birds were singing; the gulls were crying; a man, a woman and a sheep-dog climbed the road over the hill opposite and vanished; a small train puffed past in a cloud of steam and whistled; and, out at sea, a yacht with white sails spread, slid quietly round the granite spur of Langness and was gone.

Littlejohn pushed his hat on the back of his head, rubbed his chin, and smiled.

"My wife's last words were 'Keep out of mischief,' " he said. "By which she meant, I always seem to run into trouble if I go on holidays without her."

Parson Kinrade tapped his pipe on the wall.

"Oh, come now. I'm not intending this to be a busman's holiday. You're here because I wanted to see you again. But whilst you're with us, I thought you might perhaps help and advise a good man who's in trouble."

"Only my joke. Of course, I'll do anything you want. But aren't the local police good enough? They might take it to heart if—how do you say it?—if 'a fellah from over' started trying to teach them their business."

The vicar patted the moss on top of the wall and then turned his far-seeing eyes on the Inspector.

"This is only a little island, Littlejohn. News travels fast. They love a little gossip and the police aren't above joining in. Once it got abroad that somebody was out to murder a Deemster, where would he be? The law is above everybody else. It's safe and impregnable. Or that's the illusion that's to be created about it if people are to respect it. 'That's the man somebody's after murdering,' would think every malefactor brought before him. It just wouldn't do, Littlejohn. That's why Deemster Quantrell's told nobody but me and I said you were the man to share the secret and put it right in secret. Understand?"

"I understand. How did it happen?"

"Simply enough. His Honour drives his own car. The roads are good here and one tends to develop a fair turn of speed. Even Teddy there... The hills are pretty steep and there are bends and drops at the bottom of them. Fortunately the Deemster's steering went wrong too soon. It broke as he drove it out of his garage. Whoever'd sawn into it, did it a bit too much..."

"*Sawn* into it? Are you sure?"

"His Honour's no fool. In his young days he mended his own motor-bike and then his car. It was sawn, all right. He guessed then that somebody was up to no good. He kept it quiet for his wife's sake and, lest some local tittle-tattler should get talking, he sent for new parts and a mechanic from the mainland to fit them."

"But who could have wished to...?"

"That's just it. Who could? Deemster Quantrell's a member of a very old Manx family, always highly regarded, which has given to this land dozens of fine men; deemsters, doctors, lawyers, parsons. Everybody loves the Quantrells. And as for criminals he's sentenced... Do the mainland judges get murdered for their judgments? No, they don't. And any fierce sentences Deemster Quantrell ever gave were in the past, long ago. There hasn't been a murder trial here for untold years and most of the real bad criminals go across to the mainland and commit their evil deeds and get their just dues across the water..."

"What about the second attempt, sir?"

"Two bricks off a block of property being pulled down in Douglas. *Two*, I said. Like the barrels of a shot gun. Bang down comes one and misses His Honour's head by inches. Then another. And nobody up on the building, because it's dinner time for the men."

"Is he sure it was deliberately done?"

"No wind blowing; no children playing on the site. Just nobody about. Deemster Quantrell sent a policeman to look into it. He said he'd seen something fall down. He didn't tell the officer it had nearly fallen *on* him... That settled in his mind that some-body was out to give him trouble, to put it mildly..."

Littlejohn knocked out his pipe and shook his head.

"It looks like deliberate attempted murder. It's as well we're going to meet the Deemster. Maybe I can do something."

"I'm sure you can. Quietly, circumspectly, you'll put things right. We'll talk it over after dinner, and then you can decide what to do for the best. Well... I see Teddy's getting mad at the thought of his unmilked cows. Let's be getting along."

They followed the undulating road, with broad panoramas of hills and the sea until, with a quick turn, it joined the main highway to the village of Ballasalla, beyond which the view opened to reveal the ancient island capital of Castletown with its old granite castle standing like a bastion ahead of them. As they slowed down to pass the busy airport of Ronaldsway, the parson gripped Littlejohn's arm and pointed ahead.

On the topmost tower of Castle Rushen stood a flagstaff, and they were slowly hauling up the flag.

Teddy Looney turned in his seat.

"They seem to be celebratin', sir..."

"Wait!"

The limp flag had stopped half-mast and a puff of wind caught it, revealing the emblem of the Island, three legs, in armour, and spurred, in gold on a red ground.

"Half-mast?"

"Hurry ahead, Looney," cried Parson Kinrade. "I hope it isn't, but it looks as if... as if..."

"Half-mast for the Deemster, sir?"

Littlejohn finished it for him, and they sat in silence until Looney braked at the roundabout leading to the by-pass road at Castletown.

"Go along into the town, Looney..."

But the parson needn't have said it. Standing at the junction was a policeman with a bicycle, who jumped with interest at the sight of Looney's car. He hurried across and held up his hand. He saluted smartly as he saw the Rev. Caesar Kinrade.

"Afternoon, Archdeacon. The sergeant said I was to look out for you on your way back from Douglas, and say he'd like to see you, if you don't mind..."

"I was coming in any case... I promised to pick up the Deemster..."

The constable's face assumed a look of reverent awe, as though he were already marching in the funeral procession.

"The Deemster died half an hour since. That's what the sergeant said he wanted to see you for... And..."

The bobby turned to Littlejohn, gave him a look of admiration and fellow-feeling, and saluted again, a feat which required considerable contortion, because the officer's head was thrust through the open window of the car.

"And are you Inspector Littlejohn, sir, of Scotland Yard?"

He uttered Scotland Yard in tones a pilgrim would use of Mecca.

"Yes, Constable..."

"I was to bring you along, too."

"Why?" asked the parson curiously. "Nobody knows he's here... Or do they?"

The constable cleared his throat.

"Beggin' your pardon, Archdeacon, but I shouldn't be talkin' like this. The sergeant said to bring you right away... But they found a note the Deemster must have just started to write before he died. It said, 'My dear Inspector Littlejohn. . .' and then it finished. So the sergeant said you was to come as well, *if* you please..."

He flipped a thumb at Teddy Looney to indicate he had better be driving along, and mounted his bicycle to escort them.

"Here, here," called the Archdeacon. "How did he die? Was he murdered...? Shot...? Stabbed...? What?"

He couldn't wait.

The constable looked at the ancient whiskers reproachfully.

"Oh, come, sir. Not that. He had a seizure in his room in the court. They found him dead when they went to call him after the lunch adjournment... They thought at first he was asleep..."

And to speed up progress, the bobby put on a spurt, pedalled ahead, and waved to Teddy Looney to get a move on.

2

HEARING ADJOURNED

As Littlejohn was embarking for the Isle of Man, the court held in Castle Rushen, Castletown, was opening. There was a short list for Deemster Quantrell, but some of the cases looked like taking a lot of time. They were civil actions, giving rise to many opportunities for argument and patience.

One by one, the officers and advocates gathered in the sunlit room. It was a lofty, well-lit, old-fashioned place, used for many purposes, from magistrates sessions to high-court suits. A constable started to adjust the ventilation in the roof lights to please a barrister who had started sneezing. He self-consciously tugged at the cord, growing redder as it resisted...

Members of the Manx bar and their clerks opened their brief-cases and scattered papers on the long table which dominated the well of the courtroom. Two pressmen sauntered to the desk behind the lawyers and opened their notebooks. There was nothing exciting in the day's programme and the atmosphere was flat and prosaic. There was a lot of shuffling and whispering; the clerk to the court entered and took his place under the bench facing the advocates. On the raised dais behind him, four small chairs, upholstered in red, with a fifth, larger one, in the centre under the Royal arms. The two chairs on each side of the heavier one were all used by magistrates in petty sessions. To-day, the Deemster would sit alone, with a jury.

Two or three holidaymakers tiptoed in and a small wiry man with a heavy moustache and a pale wrinkled face followed them. He was the town undertaker and when trade was slack he haunted the courts or the swing bridge over the river where the boats tied-up. The sightseers looked amazed at coming upon the light intimate courtroom in the midst of the huge stone mass of the castle. They had arrived there through dark, chilly passages and worn stone staircases to the ramparts, and then through the small door into another cosier and more civilized world, albeit an old-fashioned, Georgian one.

The Coroner, a necessary part of this Manx institution, walked in, heavy-footed, workmanlike, chubby, benevolent, mainly concerned with process-serving, but filling few of the more imposing forensic offices of his namesakes on the mainland. In some cases, he could, for a fee of 2/-, represent accused persons, who needn't attend the court at all, and whose fines he would later collect if they were imposed! He looked round the place, counting the occupants, nodding here and there, and took his seat in a small pew near the back, next to the dock reserved for prisoners in days when criminal as well as civil cases came to Castle Rushen.

Along the right side of the well of the court ran a jury box, and behind this, a passage, hidden from view and leading to a private door, whence a dark spiral staircase ran down to the Deemster's private quarters. All ears now seemed cocked in the direction of this passage; it was five minutes past the hour of opening...

The occupants of the courtroom began to shuffle one by one to their feet, the Deemster's pattering footsteps sounded, and a tall, wiry lantern-jawed man appeared on the dais, bounded to his chair and faced the court. He wore black robes and a bob-wig and carried a sheaf of papers. The bar bowed to him and he acknowledged the salute with old-world grace and a wry little smile of the thin lips. He seated himself with a rustle of his gown, cleared his throat, and slipped a pastille in his mouth.

Deemster Quantrell was in the last year of his office. At the end of that time, he would retire from being first judge, deputy-Governor and second civil officer of importance on the Island, and sink to the level of an ordinary citizen again. That did not bother him much; his chief worry was the fact that his income would fall considerably when he took his pension. He was a poor man, owing to calls on his purse not only arising from his rank, but from elderly members of his family whose fortunes had declined. His shrewd dark eyes glistened as he settled himself. There was ironic humour in his thin mouth, wisdom in his broad, clever forehead, worry in the lined pale face, and parsimony in the long, narrow nose. He glanced at the Coroner, who rose and coughed behind his hand.

"I fence this Court in the name of our Most Gracious Sovereign Lord the King. I charge that no person do quarrel, brawl or make any disturbance and all persons answer to their names when called... I charge this whole audience to bear witness that this Court is now fenced..."

The Coroner intoned it slowly and solemnly, like someone tasting the sweets of holding the stage for a brief moment. The court was in session. The jury were sworn without a hitch.

Willoughby *versus* Cooil.

Somebody had been having a garage built and now refused to pay for it, because it wasn't what he had ordered... Or so he said.

The advocate for the plaintiff rose, hitched his gown on his shoulders...

Outside, the custodian of the Castle looked glumly at the sky from the office at the main gate. It was a poor day for visitors; too sunny and soft out of doors to tempt them to inspect dungeons, royal and lordly apartments, and prisons which had housed epis-copal dignitaries. People nowadays didn't seem to want to learn anything. Once upon a time, he had been kept busy all day and every day with crowds who asked a lot of questions. Now, all they wanted was to whizz around in motor-coaches, gape round the town, eat large quantities of ice-cream and candy-floss, and career about on the dodge'ems on the fun-fair. He sighed...

"Will you show us round, mister?"

Suddenly, as from nowhere, three boy scouts clicked their way through the turnstile. Their eager faces glowed with admiration at the peaked-capped, uniformed official, with bristling white moustaches and haughty manner. They thought he owned the place!

At one, the court adjourned. The Coroner cleared his throat. He had been snoozing, lulled to sleep by the hot autumn sunshine falling across his large bulk through the windows, and by the droning of the lawyers at the bar and the blow-flies on the window-panes.

"By order of His Honour the Deemster Quantrell this Court stands adjourned..."

They all rose and the bar bowed to the Deemster and he bowed back to them and withdrew. The occupants of the room gathered in groups and sauntered away to lunch. His Honour had looked preoccupied, they thought, returning with a jerk from time to time to the case in hand, but never once losing grip of the thread, delivering his judgments with dry, impeccable precision and complete grasp of the facts and the law.

The custodian of the castle was sitting down to fish and chips in his quarters and the Deemster was opening a packet of sandwiches in his room. A policeman deferentially brought in a tray of tea.

"Thank you..."

Without his wig and gown, His Honour seemed less like a corpse. Deprived of their black and grey background, he looked healthier and bore the pink of his outdoor jaunts in the small yacht he kept. He always ate sandwiches; his stomach wasn't so good and he was faddy about where and what he ate. There was no canteen here at the court... Some said it was all an excuse of the Deemster's to save the expense of a full-course meal.

He ate and drank thoughtfully, hardly aware of what was passing his lips. There were books of law on the table before him, his papers at his side, journals and the daily newspapers, but His Honour did not bother to read. He was lost in his own thoughts, scarcely troubling to watch the tea as he poured it from the silver teapot into the cup at his elbow.

The room was dark and musty and smelled of stone and damp soot. A small fire burned in the old fashioned grate, for even in mild weather, the old building seemed to hold cold and moisture in its grip. His Honour was dining at the head of a large table, the top covered in green baize cloth, with two chairs on either side of him. The bow window facing him in the wall ahead, lighted the place and gave views of the town, of a corner of the bay and little port, and of the gaunt slated gables of Bridge House, once a bank, now an auction-room. The fire flickered and the glass of the framed SPY cartoons on the walls cast back the reflection of the flames. Near the window another door led to a spiral staircase and a private entrance, which was locked.

Nobody intruded on the silent man eating his simple meal. He had a fixed routine at the luncheon adjournment wherever he went. He ate his food and then took a nap of forty minutes. He didn't like it if they disturbed him. At 2.15, the constable would call him for the afternoon session...

Deemster Quantrell wiped his fingers on his napkin, very slowly, meticulously, one by one, and flung it back on the tray, which he pushed away at arm's length. At close quarters, his eyes were pouched and tired. Inch by inch, it seemed, he had, over forty years, made his slow steady course from the bottom to the top of the legal ladder. He had started without money or any influence save the good name of his old family and his personal integrity. He had established a practice, nursed it into becoming the most prosperous in Athol Street, Douglas, the street of advocates. He had married the girl he had always loved and they had been happier than most. He had brought up two nice daughters and seen them married to good men. Then he had been elevated to the bench with everybody's approbation and good wishes; he had risen to first Deemster. On the mainland, as well as on the Island, he was regarded as a wise, reasonable, sound judge and the King had honoured him. Before him stretched years of retirement and leisure in which to write his book, sail his boat, pursue his love of Manx antiquities, amid the friendly and approving people of his own land... Now...

He sighed and taking off his black-framed spectacles, passed his hand over his brow and rubbed his eyes vigorously, boring into the sockets with his fingers as though he were blinded by his thoughts. Then he opened the drawer above his knees and took out paper. He dipped the pen in the ink and with firm vigorous strokes drove it before him.

"My dear Inspector Littlejohn..."

And then the nib broke.

With a gesture of impatience, His Honour screwed up the paper, flung it in the direction of the waste paper basket, took out his fountain-pen, and prepared to begin again. He also began to cough...

Deemster Quantrell's cough mixture was a standing joke. In winter, when his chest grew worse, he had his medicine on the bench with him and spooned it in his mouth as required. Now, when his spasms were intermittent, he took a dose before he entered the court, sucked lozenges of the same brand during the hearing, and then more liquid after his meal. His cough was a legacy from the first world war, when he had served in the Navy, and had spent a day in the water after a submarine had dealt with his small craft.

Brandywine's Electric Linctus. That was it. It was a fad of the Deemster's. Nothing else did him so much good, he said. He rose, took the bottle from his overcoat which hung behind the door, and after shaking the mixture, poured a dose in the spoon provided for the purpose on the tray. Then, he sat down to resume his letter...

The constable found the Deemster sprawling in his chair when he came to wake him. He wasn't a pleasant sight, with his staring eyes, contorted features, and his hands gripping the table before him. At first, P.C. Lace thought His Honour had had a seizure. In fact, he told everybody that, even after he found the judge was dead.

As they moved the body, they saw the spoiled letter to Littlejohn at the Deemster's feet, where it had rolled after his bad shot at the paper basket.

That was why they were anxious to see Littlejohn, who had no idea what it was all about and, as Looney's tumbledown chariot trundled over the swing-bridge and along the roadway under the grim walls of Rushen Castle, he felt suddenly like one in a dream, transported to a Kafka world of castles and towers where strange things happened.

But ahead was the police-station with a man on the doorstep in a helmet and uniform waiting to receive them. The Inspector snapped back into the familiar mood and surroundings of work again.

A knot of men had gathered in the police-station, a little stone building with a pepperpot tower, admirably in keeping with the ancient town and the great castle which faced and loomed over it. This sort of thing did not happen every day. In fact, murders were rare indeed on the Island and when they did occur, were the work of cranks or crackpots. That of a Deemster was unprecedented. There was no babble or fuss; only bewilderment and grief at the event and a grim determination to avenge it, though how to start had not yet become apparent.

The police surgeon had stated that Deemster Quantrell had died from a dose of cyanide. How it had been administered, he had yet to find out, and there was to be no delay in the autopsy.

But it was cyanide of potash, or prussic acid... no doubt whatever about it. You could still smell it faintly on the air around the body.

The police—two uniformed constables, a sergeant and a plain-clothes man—greeted the Archdeacon civilly and he introduced them to Littlejohn. They didn't know what to say. Shyness over-took them in the presence of a distinguished member of Scotland Yard. There was a sickroom atmosphere about the quiet, plainly furnished office; you might have thought Littlejohn was a special-ist, there to consult with a group of general practitioners about a patient. And that he had brought with him a parson, just in case they couldn't do the victim any good...

The officer introduced as Sergeant Cregeen was temporarily in charge. They were waiting for the Chief Constable to arrive from Douglas. The sergeant was a good, rule-of-thumb officer, who went by the book. And as the book contained no reference to "Deemster, death of...", he was rather at a loss. They had left everything as it was; even the body. The photographers and finger-print men were on the way and due any minute. Mean-while, they looked to Littlejohn for a lead. "Did you have a good crossing, sir?" asked the sergeant, after clearing his throat behind an enormous hand. He wished to show he was friendly and co-operative.

"Yes, thanks..."

"Nice weather we're havin' for the time of year..." He paused and then thought he had better show willing about the case.

"Maybe you wouldn't mind waiting till the Chief Constable arrives, sir?"

Littlejohn nodded. "Of course, sergeant." They grinned at each other and the tension was eased.

Outside, the afternoon sun was shining and the town seemed charged with expectancy and curiosity. Knots of people gathered silently around the castle and police-station, shopkeepers stood at their doors, a party of men demolishing a building had ceased work and were discussing the news.

"Never knew the likes of it..." one was saying and in the quietness he sounded to be shouting.

The flag above the castle tower hung torpidly in the still air. Littlejohn looked out and took a turn in the narrow street.

On the right, the little port with a small coaster tied-up in the river and seeming huge in its surroundings. A pair of swing-bridges, a customs house, and beyond, a small riverside promenade, bordered by old artillery pieces with muzzles buried in the concrete to serve as a palisade. Then a little harbour, a lighthouse, rocks beyond, and a sweep of bay, with a steamer passing on the skyline. A group of large, old houses and a brewery in the foreground...

To the left, the town-square, with grey stone houses or stuccoed imitations of those in London, copied and erected, it seemed, with a certain nostalgia, by the English garrisons exiled in the capital of the Isle in days gone by. A church with a curious rococo front, square tower, plain glass windows and a view over a wide sweep of the bay. In the centre of the square, a tall sandstone memorial, like a weathered, fluted candlestick, to Cornelius Smelt, one-time governor of the island.

The town centre was large and dominated, as was everything else, by Rushen Castle, with its one-handed Elizabethan clock, grassy, filled-in moat, sundial and palm trees. The surrounding town houses of past gentility filled two sides of the square, in different colours and styles, still elegant in their shabby way, with a monstrous modern shop-front defacing the façade of one of them, which, until the outrage, must have been a little gem of its kind. The whole setting, the streets, the square, the river, the port and the people standing around reminded you of the first act of a Verdi opera, where, in a medieval, sunny town, the chorus and the supers hang about, woodenly waiting for the principals to enter and bring with them life, excitement and the first stirrings of tragedy.

You could tell things were warming-up by watching the movements of the spectators on the road to the town along the river-side. A large red bus full of sightseers and sensation-seekers halted at the brewery and the passengers eagerly alighted and started asking questions of those loafing there. They had heard things were happening in Castletown and had rushed in hot-foot for news and whatever they could see of horror and of the law steadily and relentlessly functioning. Suddenly, a spasm of attention rooted them where they stood. Then they stirred, craned their necks, and ran to witness the approaching procession.

"They're here..."

Seven cars and a van, containing police-officers, reporters, technicians, doctors, lawyers, representatives of the family and a film unit stationed on the Island to produce a thriller. They crossed the swing-bridge, drove one after another along the causeway under the walls of the castle, and into the public car-park near the church. One by one... Like the motorcars on the fun-fair. You almost expected the accompaniment of a steam organ and a wooden hobby-horse, ridden by raffish excursionists, to leap in the midst of them by way of a change. The tailpiece of the procession was an alien red brewery lorry. "Kinnish's Conister Ales!" The driver stolidly held his place, broke from the procession at the memorial candlestick, pursued a wild course down Malew Street, and away, contemptuous of a lot of fuss, and eager to be rid of his barrels of beer...

The cars emptied themselves, and their occupants formed a ragged procession to the police-station. Somewhere, at sea, a steamer hooted, and a child in a perambulator outside a shop began to wail dismally.

3

THE NEW APPRENTICE

I thought he'd had a stroke. I tried to give him a drink of water... There was a bit of a smell of almonds, but I thought he'd been eatin' nuts..."

The constable who had found the murdered man kept telling it first to one, then to another, over and over again, as though trying to clear himself of suspicion.

"How was I to know he was murdered? Would *you*...?"

The photographers had taken their grisly pictures and gone and the finger-print experts from Douglas had dusted and examined various articles of furniture and parts of the room, and now had carried off their films to be developed. Littlejohn, the Chief Constable, the sergeant and a plain-clothes man or two were left, with Archdeacon Kinrade hanging on the fringe, curious to watch an investigation start and as eager to learn as a young man.

The Deemster's retiring-room yielded little. Such clues as gave some idea of His Honour's behaviour just before his death were spread on the green baize cloth of the table, together with the belongings taken from the pockets of the body, which had now been removed to the mortuary. The grease-paper packet which had held the sandwiches, the broken pen-nib, the ball of crumpled writing-paper picked up at the dead man's feet...

My dear Inspector Littlejohn...

"He must have had some reason for writing urgently to you. Something that couldn't wait until he met you this evening. Or maybe, he was afraid something might happen before you came. It looks as if he began to write a letter, spoiled it when the pen-nib broke, and then started another one... The murderer must have carried that one off..."

The Chief Constable was an ex-army man, practical and alert. There was no professional jealousy in his makeup and he made it clear that it must be all hands to the pumps to find a quick solution before the tracks of the killer grew blurred.

"I know you're here on leave, Littlejohn, but, you are in a way, involved, you know. The dead man seems to have specifically singled you out to solve his problem. I hope you'll help. I'll make it right with Scotland Yard..."

So, the Inspector was virtually in charge of the case.

Archdeacon Kinrade drew near as the Chief Constable spoke of his theory about the letter. He was anxious not to miss a thing and, as the best logician of his year at Cambridge, long ago, he tested every word for truth and meaning.

"I thought he'd had a stroke..."

The constable was telling a reporter outside the room all about it.

"What would *you* have done if *you'd* thought he was ill? You'd have given him a drink of water, wouldn't you...?"

The police surgeon had rebuked him. Here was a man, poisoned, and he was given a drink from a bottle on the table! Suppose the water had been the vehicle for the poison. His Honour might thereby have been given a second dose.

"The doctor said..."

But the water was untainted. The doctor had smelled it and even tasted a drop of it and carried it off to the analyst, sure he wouldn't find anything. He had also taken away the bottle of cough mixture from the Deemster's coat pocket. He didn't taste that and, as for smelling it, it gave off so many strong aromas that you couldn't tell one from another. But if you left it uncorked for a bit, you got the smell of almonds.

The contents of the pockets contained the usual coin, cigarette-case, matches, lighter, silver pencil and fountain-pen carried about by most men. There was four pounds ten shillings in notes in a note-case, and a wallet stuffed with papers. The latter interested Littlejohn, but he obviously could not begin to pore over them then and there. Instead, he asked if he might take the lot and examine it at his leisure during the evening. The Chief Constable agreed and seemed surprised at being asked. It was obvious that the case was under Littlejohn's command.

Littlejohn wished he had Cromwell there to keep up his morale and sense of humour. These were very friendly and considerate folk, but the Inspector felt entirely on his own. Cromwell was always a good foil for him, solid, humorous, sane in counsel, a terror for work, an expert in getting what he wanted from all types of people. But the sergeant was also on holidays, with his nice wife, three kids and his mother-in-law at Truro...

The Chief Constable must have read Littlejohn's thoughts. He put a kindly hand on the Inspector's shoulder.

"I know you Scotland Yard Inspectors usually work with a detective-sergeant. You may have one you'd like me to send for. If so, I'll do it with pleasure. Otherwise, I'll assign one of our own men to you and he can do the routine and local work for you. We have a young sergeant who's up-and-coming, intelligent and ambitious and he'll be delighted with the chance to study the methods of Scotland Yard. It'll be a godsend to him... What do you say, Inspector?"

Littlejohn said he'd be grateful for the help of the detective from Douglas.

The Chief strode to the door.

"Knell... Knell... Please come here..."

Detective-Sergeant Knell was on the top side of thirty, earnest-looking and rather overwhelmed by his new job. He wore a raincoat and soft black hat with a snap brim. He'd worn the brim turned up all round until he'd seen Littlejohn's style, and then he'd turned it down all round. "You look like a real detective now," one of his colleagues, who was a bit jealous of him, had said. In the force, on account of his lugubrious name and his fair pink complexion, he was known as "Nellie", but only in private.

Knell entered, removed his hat and revealed a long head, thatched in silky dishevelled hair, which he combed into order with his fingers. He had a Roman nose, blue eyes and a good forehead. His cheeks were a bit sunken and tapered down to a pointed chin. When he grinned, which was rarely, he revealed a double row of strong large teeth almost like the keys of a piano.

"This is Detective-Sergeant Knell, Inspector. You'll find him a very helpful man..."

"Well, Reginald, your chance has come at last..."

Archdeacon Kinrade pumped Knell's hand up and down with both his own and explained to Littlejohn that Reginald Knell had been born in the parish of Bride when he himself was rector there, that he had christened him and prepared him for confirmation, and that he hoped one day to marry him at Grenaby and baptise his children there.

Knell blushed and looked here and there as though seeking a bee-line of flight or else wishing the ground would open and hide him. He had been courting a girl for a number of years, but had not yet brought his mind to leading her to the altar at Grenaby or anywhere else.

Littlejohn shook the sergeant's hand, which was perspiring heavily from his emotions. Knell was about six feet tall and a conscientious officer. He had once arrested an armed burglar, over-powered an Indian juggler who had run amuck on the funfair and started to perform a knife-throwing act among his audience, and he had at one place and another rescued four people from drowning. Ever since Littlejohn's arrival, Knell had been watching him closely with a sort of dumb adoration, listening, pondering. The blue eyes fixed themselves on the famous Scotland Yard man like the all-seeing Eye on certificates issued by secret societies. He had been expecting Littlejohn to take out a book and make notes of things in it and whip out a magnifiying lens and go down on his knees and creep around for clues...

"Pleased to meet you, sir."

This was beyond Knell's wildest dreams. When he'd been told at Douglas to go down to Castletown with the murder squad, his heart had missed a beat. Murder! In his modest way, he thought they'd just need him to hold the crowds back... And now...

As he hung around waiting for orders, people he knew had started to quiz Reggie Knell.

"Inspector Littlejohn from over at Scotland Yard's on the job. He'll be questioning everybody," he had answered and set Castletown in a bit of a panic. Now, it would be himself, Reggie Knell, doing it! His uncle, Knell the Shoe, who kept a bootshop in Arbory Street, was in the pub already, standing drinks to all who came.

"Our Tom's Reggie's on the case, with a high-up expert from London... Somebody had better look-out." And when they told him later that his boast was really true, he got properly drunk, and went home to his shop where he soled a lot of shoes that only needed heeling and heeled a lot that needed soles...

"I'll see you in the morning, then, Knell. I'd like to get settled in at the Archdeacon's place first and just think things over and have a talk with Mr. Kinrade about the Deemster's background. Shall we meet here...?"

"He'll call for you, Inspector," said the Chief Constable. "There's a police-car at your disposal and Knell can drive you..."

They all hung about a bit, hesitating what to do next. Little-john felt sorry for them. In the small community, the murder of a Deemster was a shocking blow and a personal loss for all of them.

Teddy Looney entered, beaming, unperturbed by the presence of so many police. He'd milked his cows and now he could face life with an easy mind again. The party broke up and Littlejohn joined the Archdeacon in Looney's old car, which now bore on its bonnet a number of large white exclamation marks, made by Teddy's hens whilst he milked the cows... They trundled along into the country and Littlejohn recognized the old road to Gren-aby, the stone bridge where the man in dark glasses had once tried to murder Parson Kinrade, and a little farther along, the houses in which the killer had confessed and died. They turned in at the lane leading to Grenaby parsonage and soon were taking tea and talking by the fire. It was mild for the time of year, the windows were open, and the sun was beginning to set over the mountains in the direction of Peel. The birdsong, the whisper of the trees, the smell of wood-smoke on the air, a dog barking far away... So unreal and remote from the world and the dead man whose killer Littlejohn must now find before he could really enjoy his holiday. He took the Deemster's wallet from his pocket, carried his chair to the table and emptied out the contents.

A driving licence, stamps, return tickets on railways and 'buses, the titles of some books on a slip of paper, a recipe for plum-cake—of all things!—and some snapshots of family groups and children.

"Those are of his two married daughters and his grandchil-dren," said the parson, who had drawn up his chair as well and was peering among the papers through a pair of spectacles he had put on.

Littlejohn hardly heard what he said. He was looking through some newspaper cuttings, one in particular of which interested him. It was an editorial or columnist's note marked 'Times', with the date.

We have it on good authority that the banks on the Island have been troubled by a number of spurious notes this summer. It is to be hoped that these are only odd cases, for an organized effort of this kind on the Isle of Man during the season would tax the ingenuity of the police to the full. Not only is there a moving population of hundreds of thousands of people holidaymaking here, but banknotes of English, Scottish, Irish and our own insular banks circulate freely and without being questioned. In fact, during the high-season, the Island might be called the counterfeiter's paradise!

"Which is true," said the parson after they had read it. "Easier than a racecourse... But why's the Deemster bothering about it? Does he think he might get the very criminals to his own court for judgment...?"

Littlejohn passed over the last articles he'd extricated from the wallet.

"I don't know; but have you seen these?"

There were five banknotes, all on different banks, and a pound each in denomination. Bank of Mann, Bank of England, Bank of Scotland, Bank of Ireland, and Home Counties Bank in England. The parson put his finger on the last note.

"You'll observe, that whilst the English banks, other than the Bank of England, aren't allowed to issue notes in their own country, they can come over here, open a bank, and issue them on the Island."

"I wonder if these are genuine, or spurious. The Deemster had a note-case with some other notes in; these seem to have been kept apart and tucked away for some reason."

"Yes... And all of different banks. We'll see what the bank at Castletown says about them to-morrow. Meanwhile is there anything else, any clue among the rest of the stuff in the wallet?"

"No... Not that I can see. This case looks like being a tough one to crack. As you said before, Archdeacon, people don't, as a rule, murder the judge who sends them down for a term. Prison makes them respect the judge more than you'd think, although it might not prevent them coming up for another stretch. We can't dismiss the idea, but it doesn't seem a very hot one to me. You knew the Deemster well? Was he likely to have enemies, sir?"

The parson rubbed his white whiskers.

"I told you he was a beloved man in this land. Charitable, kind of heart, a public servant in more ways than one, a member of a family highly respected here for generations, a scholar, a good friend... I can't think of a single reason why anybody should want to murder him."

"Yet, somebody did, and was very determined to do it, too. There must be something good or bad, hidden in the judge's life, which has caused this..."

"It can't be bad... It must be some evil he's come across in the course of his duties which he's tried to put right, and thereby met his death."

Littlejohn expressed no views on the parson's theory. He had so many times before had to burrow into the lives of decent, respectable people to find the one flaw, the weak spot which had brought their ruin or destruction, that he never showed surprise at what he found. But he was half prepared to take the parson's word for it. Archdeacon Kinrade, although he lived at the back o' beyond, was no fool, but a clever man of the world. Maybe the Deemster...

Outside, the telephone bell was ringing frantically. They could hear old Maggie, the housekeeper, shuffling along, talking to herself about the interruption.

"All right, all right! I'm comin'..."

She looked a bit annoyed when she entered.

"It's them policemen at Castletown again, wantin' the Inspector. I told them you were takin' tea with your shoes off and your slippers on; but no... they must speak to you..."

It was Sergeant Cregeen at Castletown police-station and he

was sorry to trouble the Inspector again. But they'd *another* murder on their hands. This time a mere child, a boy scout. Could the Inspector come over...?

Littlejohn changed into his shoes and so did the Archdeacon. "I'm not missing any of this, Inspector," he said. "I feel responsible for you and, if you'll have me, I'd like to come."

"Of course... I'd be glad if you would."

This time a police-car came for them. Knell was driving and he looked to have grown a couple of inches since his appointment as Littlejohn's assistant. He told them that the custodian of the castle had found the boy as he went his rounds after closing. He had been throttled...

It was the same all over again. Crowds, the fleet of cars, the whispers, the still air of expectancy over the town. Now, there was a faint symptom of panic in it, too. You could understand a criminal going out for a judge. When all's said and done, you can't expect somebody who's suffered at the hands of a judge bearing him anything but ill-will, they were all saying. But a little lad, a boy scout over on holidays in camp... There must be a maniac at large!

In the evening light it was all a bit unreal and fearful. Long shadows fell from the castle and, inside, the gloom was ominous and the imaginative might feel the shades of past kings and lords of Mann, their soldiery, their victims of the dungeons, their watchmen rubbing past in the half-light, or the giants, said to be imprisoned in the foundations, roaring their heads off in rage. A man had once gone down a hole in one of the oubliettes and never been seen again...

Littlejohn and the Archdeacon entered by the main gate and through the tunnel they had used earlier in the day. Beyond was the stone staircase to the watchpost on the walls, whence a door led to the courtroom. In a dark part of the passage stood an old vehicle, almost like a coach of state, invented, it was said, by an island native for his comfort. Now it was part of the museum. The police were gathered round it. The good old man who looked after the place was in tears.

"I might have prevented it if I'd only known," he said.

They had not yet moved the body, and every officer who saw it gnashed his teeth, either actually or metaphorically. A harmless child, neat in his scout's uniform, sprawled in the musty interior of the vehicle in an atmosphere smelling of straw, old leather and dust. By the light of police lamps the whole gruesome scene was plain. Somebody had simply strangled the boy and now he lay there, staring eyes, clenched hands, terror all over him.

The custodian told his tale again for the fifth time.

"He came and said there was somebody in the coach. He had his two little friends with him and I was showin' them over. The court was sittin' and there was plenty of time, and no other visitors. We thought he was being funny and we laughed at him. Then we went on into the other rooms... He must have gone back, because we missed him and we couldn't find him again. The other two said he'd perhaps got tired and gone back to camp, which is two miles along the Douglas road... They both said he didn't like to be laughed at and was inclined to sulk. He'd done it before and run off when they pulled his leg a bit..."

So, with that, the keeper had finished the round with the remaining pair and seen them off the premises. There had been no more visitors. A slack day and then, after the murder of the Deemster, the castle was quarantined, as you might say...

Just before official closing-time, the scoutmaster had rung up the police-station. Young Willie Mounsey, the missing scout, hadn't turned up... They were a party from a Church somewhere in Lancashire, and were there for a week. Mounsey was a quiet, respectable lad who'd never got into trouble before. And then the custodian had remembered. The police were starting to search the castle in case Willie had got lost or met some accident. On the way in, the keeper had mentioned Willie's tale about the coach and had opened the door! This was a cruel blow. Nothing like it ever before. And a little boy... ! The old man was in great distress, as though he were personally responsible for all that went on in the great pile under his charge. He refused to be comforted even by his old friend the Archdeacon.

The same party of police and their equipment were there as had been at the inquiry in the courthouse earlier in the day, but this time, little was said. There was grim silence as the technicians worked and the constables and detectives searched, measured and made their notes. Sergeant Knell kept his eye on Littlejohn, who stood beside the Chief Constable, watching the police-surgeon and the others at their jobs, quietly, efficiently, with an intensity which spoke ill for the killer if so much as a clue of his identity came to light. They all had children of their own, and in their thoughts they were identifying them with the unhappy scout now lying on a stretcher, covered by the surgeon's overcoat.

Knell looked a bit disappointed. He had expected more activity on the part of Littlejohn; a notebook and pencil, a lot of keen questions, physical activity... Like Sexton Blake and the like. Instead, he was listening to the Chief.

"The man must have been hiding in the coach until he could get a chance to go for the Deemster. And lad-like, the youngster opened the door of the coach... or else he might just have peeped in at the window. That's it. He saw the man through the window and then sneaked back to see if he was still there after he'd told the custodian and his friends. The murderer had either done the deed or was waiting to do it, and he wasn't going to have it spoiled by anybody, even a boy scout, being able to say where he was at the time of the crime and identify him. So the boy walked right into him again, and..."

"That's as I see it, too. I think you ought to give that view to the press at once, sir. If you don't, all the Island will think there's a killer out to murder all and sundry indiscriminately. It will prevent panic..."

"I'll do that..."

Shortly after, having searched the castle, dungeons, guard-rooms, private apartments and all the rest without results, the party left again. Constables remained on guard.

It was almost dark as Littlejohn and the Archdeacon climbed in the police-car for home. They sped along, the headlamps making a green tunnel of the trees on the way, the rush of water announcing the bridge at Grenaby, and then they turned left to the parsonage.

"Good night, sir..."

Knell saluted and went off in the night. The cosy glow of the lamp in the hall greeted them and the warmth of the good fire was pleasant in the chilling evening. Littlejohn thought he'd better ring-up his wife and ask if she'd landed safely in the Fens, and tell her that, as usual, mischief had been awaiting him for his holidays.

There was a lot of shouting and noise before they connected them, but it didn't take long.

"Hello... hello... Douglas. Liverpool? Give me Comstock-in-the-Fen 5599... Yes... Comstock-in-the-Fen... Hello... hello..."

Littlejohn remembered that the line went under the sea. In his mind's eye he saw it, deep in gloomy water, with coasters passing over it on the surface, and entangled amid wrecks, and shoals of strange and hideous fish with huge mouths...

"Hullo..." The pompous voice of his brother-in-law, the Canon, boomed through the fens and across the deep forests at the bottom of the sea. Soon Littlejohn was talking to Letty.

The Inspector and the Archdeacon spent little further time talking about the case. They drank some whisky, ate crackers and cheese, and then said good-night.

Littlejohn couldn't find his pyjamas, though he knew he'd brought them and, descending below to inquire from the house-keeper in the kitchen, he came upon them airing before a large fire, side by side, on a clothes-maiden, with a long white night-shirt with a collar embroidered with pink roses. The 'plane to

Ireland droned overhead, owls hooted, a dog barked, the old timbers of the house creaked as though the ghosts of the Archdeacon's vanished family were back again in the place they loved. Littlejohn fell asleep just as he was wondering what Knell thought of him, and what he expected him to do.

4

THE CANARY PULLOVER

Next morning, after the ordeals of the previous day, Littlejohn slept late and was wakened by Maggie, the housekeeper, who, he found, was the widow of a former gardener at the vicarage, called Keggin, and had three children, one in London and two in America. She shook him gently, drew the curtains, and showed him a breakfast tray containing two brown-shelled eggs and several rashers of Manx bacon, crisp and fat with streaks of lean.

"It isn't rationed here..."

She had a fine strong face, with aquiline features, high cheek-bones and a pointed chin. There was the physical strength and the fatalism of a peasant about her, and the curiosity as well.

"That young fellah from the police is here already. He's turned up in a car, large as life, and pleased with himself. Not that he's much to be pleased about, as far as I can see. He's been courtin' Will Teare's girl for it must be seven years and she's not made up her mind to have him yet..."

"Where is he?" said Littlejohn, helping himself to tea from a small teapot labelled *A Present from Ramsey*, and with a little verse engraved on it.

Ramsey town, Ramsey town, shining by the sea.
And here's a health to our true loves,
Wheresoe'er they be.

Maggie snapped her lips.

"I sent him about his business. I told him you were still asleep and, after all they did to you yesterday, they weren't goin' to wake you. You hadn't had your breakfast and weren't ready for him, so he could take himself off for a bit."

"What's he doing while he waits?"

"Following his fancy, I've no doubt. It would do him a power o' good with Millie Teare if she could see him now. He's talking with the land girl from the farm. You might have guessed...

Snaps and snails and puppy-dogs' tails,
And dirty sluts in plenty,
Smell sweeter than roses in young fellahs' noses
When the heart is one-and-twenty..."

"Whoever taught you that jingle, Mrs. Keggin?"

"My uncle William, who'd been all over the world in ships. He'd picked it up somewhere, I suppose. Don't worry about hurryin' over your food. That young chap won't mind..."

As he dressed, Littlejohn could see his new apprentice talking with a girl in a green jersey, slouch hat, and breeches. They were having a good time. The day was fine and the air smelled of damp leaves, peat and wood-smoke. Littlejohn had been given the best bedroom, full of old, highly-polished mahogany furniture, a great four-poster bed with curtains, like a ship in full sail, and windows on two sides overlooking the vast, silent interior of the Island from one angle, with Ronague, The Slock, South Barrule mountain, all yellows, greens and browns; and from the other, a mist of old trees hiding the village of Grenaby down the road.

Downstairs, relations between the Archdeacon and his housekeeper were a bit strained. It was his day for preparing his Sunday sermons, to say nothing of meeting a contractor about the hole in the church roof, but he had shown little enthusiasm for them, and had been anxiously waiting for Littlejohn to take him out.

"Chattering women and nosey old men, bring the Devil right out of his den," he had been told by his housekeeper, who ruled him with a rod of iron for his own good.

"I shan't be coming along to-day, Inspector. I've my sermons to prepare..."

"They'd better be good, parson. I'll be in the audience on Sunday," said Littlejohn, and went to disturb his assistant's philandering.

Knell had brought a copy of the police-surgeon's report. The contents of the Deemster's stomach had included sandwiches, paregoric, ipecacuanha, chlorodyne and aniseed, and enough prussic acid to kill half a dozen. The poison had been administered through the cough mixture which contained enough to kill another dozen. The aroma of the medicine must have hidden the characteristic smell of the poison until the Deemster had taken his dose. This widened the search for the murderer, of course. The poison might have been introduced at any time, thought Littlejohn.

Knell waited patiently until Littlejohn had read the document. He looked a bit more cheerful. The night before, after his excited duties of the day, he had called on Miss Teare, who, having heard of his collaboration with a famous man from London, had smiled upon him and shown herself more susceptible to his bashful wooing.

"The sergeant at Castletown thought you'd like him to inquire round about the poison being sold, so he's sent word that every chemist in the Island has to be asked about it."

He said it as though something marvellous had happened. Littlejohn smiled as he thought of what a feat such instructions would entail on the mainland, or even in the Metropolitan Police area!

"It might have been bought on the mainland, after all. You can get it for killing wasps and other vermin if you choose the place and tell a good tale."

"I never thought of that, sir. But the sergeant also told me to say, the constable who was with the Deemster before he went in court for the morning session, saw His Honour take a spoonful of his cough medicine before he went. So that narrows it down a bit. Between half past ten and one o'clock somebody must have sneaked in the Deemster's room and put the poison in the bottle in his overcoat."

"That does make things a bit easier. But why did he have to kill a boy scout afterwards? Had the lad seen him leaving the Deemster's quarters...?"

Knell thought heavily. You could almost hear his brain turning over the problem.

"Suppose, sir... Suppose young Mounsey went back to spy on the chap in the coach, saw him come out and do what he did to the Deemster's cough mixture, and then the murderer spotted him. He'd have to kill him for fear of being identified."

"That's quite likely, Knell. I think you've got it."

Knell broke into a sunny smile. Things were looking up! He nodded his head sagely and made a note to tell Millie Teare that he was having to tell Littlejohn how to go about the case.

"Let's drive to Castletown, then..."

Knell made for the car with springy steps. Littlejohn noticed that he seemed to be dressed in his Sunday best and his boots shone like polished jet. He self-consciously passed the land-girl, who couldn't take her admiring eyes from him.

"When the heart is one-and-twenty..." thought Littlejohn.

They entered the town by a new route; along a by-pass, past a derelict windmill, and down the narrow high street, where Knell had to drive part of the way on the pavement to pass an approaching bread-van. The atmosphere of tragedy still hung about the place and the three-legged flag flew half-mast over the castle. Normal life had been resumed. Sightseers, attracted by news of the previous day's sensation, were flocking morbidly to the castle and the custodian had his hands full. Among the excursionists climbing from a charabanc, Littlejohn spotted the man of the big overcoat he'd met on the boat. He had shed his heavy clothing and instead, wore a bowling-club blazer with an embroidered pocket, an open-necked shirt, flannels, a beret and a pair of rope-soled sandals he'd bought in France the year before on a trip. He looked taller and thinner without the overcoat. He touched Littlejohn as they passed.

"Hullo..."

"Hullo..."

Knell was anxious to be getting to work.

"Are we calling at the police-station, Inspector?"

The little man's jaw fell and his eyes shot out. *Inspector!* You could hear him thinking. He'd have a tale to tell when he got back to the boarding-house. The Inspector on the job's a pal of mine...

The custodian left his conducted party to tell them the time he had taken the scouts round on the day before. The whole thing tallied with Knell's theory. He eagerly told Littlejohn so. The castle-keeper wasn't impressed.

"Don't get excited! You haven't found out who did it, yet, by a long way, Reggie..."

"It must have been somebody who knew his way about the castle, Inspector. How did he know the back way to the chambers else? And he must have known the Deemster's habits with his cough mixture and also the routine of the court."

"That's right."

The custodian hurried off to join his party who were getting annoyed.

"Come on! What do you think we've paid our money for. . .?"

"Could it have been one of the lawyers, sir?"

Knell said it ominously. Although he was an officer of the law, he had a native distrust of lawyers. His uncle, Knell of Ballagoole, a farmer, had died well-off, or so they said. And all his money had vanished in family litigation...

They crossed to the police-station. As they got to know each other better, Sergeant Cregeen took a fancy to Littlejohn. No fuss and no side, he told his missus in bed after their first day. The Inspector's vast, imperturbable bulk seemed to fill the little office and gave them all confidence and a feeling of security and pride in their job. He lit his pipe as they showed him round the building and pointed out the views from the windows. Knell was showing-off a bit, too. He lit a pipe, as well, and the sergeant looked daggers at him.

"One thing I'd like you to do, sergeant. Will you inquire who was in the castle on court day? Lawyers, attendants, litigants, everybody. I'd even put an advert in the papers and ask visitors who were shown over to come forward. We want to know if there was anybody suspicious hanging around and whether or not anybody saw William Mounsey after he left his friends and the custodian. Did anybody go in or out of the Deemster's private chambers whilst the court was sitting? Was anybody seen around the private staircase leading up to the chambers or hanging around the door at the bottom?"

"I'll do my best, sir."

"The private door was always kept locked?"

"Yes, sir. The Deemsters had their own keys, of course, and we have one here, and the custodian will have one."

Sergeant Cregeen indicated a board in the outer office on which numerous keys hung from hooks. "That's the key we hold."

"If nobody were in the outer office, anybody could unhook it and take a soap or wax impression?"

"Yes. But who'd be wantin' to?"

"Ah! Somebody did, didn't they?"

"Yes. But they'd have to know which key it was."

"I said it was somebody who knew a lot... A lawyer, maybe..."

Knell puffed his pipe sagely; the sergeant gave him another black look, implying that he should be seen and not heard.

"This was the third attempt..."

They all looked amazed.

"You mean, sir...?"

"Yes. Three days ago, somebody tried to throw a brick on His Honour's head from a building they were demolishing in Douglas. Previously, someone had tampered with the steering of his car. It means that, not having succeeded, the murderer turned to his third scheme. It's probable, then, that the impression of the key has been taken this week, unless the door was open. Has anybody been here and had a chance of taking it?"

"I won't say they hadn't, sir. But how did they know which key?"

"As I said, it was somebody who knew a lot."

The sergeant went red again.

"No need to keep telling us. We know, Reggie. And it couldn't have been the keeper. He won't let the keys out of his sight."

"I suppose you've been getting the courtroom ready for a day or two beforehand."

"Yes, sir. It isn't used much, especially by the Deemsters. One of our men would go across to see that all was tidy, ready for His Honour..."

"Taking the key from the hook and going over with it?"

"Yes. But how did they know *when?* They couldn't have watched the place all the time, could they?"

"Just give it a bit of thought, Cregeen. Think, and ask, if anybody has been around a lot of late."

"I will..."

He looked worried. It wasn't going to be as easy as he thought, even with Scotland Yard on the job. A very modest, decent fellah, he told his wife in bed that night about Littlejohn.

"It's hardly an appropriate time to do it, Cregeen, but I'd like to talk to the Deemster's widow, if she can bear it. It's vital we get our information right away. The longer we take, the more like a needle in a haystack it will become, with all these people on holidays coming and going by boat and 'plane. She lives in Douglas?"

"Four miles out, sir, at a mansion called Ballagarry, in East Baldwin. Perhaps the Chief Constable could tell you if it's all right..."

The Chief soon fixed matters, after a telephone call and a brief wait. Mrs. Quantrell would be pleased to see the Inspector. He drove off in the car with Knell right away. They turned left just before Douglas, climbed a little, breasted a slope, and then the scene from the top took one's breath away. Here it was that the two valleys, East and West Baldwin converged amid soft rolling hills, their feet lost in a rich mass of trees, their slopes covered in pines, heather and gorse, until their tops showed dark where only moss and blaeberries grew. They took the East Baldwin fork, passed a cluster of cottages and a school, and then, driving through an avenue of beeches, came to the home of the Quantrells. It was known as a mansion, the Manx term for a large family house in the country. It had the long, lovely façade of an American colonial house. Two drives from separate gates met in a broad sweep before a large graceful door with a wide fanlight above it. A spacious room on each side of the porch and, on the first floor, three big oblong windows with small balconies. There was a short wing on the right, the French windows of which gave on a lawn, with a bed of geraniums flaming in the middle. At the front and sides were old established grass plots, with palms and eucalyptus trees and fuchsia hedges, relieved by flower borders and with a background of old trees.

Here the sun was shining, birds singing, and behind, in the poultry yard, hens were making wailing overtures to egg-laying. All the blinds of the house were drawn... Someone had mercilessly cut short the Deemster's joy in this gracious place and his anticipated pleasure in retiring there.

The door was opened by an elderly maid, who was so obviously expecting them, that she appeared in the porch almost before Littlejohn removed his finger from the bell. She eyed them shrewdly, sizing them up with bright dark eyes. She led them to a large airy room, took Littlejohn's hat deferentially, snatched Knell's from his hand as he showed no inclination to give it up, and left them.

The drawn blinds darkened the place, but you could make out, in the firelight from the broad open fireplace, the fine old furniture, the easy chairs on either side of the grate, the Hepplewhite chairs by the walls, a mahogany sideboard and bookcases, silver and porcelain figures here and there, and heavy pictures on the walls. Over the fireplace, a large oil-painting of the Deemster in his red robes and full-bottomed wig...

The lights were switched on, and a young man in a canary pullover, check jacket and corduroy trousers stood in the doorway. Littlejohn instantly disliked him. He was short and thin, with small hands and feet, and his head was long and narrow, with brown hair brushed back from a high forehead and growing long and shaggy at the back. The nose was snub and flushed, and the brown eyes set too close together. He advanced to meet them with studied nonchalance savouring of impudence.

"I'm Jeremy Lamprey and Mrs. Quantrell is my aunt. I'm staying here for a bit and luckily hadn't gone back to the mainland. My aunt's not in very good shape. You'll appreciate that. I wouldn't want her upsetting..."

"I understand, sir, the Chief Constable has already spoken to her, and she doesn't mind sparing a minute or two of her time."

Lamprey screwed up his face in a nervous gesture which might have meant annoyance or impatience.

"I know it's important that you Island police should get to know as much as you can, but..."

"I'm not the Island police. My name's Littlejohn and I'm from Scotland Yard. Will you kindly give your aunt my card, sir?"

The pink left Lamprey's cheeks and he gave Littlejohn a queer, half-fearful look.

He's done it, thought Knell to himself. He's scared stiff of the Inspector!

Without another word, the canary pullover hurried to the door and you could hear the rubber-soles of his suede shoes squeaking on the polished floor of the hall.

The police officers waited. In the light of the electric chandelier, the room looked even finer and the furniture shone and glowed with age and expert polishing. Littlejohn's eyes turned to the bookcases which filled the alcoves on either side of the fireplace. This was a natural attraction, for the colouring of their contents was vivid and clashed with the rest of the room. At least half of the books were still in soiled and battered publishers' jackets. The Inspector approached and examined them. Almost without exception, they were crime stories, ranging from Edgar Allan Poe and the Mysteries of Udolpho to modern classics of detection and humbler English and American whodunits.

"The Deemster seems by way of having been a bit of a detective himself..."

"He was very interested..."

Littlejohn turned. Mrs. Quantrell had entered the room without his hearing her. Knell blushed and moved first on one foot and then on the other. She made straight for Littlejohn, after raising the blind of a side-window.

"You are the Inspector from Scotland Yard my husband talked of...?"

They shook hands. She was Manx and obviously of a class of gentility now rapidly dying-out. She was medium built, dark eyed, with a good complexion, and must have been much younger than her husband, perhaps in the middle forties. The high cheek bones, the straight nose, and the bone formation of the face must have made her a local beauty in her time. Before tragedy overtook her, she had been a happy woman, looking forward to spending the rest of life in the company of her distinguished husband in their lovely home. Even now, under the grievous blow she had suffered, she was making no fuss. Her breeding, her beliefs, her pride forbade any dramatizing of the situation. She was strong enough to bear her grief alone and in secret. At once, Littlejohn knew how it had been possible for a man to rise from early penury to the highest post in the community with such a helpmeet to support him...

"Your husband was interested not only in the judicial aspect of crime, then, but in its detection, too, Mrs. Quantrell?"

"Yes. It was one of his main diversions..."

"I'm so sorry about all this. I do offer you my deepest sympathy..."

Knell cleared his throat.

"And so do I, Mrs. Quantrell..."

"Thank you both... I heard you were helping the Inspector, Mr. Knell. Your mother will be very proud... How is she?"

"Middlin', madam. Middlin'. She's nearing eighty, now."

"She must be. I remember when she used to bring eggs and butter to us when I was at home... That seems a long time ago..."

Hers was a native courtesy, which forgot its own troubles.

"But this is not helping you, Inspector. Here you will find us fond of a gossip, telling tales of old times and the like. Very exasperating to people in a hurry... What can I do to help you?"

"If you would prefer to leave rather a painful interview until later..."

"No, Inspector. Let's get it over. Do sit down, the two of you."

She offered them cigarettes from a box. Knell, who only smoked a pipe, accepted one and started to puff it with heavy breath, surrounding himself with a fog of smoke.

"Where were you when the news reached you, Mrs. Quantrell?"

"I was calling on Mrs. Christian at Ghlon Crusherey... a

meeting and tea for the effort at Braddan Church. They telephoned from here to tell me."

"It may seem an absurd question to you, madam... but do you know anyone who might have wished the Deemster's death?"

She seemed amazed.

"Martin...? Anyone to wish him dead...? It does seem absurd. As a judge, of course, those who were punished at his hands might dislike him; but murder him... indeed no. In fact, many of the hardened criminals he dealt with were very fond of him. They even doffed their hats to him when they passed him in the street. I don't think we have any really bad criminals over here, judging from the court cases. It is said, of course, we export them to the mainland..."

She smiled sadly.

"Did your husband not tell you that anyone was trying to kill him?"

Mrs. Quantrell looked horrified.

"No... But then nobody wanted to, did they? You don't mean. . .?"

"Yes. There had already been two attempts on his life."

"But he didn't tell me..."

"He didn't wish to alarm you, madam. First of all, someone tampered with the steering of his car; and then, when that didn't work, they tried dropping a brick on his head from an old building in the town. He merely told his old friend Archdeacon Kinrade, and that is one of the reasons why Mr. Kinrade asked me to come over here."

"My husband said you were coming and that he was dining with you at Grenaby parsonage. But I understood that was because he was interested in detective work. He said it would be great fun meeting a famous detective in the flesh."

"I was going to try to get to the bottom of the two attempts. I'm sorry, I was too late."

GEORGE BELLAIRS

"He should have told me, though. That explains his anxiety over the past months, then."

"Months? But the attempts have only been made over the last fortnight, Mrs. Quantrell. Had the Deemster seemed upset for longer than that?"

"Much longer. He's been very preoccupied since early summer. Something has been on his mind and he's been unduly excited and has spent more time out of doors doing things he'd not told me about."

"Have you any idea what it was?"

"No. He has gone out in the car and people have seen him driving about the Island. I thought it had something to do with his antiquarian work. He was very interested in the prehistoric remains in which the Island is so rich. I asked him, but he was very elusive about it."

"Did those who saw him out on his expeditions say where he was?"

"Mainly in the north of the Island. He was seen at The Lhen, which is almost at the northernmost tip, and in the Curraghs, which are what you call fens on the mainland and lie north of the main road from Ramsey to Ballaugh. But what he was doing there was a mystery."

"You say the judge was interested in the detection as well as the punishment of crime, Mrs. Quantrell?"

"Yes. He planned to write a book on it. He was collecting material for when he retired. He had a theory that in the detection of crime, much more of the psychology of the criminal came to light than did in the law courts. He thought such background was valuable in matters of curative or preventive detention, and in the very sentence itself. We had planned to do it together, and I had learned to use a typewriter and be his secretary..."

She gave no sign of sentimental emotion, but in the forlorn little smile as she said it, there was grief too deep for tears.

"Do you think he tried his hand at detection, Mrs. Quantrell? I

48

mean, in the course, perhaps, of experiments, it is likely that the Deemster might have unearthed a hornet's nest of crime and set some dangerous criminals on his track?"

"That might account for his preoccupation of late, but what on earth could he have found in a little place like this?"

"Did he ever mention forged banknotes to you?"

"Why, yes. I think it was I who first raised the point. I sold some old furniture to an antique dealer in the town and was paid in pound notes... One was returned from the Bank of Mann as a spurious one. We had to let the police have it, but my husband went to see about it. He was interested in how it had got to the Island.

"I'd better know the bank and where you got the note from originally, if you don't mind."

"My bank is the Bank of Mann, Victoria Street, and the antique dealer is Mr. Irons, in Duke Street..."

Littlejohn made a note of it on the back of an old envelope. Knell regarded this with disapproval, for he had been expecting answers to all the questions to be written down in an official black book. Furthermore, why wasn't the Inspector looking round the place for clues? There must be plenty for the finding. He almost asked if he could borrow the magnifying glass which Littlejohn must surely carry, and set about it himself.

"Yes, Knell? Did you want to ask anything?"

He met Littlejohn's kindly questioning eye. He gave a start. The man must be able to see right inside him!

"No, sir. I just thought... Well... If you've anything you want to take down, I might write it in my book. I've got one with me. Save you the trouble, like..."

He giggled nervously and produced a fat notebook with a shiny imitation-leather back, the pages held in place by a thick elastic band.

"Of course. I'm sorry if I'm neglecting you. Take down the addresses then from this bit of paper..."

"You'll soon have the task of going through the Deemster's papers, Mrs. Quantrell. Are you the executrix?"

"No. The bank are looking after that. Were you wanting to search for anything?"

"I thought there might be some indication among them which would throw light on the Deemster's recent state of mind."

"They are all locked in his desk in his study. He was a very neat and methodical man. When we open them, you can be there, if you wish, Inspector. It will be after the funeral, of course. They will not be touched until then. I could let you know when the bank and the advocate are calling to go through them."

"That would be very kind of you. I'll wait till I hear from you, then... What a lovely view you have from here!"

Knell's head flew up with a jerk from his labours in his note-book. Lovely view, indeed! And them hot on the track of the Deemster's murderer! Knell felt like weeping with despair. He was a great follower of Sherlock Holmes, to whose methods he had graduated from Sexton Blake in schooldays. With as much to hand as Littlejohn had, Holmes would have solved it all!

Littlejohn strolled to the side window to look out at the hills showing through a gap in the trees. The window was opposite the door of the room, which stood slightly ajar. Littlejohn glanced at the door instead of the view, strode to it, and flung it wide open. Jeremy Lamprey was sitting silently on a chair in the hall, listening to all that was said. He rose, slightly flushed, and tried to make light of it.

"Didn't want to disturb you all... Just waiting for my aunt. I've got to look after her you know. Don't overdo it, Inspector..."

He was recovering his aplomb as he talked and made excuses.

"Come in, Mr. Lamprey. No sense in sitting outside like a stranger."

Littlejohn felt like planting his foot in the corduroy backside of this little snivelling ass, who now entered the room, swaggering to show he wasn't put-out by being discovered eavesdropping.

"Why, Jeremy. Where were you?"

"Sitting in the hall waiting to get in a word. I wanted to say I'm going out for a bit. It's cleared up so I'll go and do some more painting. That's all. S'long..."

He flipped his hand at them all and went. He had been drinking and left a reek of whisky like the exhaust of a car in his wake. They saw him shambling to the front gate loaded with an easel, a canvas and a box of paints.

"I'm sorry I hadn't time to introduce you, Inspector. Jeremy is the son of my late sister. He lives in Chelsea and paints for a living. He's not been well lately and has been spending rather a long holiday here. He comes over between jobs and paints and does etchings of the Island. His main work is advertising art. You've doubtless seen some of it on the hoardings on the mainland... It is rather a comfort to have someone of one's own flesh and blood here at a time like this..."

She said it without much enthusiasm, and Littlejohn could well understand it. Lamprey was evidently a sponger who came over for the Quantrells' hospitality when he was hard up or didn't feel like work.

"Is there anything more, Inspector?"

"Not at the moment, I think. You have been most kind to see us at such a time. I hope it hasn't been too upsetting."

"Not at all. I do want this affair clearing up, please. And I'll let you know about the papers..."

She showed them to the door herself and returned to her loneliness.

Littlejohn and Knell entered the car and drove back to the main road. On the way stood a red telephone kiosk in which someone was telephoning. He had his back to them but there was no mistaking the check sports jacket. It was Jeremy Lamprey.

"Did you see who that was, Knell?"

"Lamprey?"

"That's right."

Knell breathed deeply with elation. Things were moving. He was keeping abreast of Scotland Yard. If it went on like this, he'd be solving the mystery on his own.

"Just stop here, go inside, then ask, as a police officer, to use their telephone..."

They pulled up at the drive at a hospital, with outbuildings sprawling over large gardens, and a lodge and inquiry office almost fronting the road.

"Telephone to the Douglas police and ask them to find out, at once, from the telephone exchange, where the call from the box at the cross-roads there was for... I'll wait..."

"Lucky it isn't on the automatics, eh?" said Knell jauntily, and with sprightly official feet, he pranced away. Littlejohn filled his pipe, lit it, and took a stroll. He wasn't even thinking deeply about the case; he was enjoying the air and the view. A man cycled past with a creel and fishing tackle on his back; then another with a gun and a dog at his heels. The Inspector wondered if he'd get any sport before the time came to go home... At Braddan Old Church, down the hill, a funeral procession was approaching; the cars drew slowly along, halted, and a crowd of men got out and formed a ragged procession. They were lifting out the coffin...

"Something and nothing, sir..."

Knell was back, making light of his investigation.

"What do you mean, Knell?"

"The Douglas police were on it like a shot when I mentioned your name, sir. But it won't help much. Lamprey was just 'phonin' to Alcardi, at the art stores on the Promenade. Alcardi is an Italian, interned durin' the war, and he settled down here selling pictures and statues and souvenirs when it was over. The telephone exchange didn't listen-in, of course, but that's where Lamprey was ringing-up. Likely as not, he was trying to sell a picture. What else could it be? Only natural..."

Knell climbed inside and started the engine.

"Let me give you a bit of advice, Reggie..."

Littlejohn said it in his kindliest tones. Knell blushed. Reggie! Things were looking up!

"Never dismiss anything in a case as something and nothing. When you've lived as long with crime as I have, you'll find out that the little things are often the most important and a lead like this may save weeks of work..."

"But I only..."

"I'm not ticking you off. Just put down *Alcardi* in your little book, and don't forget him... And now, drive on to somewhere where we can get a good lunch and after that we'll call at the Bank of Mann, and then have a word with Mr. Irons..."

At the church down the road, they were singing the favourite hymn of the dead man at the graveside, as was often the custom. Knell slowed down.

"He must have been a sailor," he said as he took off his hat.

A great surge of song filled even the little police-car.

> *Our wives and children we commend to Thee,*
> *For them we plough the land and plough the deep,*
> *For them by day the golden corn we reap.*
> *By night, the silver harvest of the sea.*

Knell even joined-in himself, as he drove slowly past, unconsciously drawn by the native tune. It was very moving and Littlejohn liked his colleague all the better for it.

5

THE COUNTERFEIT NOTES

The marble portico of the Bank of Mann, Victoria Street, stood magnificent and aloof between a shop selling rock and an eating-house in the window of which the menu for the day was written in chalk on a blackboard. Once through the bank doors and you got a surprise. It was like one of those hidden ancient city churches which spread their glories behind a misleading and commonplace façade in which the vulgar things of life have jostled away the holy. Marble pillars, mosaic floor, and stained-glass windows ornamented with emblems of agriculture, fishery, and commerce, with the Three Legs of Man frequently repeated. The light entered through two great domes, which cast upon the clients below strange purple, yellow, scarlet and green hues, which gave misleading impressions of their states of health. The counter was long and divided into about eight sections by partitions, which formed a series of small cubicles in which deposits and withdrawals could be carried on in secret. Three cashiers were attending to the queues of customers and popped from cubby-hole to cubby-hole, like creatures seeking a place of rest and unable to decide which they preferred.

When Knell and Littlejohn entered through the revolving doors a wave of curiosity and expectancy broke over the occupants of the bank. They all knew Knell, and swift rumour had told of his new job. The eyes of those in the queues all focused on the policemen, and the heads of the cashiers were raised expectantly. The faces of clerks appeared over the carved screen which divided the public from the secret workings of the bank. Knell made his way to the head of the first tail of clients.

"We'd like to see the manager, Mr. Mylecraine..."

The chief cashier gave Knell a stony look. In the male-voice choir where they sang together, it was 'Bill' and 'Reg'. His new job had evidently turned Knell's head already!

"Very well, *Mister* Knell."

Mylecraine slapped a passbook on the top of the partition, and the head and eager eyes of a junior clerk popped up like a dummy on the Aunt Sallies of the fairground. His hair had been over-anointed with oil which shone on his forehead and ears as well.

"Tell Mr. Kerruish the police want him."

"Very good, sir..."

There was a mild commotion on the public side.

"Mr. Kerruish!" They said it in amazement to one another. They could only, in their ignorance, think that the manager must somehow be involved in the murder of the Deemster. Churchwarden, Justice of the Peace, Member of the House of Keys, Treasurer of half the charities and institutions of the Island...! Some of them looked ready to withdraw all their money and cause a run on the bank and then, turning their eyes from Knell to Littlejohn, they changed their minds. The man would never look so cheerful if he'd come to arrest anybody!

"Don't do that in front of a crowd, Knell. You might start a run or a riot. Always give them your card," Littlejohn advised the sergeant later.

"I haven't got any cards..."

Mr. Kerruish emerged from a door at the end of the banking hall and hastily ushered the policemen into his room. He was a small man with a bald head and a fringe of light hair round it. His kind eyes sparkled behind gold-framed spectacles and he wore a close-clipped beard. He was clad in good, dark Manx tweed and his head emerged from a wing collar held by a sober tie threaded through a gold ring.

"Well, sergeant, and what can I do for you?"

Knell, rather overwhelmed by his duties, introduced Littlejohn.

"Sit down, both of you..." Mr. Kerruish flipped open his gold hunter watch suspended from a large gold chain strong enough to hold a dog, and then snapped it shut again.

"I've just ten minutes before the board meeting..."

He was at everybody's beck and call, chasing here and there as fast as his short legs would carry him, respected, universally imposed upon, good natured, everybody's friend...

"The late Deemster and his wife banked here, I gather, sir?"

"Yes... A shocking blow. I confess a number of us wept openly when the news was broken..."

He took out a folded white handkerchief, shook it out, and trumpeted in it, as if to show he was ready to weep again if provoked.

"There was some trouble a few weeks ago about some spurious banknotes, I'm told."

"Yes... Mrs. Quantrell paid-in a forged note which was returned. It was handed to the police over here, and I believe they lent it back to the Deemster, who was interested. He also borrowed three other forged one pound notes on other banks and one on this bank. They'd all been handed to the police, who said he might take them..."

"Why? Was he interested in trying to bring the counterfeiters to justice?"

"He was interested in detection in an amateur way... The police were naturally glad to have the help of such an eminent authority on crime."

"Have you had many forged notes in the town of late?"

"About a hundred pounds' worth spread over the various banks, have appeared over the last month. As soon as the first one appeared at the Home Counties Bank, the manager there passed word round. We all started to watch our notes carefully and the result was we found quite a few were spurious..."

"They were obviously bad, were they?"

"Yes. The paper wasn't right, although the plates must have been done by an expert. It's rather easy to tell if the paper is wrong. One gets used to the feel of it..."

Mr. Kerruish rang the bell on his desk and Mr. Mylecraine arrived at once.

"Mr. Mylecraine... Please bring us a new genuine pound note of our own, and one of the fake ones you hold..."

The cashier soon returned with a magnifying glass as well.

"Feel that, Mr. Littlejohn... That's the real article..."

Mr. Kerruish passed over a pound note.

"Now this... That's one of the fakes..."

Littlejohn rubbed them both between his finger and thumb. "The dud one feels more like rag than your own. Probably there's more size in the paper..."

"Exactly... And notice, when I put the notes up to the light... The watermarks are almost alike, but they've missed the spurs from the heels of the Three Legs of Man... See...?"

Knell handled them a bit timidly, like an apprentice who hasn't yet got used to the job. Mr. Mylecraine smiled a superior smile at him.

"All part of the job, *Mister* Knell."

"Was it the same with the other banks, too?"

"More or less... yes. Of course, one or two might have slipped back in circulation before we were properly on our guard. In which case, we'll doubtless be seeing them home to roost."

Mr. Mylecraine departed to look after his customers and Mr. Kerruish showed signs of wanting to get to his board.

"Just another question or two, sir," said Littlejohn taking up his hat.

"How do you account for the fact that so few notes have been circulated, and that most of them have been detected?"

"The Deemster had a theory which he gave us when the local bankers met the police, who, at his request, asked His Honour to be present. Deemster Quantrell's idea was that whoever made the faked notes had been working against time to get them in circulation during the full holiday season. There would be thousands of strangers on the Island, money would pass from hand to hand more rapidly without coming back to the banks, and, finally, among the crowds, there were greater facilities for passing-off the bad notes..."

"Yes?"

"For some reason, there was delay. The holiday season was over before they got down to making the notes and putting them into circulation. Perhaps they hadn't got the right paper, perhaps the plate was delayed... Who knows? But they were too late. Their chance for this year had gone. The Deemster thought that next year, at high season, they might try to flood the Island with false notes again. The thought of it is a nightmare. I believe the police have no idea where to look. Of course, they might be making them on the mainland. During the winter, unless an arrest is made, the banks will need to have new plates and entirely new notes issued. That, of course, is strictly confidential. The new notes will suddenly appear, the old ones will be minutely examined, but even then... I shudder to think of it!"

Mr. Kerruish raised his hands and eyes to heaven as though praying to be spared such a calamity in the last year of his office, for he was due to retire in twelve months.

Knell looked distressed at the very thought of Mr. Kerruish's misery. The banker had taught him at Sunday School when he was a boy.

"We'll do our best, sir," he burst out, and then blushed.

"That's right." Littlejohn clapped him on the shoulder.

"Do you think the Deemster might have had some idea of who was at the bottom of this forgery racket, Mr. Kerruish?"

The banker looked startled.

"I've no idea... Oh! You don't mean he was murdered because... because..."

"It may be so... We'll have to find out."

"Oh, dear. Most disconcerting... Most..."

A buzzer at the manager's elbow rattled twice.

"Yes? Oh, dear... Coming..."

He gathered his papers in trembling hands.

"The board! The board! There'll be reference to the Deemster's untimely end... May I say you hope to make an early arrest, Inspector?"

"Yes..."

"I'm so glad. Well... Good-bye, and call again if I can help... Good-bye... good-bye..."

He let them out by a private door to the street.

Knell looked crestfallen.

"I'm sorry, sir, but I must be a bit slow. You said about making an early arrest... I'm only a beginner, and I don't know how it's done, yet. Will you...? "

Littlejohn affectionately took Knell's arm.

"I said we *hoped*, and we *do* hope, don't we?"

"And you haven't got your eye on the guilty party yet, sir?"

"I've not the faintest idea. But if Mr. Kerruish spreads that news among his board of prominent men, they'll tell their wives over dinner later, and the tale will be all over the Island to-morrow."

"Somebody will be disappointed when..."

"Somebody will be rattled, as well. One way of making progress is to get the guilty party to make a false move. There's more chance of that if he gets rattled. We'll see. And now, for Mr. Irons. Where's Duke Street, Knell?"

Knell piloted them across the street and down a narrow shopping thoroughfare. Between a tobacconist's and a fruit shop which advertised Manx kippers for export by post, stood a large double-fronted shop, with a mixture of good and bad jewellery and old silver in one window and porcelain and antique furniture in the other. There was little attempt at order. It looked as though the owner, having bought his stuff, dumped it in a vacant spot indoors and trusted the buyers to do the rest. A. IRONS, JEWELLERY AND ANTIQUES. They entered.

The shop was empty and they had to make their way through a mass of old tables, regency chairs, commodes and a Sheraton cabinet or two. Every available space, on furniture or elsewhere, was cluttered with china, tea-services, figures in Dresden and cheaper makes, gallipot lids, framed miniatures, lustre jugs, and, on the top of an old oak beer-table, a whole orchestra of monkeys in Dresden ware. There were cabinets of old silver, too, and flat counter cases, filled higgledy-piggledy with brooches, bracelets, ear-rings, signets, dressrings, all kinds of knick-knacks which tempt holidaymakers with money in their pockets and appetites like a lot of jackdaws after anything that glitters.

There was nobody guarding all the wealth of the shop. From a room in the rear, however, came the sounds of music on the radio. Elgar's *Enigma Variations*...

Knell stamped hard on the floor with his regulation boots. The music ceased suddenly and shuffling footsteps approached. Alexander Irons stood in the doorway. He was small and very fat. So fat that he had the look of leaning backwards. His legs were so swollen that he had to walk with them wide apart to prevent their rubbing together as he moved. He was either bald or his hair was clipped right down to the skin, his eyes were black like shoe buttons set in blue whites, his nose snub and broad, his lips fleshy with the bottom one hanging, his large ears lost in the flesh of his chaps, his three chins falling in tiers to his thick neck. He was in his shirt sleeves and wore an old cap. He seemed to have all worldly experience, sorrow and joy in his heavy, sad eyes. He was not fifty, but looked over seventy.

"Good morning, gentlemen. Fine day. Sorry I wasn't in the shop. I was listenin' to *Enigma Variations*. They remind me of men I know. I like to think of myself as Nimrod... Heavy, slow, distinguished..."

He laughed a throaty, wheezy laugh and his jowls shivered like jellies.

He's got a nerve, thought Littlejohn, and grew anxious to get it over and the Jew from Scotland out of his sight. Nimrod indeed! Irons spoke Scotch with a lisp. First impressions of him were always the worst. In the trade, his reputation was high. His name on the bills was a certificate of authenticity to buyers of antiques.

"I'm glad the season's finished. It's getting cold and raw here. Two weeks and I'm off to Nice..."

He knew Knell and he recognized the official in Littlejohn. Irons was waiting and killing time until they told him what they wanted.

"Morning, Mr. Irons..."

"Good morning, Mister Knell..."

"This is Inspector Littlejohn, of Scotland Yard. He's over on the Deemster Quantrell case."

"Glad to meet you, Inspector. Scotland Yard! This is an honour to the Island... An honour indeed. And the poor Deemster... a good man..."

He fixed his sad heavy-lidded eyes on Littlejohn.

"Did the Deemster call on you not long ago about a forged banknote you paid out to his wife for some furniture you bought from her, Mr. Irons?"

Mr. Irons sat down on an old oak bench with 1672 carved in a panel on the back.

"I'm no expert on banknotes, Inspector. Good ones or bad ones, they're all the same to me, sir. It's only the bank that finds 'em out. I said I'd pay back to Mrs. Quantrell when I got the bad one returned. And I will pay back when it comes. I can't do more than that, can I?"

"That's not just the point, Mr. Irons. I want to find out where you got the note from. Any ideas on the subject?"

The antique dealer shrugged his shoulders and raised the palms of his fat hands, their fingers spread like sausages.

"I've had a very busy season, Inspector... Very busy... Money comes and money goes. I've no idea. The Deemster called to ask the same question. I told him the same thing."

"This happened weeks ago. Haven't you given any more thought to it since Deemster Quantrell raised the point?"

"I have, my dear sir, I have... I've given a lot of time and thought. I can only say, in a general way, that a visitor paid me... I can't do more..."

"Please look up the date when you bought the furniture from Mrs. Quantrell."

With a sigh, the dealer rose and consulted a ledger which he kept in the drawer of a mahogany claw-legged table. He gave the date late in August.

"Did you sell much that week. Look in your book..."

"It might not be here..."

He started to run his finger down the pages. Littlejohn guessed that Income Tax might be the cause of certain omissions.

"It was a new note..."

"I know. The Deemster showed me."

"Well... Any ideas, sir?"

"I did no deals that week. It must have been over the counter... I was busy... I don't remember any more details..."

Littlejohn looked at the man. There was sweat on his upper lip.

"Very well, Mr. Irons. We'll leave it at that for the time being. If you should chance to think of anything, let us know at the police-station, will you? It's rather important. Whoever passed that note on you is probably connected with the murder of the Deemster..."

Irons' breath caught in a hiss and he made a choking noise.

"What is it, Mr. Irons?"

"Nothing, nothing. I didn't say anything... I'll think it over again... Good day, gentlemen..."

He slowly shambled back to his quarters.

"You'd better put a man on watching old Irons, Knell. He's not told us all he knows. And get a record kept of the calls he makes. Work fast... As likely as not, he'll contact someone... I'll get along and see Alcardi on the promenade about his friend, Lamprey. Meet me there, please, after you've fixed things..."

The promenade was thronged with visitors still wearing summer clothes, delighted by the unexpected hot sun in September. The tide was at the ebb and children and dogs were playing on the wet sands. Out at sea, a destroyer was lying at anchor and a small motor launch put off from her and made for the harbour. Flowers still bloomed in the formal gardens of the promenade and a show of dahlias was at its best. Charabanc touts were busy trying to collect passengers for an evening tour. The siren of the departing afternoon boat sounded and echoed over the town and was cast back by the hills beyond. The water of the vast lovely bay between Douglas Head and Onchan was like green glass. A small tramcar, like a large toast-rack and pulled by a well-fed horse, trundled slowly past...

Littlejohn lit his pipe and made for the arcade of shops in which Alcardi rented a small pitch. The bracing air and the jaunty style of passers-by made him feel in holiday mood himself. He felt like taking off his coat and throwing it over his arm like many others, but remembered he had on his braces. A hungry-looking youth in shabby flannels, seedy sports jacket and down-at-heel shoes, took his photograph and handed him a ticket. *Catch-U Studios. Snaps finished same day before seven...*

As he neared Alcardi's address, a little dark man, plump and going to seed physically, hurried from the arcade and made off in an old car parked on the promenade. The shop was closed when the Inspector reached it. In the letting next door, a woman told Littlejohn that Alcardi had just left.

"He must have passed you... His car was parked just opposite..."

The occupant of *The Chocolate Box* had little to do. It was nearing month-end and everybody had spent their sweet-ration coupons. She was middle-aged and plump with heavily powdered cheeks and dabs of rouge here and there. Peroxided hair and a lot of rings on her fingers and bangles on her wrists.

"Does he spend much time in the shop?"

The woman's prominent hungry eyes examined Littlejohn from head to foot. She couldn't quite make him out. Finally, she decided he was a Corporation official after the rent.

"I don't know how he makes a living. He's hardly ever in. About two hours a day... And look at the stuff he tries to sell!"

The small window was filled with holiday souvenirs, mainly of a bogus, arty-crafty kind. Homespun scarves, brooches made of gilt wire with the Legs of Man twisted in them, egg and tea spoons with the coat of arms of Douglas on their handles, plaques decorated with plaster fruit and country scenes in poor quality relief. A lot of cheap-jack, catch-penny stuff. Lying in the bottom of the window, two or three framed etchings of island scenes. These were decidedly better... Clean in line, well drawn, clearly processed. The work of someone who knew what he was doing. They were signed *Alcardi*.

The woman in the sweet shop obviously didn't like her neighbour.

"I don't know how he manages. Of course, these foreigners can live on next to nothin'. I wouldn't be surprised, though, if he didn't vanish on the midnight boat one of these days, owing a lot of money. I've known plenty like that..."

"He's Italian?"

"Yes. He was interned here in the war and stayed on. I suppose he thought it was an easy living. It's not good enough, lettin' all these foreigners come over fleecing visitors with their rubbish. Not that I see much bein' bought, I must say..."

"A bar of chocolate turkish delight..."

The woman regarded the small importunate child impatiently and her lips curled at the proffered ten-shilling note.

"Well, I never! Who gave you all that to spend?"

Littlejohn thanked her and withdrew. Her bangles jingled as she counted out the change...

On the promenade again, Littlejohn collided with Knell, almost running in search of him and full of news and zest.

"Irons rang-up Alcardi... They didn't know at the exchange what he said to him, because I hadn't had time to warn them, but that's what it was..."

He could hardly speak through hurry and excitement.

"Hullo, Reggie..."

A passer-by greeted the sergeant familiarly.

"Huhu..." He hadn't time to reply.

"Irons scared him out, Knell. He left in his car just as I was in sight. That direction..."

Littlejohn pointed to the left.

"Onchan. Any good following, sir?"

"I don't think so. Better warn the port and airport police all over the Island to keep an eye open for him. He may try to bolt. Detain him."

Knell couldn't get in a 'phone box fast enough; then he had to come out again because he had no change for the call. Eventually, he poured out his tale to headquarters. He was enjoying himself, like a sea-lion performing in a circus; vigorous, enthusiastic, full of zest, and pleased to do anything he was told.

"We'd better call on Mr. Irons again, now..."

The antique dealer was also shutting-up shop, but, unlike Alcardi, he had a lot of valuables to stow away. They found him palsiedly shovelling rings, watches, trinkets in a large safe, niggledy-piggledy.

"I'm not so well... I think I'll go right away to the South of France. The season's finished..."

He thought some explanation was due. His sad eyes ran over the features of Littlejohn and Knell alternately, trying to fathom why they were back.

"Why did you telephone Alcardi after we left you, Mr. Irons?"

Littlejohn removed his pipe and spoke in friendly tones, as if he might just be asking what part of the Riviera Irons was going to.

"Me? I never..."

"Come, come. The police know you did."

Irons tried to bluff it out. His voice rose and he cast up spray in his excitement.

"The line was tapped! That's illegal. I'll..."

"You'll answer my question. Well...?"

Irons looked round as if seeking a place to bolt to, and then shrugged his shoulders.

"Alcardi owes me money. Two hundred pounds. I want my money. I'm closing down and going to Nice. I want my affairs straight."

He smiled, hoping that would suffice.

"Very likely. But you also got at least a part of your debt paid by a dud note, didn't you? Why didn't you tell us the truth, Mr. Irons?"

"I swear I didn't..."

"Very well. You'd better come along with us to the police-station. You'll be charged with passing counterfeit notes."

Irons went right to pieces. It was evident he'd been under

considerable strain for some time. Now, he sat down heavily and tugged at his collar.

"Well...?"

Irons licked his lips.

"I did know. I admit it. Now are you satisfied?"

"No. Why didn't you tell us at once, instead of lying and then warning Alcardi. He's bolted as a result, and I hold you responsible. What did you tell him?"

A man and a girl were making for the shop door, evidently interested in something in the window. Littlejohn shot the bolt to keep them out. They made faces at him through the glass.

"Don't be hard on me, sir. My health's bad. My heart... I get all of a tucker. I didn't tell you, because... well..."

He burst forth like a torrent, weeping, waving his thick arms like windmills round his head. He sniffed back his tears.

"If a man owes you two hundred pounds and you get him put in jail, just for a phoney five pounds, where's your other one ninety-five coming from while he's doing time? I'm a poor man, sirs, and my health's bad. I gotta get to a warmer climate for the winter, or I'll die. I was only thinking of my other money."

"But why, having lied and got rid of us, did you ring up Alcardi right away?"

"I told him I wanted money, right now."

"How came he to owe you all that?"

"Furniture for his shop... a few souvenirs to sell..." He made gestures in the air.

"Is that all?"

Irons raised his eyes, still floating in tears, to Littlejohn's face.

"What else could it be?"

"Are you mixed up with this shady money racket?"

That raised another storm. Irons swore by all his gods, his father, his mother, his more remote ancestors, his own honour, by all the holy books he knew...

"That will do. If you've lied a second time, I'll soon know. Did you tell Alcardi the police were after him, or on the track of the false notes?"

"I just mentioned it in passing."

"You told him unless he paid what he owed you in good hard cash, you'd split on him, you mean..."

"I never. I said I knew him dishonest and wanted my money."

"So he bolted."

"With my money!"

"Whatever he bolted for or with, you sprang the trap, Mr. Irons. We'll see you later."

"I can go to Nice, now?"

He looked ready to start packing and be gone at the word.

"No. You're not to leave the Island until we say you can. My colleague here will make arrangements for you to be stopped at the ports if you try to get away. If you *do* try, you'll be charged as an accessory..."

"But I haven't done nothing. I'll die if I stay here in the cold..."

"You'll have to die, then, Mr. Irons."

"*And it isn't cold!*" Knell, eager to support Littlejohn, yelled it at Irons enthusiastically.

"Don't try to leave the Isle of Man, or you'll spend your holidays in jail."

They left him, dazedly stowing the porcelain monkeys' orchestra in a box. He was closing down, ready for the word *Go*.

Littlejohn and Knell made for the police-station. There was no recorded trace of any outward calls from Alcardi's shop. He'd been too cunning for that and must have bolted as soon as Irons warned him. They sent out an all-stations call to search for the Italian and then Knell drove Littlejohn back to Grenaby, where, in the quiet of the vicarage, he wanted to do some thinking, set his day's work in order, and chat with his host.

The Archdeacon was waiting for Littlejohn on the bridge and gossiping with his parishioners in the early evening sunshine. He waved at Littlejohn with eager joy.

"Back again! There's been a man after you, Inspector. About an hour ago. He drove up in an old car and was very put-out when I said you weren't home. I'd say he was a bit terrified..."

"Did he give any name, sir?"

"No; but I know him. Met him when I used to visit the camp in Douglas. An artist fellow, interned here. What's his name...? Italian. Let's see. Alberti? No... Alcardi; that's it. Alcardi..."

6

JIMMY SQUAREFOOT

I wouldn't go off in pursuit of the Italian, if I were you," said the Archdeacon. "He'll come back..."

The Rev. Caesar Kinrade seemed prophetically sure of Alcardi's return and Littlejohn, hungry, eager after a tiring day for the vicar's cosy study and his genial company, and assured that the Italian could not get off the Island, was inclined to agree.

"It might be like hunting for a needle in a haystack, too," added the parson. "He went off in the region of the Round Table. Now that's a spot for a wild-goose chase. Roads, old and new, all over the place. A wilderness where anyone might hide for weeks on end. Leave it till morning and then start fresh. Maggie Keggin's been cooking all the afternoon for your supper and grumbling, too, because you didn't say when you'd be back. Far better wait till to-morrow..."

"Aye. Far better wait..."

The endorsement came from a tall, wiry old man of uncertain age, with a heavy ragged moustache, a cloth cap with a wrinkled face beneath it, and deep-set grey eyes. He was in his shirt sleeves and wore a celluloid collar without a tie. A bright brass stud shone under his prominent Adam's apple. His name was Joe Henn.

Mr. Henn had retired to the Isle of Man twenty years ago from somewhere in Lancashire. He was more Manx than a Manxman and tried to make out to strangers that he was a native. He lived in a large tumbledown old house on the far side of the bridge.

"I'm sorry I didn't meet you when you was over before..."

Mr. Henn leaned his elbows on the top of the police car, so that Knell dared not start for fear of dragging him under the wheels, or projecting him flat on his face in the road.

"Heard about it all... pity I missed it. Man killed himself, didn't he? Proper bad lot, I believe. Well, well. Ain't offen we 'ave violence in these parts. Would say that Grenaby's a very peaceable spot. Peaceable as regards the yooman population, if you get what I mean. There's disturbances from the unseen world, at times, as the parson 'ere'll confirm..."

Mr. Kinrade shook his head, but said nothing. He wasn't going to be drawn into an argument and besides, he was anxious to be getting to his study for a report on Littlejohn's day.

"We'll have to be going..."

Mr. Henn dug his thin elbows more firmly than ever through the open window of the car.

"Of course, there's been a bit of excitement now and then. A woman once tried to drown herself in the river. A visitor, she was... a come-over. But there was only a foot of water runnin' at the time, so all she got was a bad cold. And two tinkers once had a fight on the bridge there and one stabbed the other in the arm with a potato knife. For the rest, it's a peaceful place, yoomanly speakin', that is."

Archdeacon Kinrade climbed in the back seat of the car to show he was ready for off, but Mr. Henn declined to take the hint.

"By night, of course, it's a bit different. *Things 'appen down 'ere*. Three streams meet just by the bridge. The Silverburn, the Awin Reash, and a bit of a river from Ballalonna. Wherever you get waters meetin', you get queer goin's-on. There's bin a yewge cat, a black 'un, with terrible big eyes haunted the field behind my 'ouse for as long as people remember and..."

Knell started the engine. It looked as if he was going to risk disaster to Mr. Joe Henn, who, however, ignored the hint.

"I'd like you to come an' see my garden, Inspector. I'll show you where the cat comes. An' besides, I've just built myself a wood hut, a summer-'ouse there, too. Come an' 'ave a look at me 'ut..."

"Is that the postman?" said Knell.

Mr. Henn turned inquisitively.

"Plenty of time, 'ere. Wot is it we say in Manx. . .? *Traa dy Liooar*... Time enough... Come and 'ave a look at me summer-'ouse..."

Whereat he removed his elbows from the car, the better to look for the imaginary postman. Knell and his passengers had reached the vicarage turning before Mr. Henn realized what had happened. He stood in the road, a gaunt scarecrow, pointing after them, like a wizard reciting a curse...

Knell left his party. He was anxious to press his advantage with Millie Teare. If the case went well, he hoped to be asking the vicar of St. Mark's, where Millie lived, to put up the banns for them before Christmas. On the way back, he took his hands from the wheel momentarily to rub them together in glee. He decided to risk going to St. Mark's in the police-car. After all, an extra hour wouldn't matter and a bit of swanking might improve his suit. He might even take Millie to the pictures in it...

The old housekeeper made them a substantial meal and after it, the parson and Littlejohn drew up to the log fire and talked. Here in the last light of day, in the cosy study, the fire dimly lighting the Hoggatt picture over the mantelpiece and shining on the well-polished furniture, it was difficult to believe there was a murderer at large and that Alcardi, scared and perhaps in fear for his life, was wandering somewhere on the central wasteland of the Island. Littlejohn and the vicar talked of the day's events. Mr. Kinrade was able to add little to the knowledge Littlejohn had gleaned. They dozed before the fire over some very nice port the vicar had unearthed and, after the Inspector had again telephoned to his wife in the Fens, they ate crackers and drank coffee and then retired early...

Littlejohn turned over in bed, which, with the feather mattress, was like a feat of swimming. The windows were wide open and the curtains of the four-poster rustled around his head. Had he really been asleep? he wondered. He ought to have known better than to drink three cups of Mrs. Keggin's excellent coffee last thing at night. It was always the same with coffee when he was keyed-up on a case...

He struck a match and looked at his watch. Two o'clock. He must have slept... and something must have wakened him. He listened. Absolute silence in the house. Outside, the trees rustled and, in the distance, he thought he could hear the water rushing, squeezing its way under Grenaby Bridge.

Littlejohn revolved the events of the day in his mind. In the dark and stimulated by overdoses of strong coffee, he saw the characters exaggerated.

Lamprey. He reminded you of a goat. He even sniffed about like one. The twitching nostrils and the receding sweep of forehead, whence you might imagine a pair of horns sprouting. What was Lamprey up to? No good, you could bet. His shifty, alcoholic eyes; the mean, greedy look. Like a goat... ready to devour all he came across.

And Irons, the rhinoceros... A great hulk of primitive beastliness. Where did he come in? Were he and Alcardi and Lamprey in league and had the mysterious Alcardi taken fright suddenly and decided to turn King's Evidence? Why had he sought out Littlejohn, if not for that? A coward, or perhaps a rogue with a streak of decency, who didn't mind with his skill, engraving a banknote plate or two, but who drew the line when it came to murder.

Who was the ringleader of the trio. . .? Or were they mere pawns in a game played by someone bigger?

Littlejohn turned from side to side.

He must have slept again, for when next he stirred, he was aware of dawn faintly showing through the windows and the grandfather clock in the hall striking four. He didn't feel very good. The port... The coffee...

Suddenly, his senses were broad awake. Someone was moving on the landing outside his door. Footsteps softly climbing the stairs, then past his room, and he heard another door softly creak and close. It must have been Mrs. Keggin, as the vicar's room was on the other side of Littlejohn's...

Then there was a commotion in the outbuildings at the side of the house. Someone sounded to be beating something. Or maybe it was a pony kicking its stall. He must ask the Archdeacon to-morrow if he still kept a pony and trap... Then, a crack, like a whip, or like a stick breaking. Or a revolver shot...

Oh, come, come, said Littlejohn to himself. This is Grenaby, not Soho... His mind was playing tricks. All the same, he got out of bed and looked through the window.

The first signs of day were showing over the rising ground behind the vicarage; a bright blush of diffused sunshine from over the sea beyond, and a keen draught of clean air, with the tang of seaweed and salt from as far away as the coast. The forlorn garden and the coach-house and stables were visible from where the Inspector was standing with his hands on the sill. They looked derelict and untenanted. He passed his hand through his hair. This wouldn't do... He couldn't be jumping out of bed all night and every night at every little sound. Things happened like that in the night in old places such as this, deep in the country. That scarecrow, Joe Henn, had said that at Grenaby *things happened in the night*... Large cats... Come an' 'ave a look at me 'ut... Littlejohn smiled, yawned and climbed back in bed. A cock crowed... Some-where in the distance in the garden a blackbird uttered a wild cry of alarm...

There was a scent of coffee again... the roasting of fresh beans, when he awoke. It reminded him of his boyhood. The old home often used to smell of coffee and it was his job to grind it at the mill when his mother had finished roasting it. He looked at his watch. Nearly seven o'clock. His wife would already be up and ready for off to Rugby by now. Last night, she had told him over the telephone that the furniture had arrived in the Fen, the beds were up for the family, and to-morrow she was going to Rugby to gather together the Canon's quiverful of children from up and down the parish they were leaving, where kindly folk had put them up for the night, in parties of one or two. She would take them all, like a circus, to their new home, where their again enceinte mother was already having hysterics at the size of the new vicarage. Dear Letty! He must write to her to-day, murder or no murder!

The noises in the night... He couldn't get them out of his mind. He knew he was expected to stay in bed until breakfast came to him, but he didn't feel like waiting. He slipped on his shirt and trousers, splashed water over his face and neck from the ewer, brushed his hair and put on his silk dressing-gown, with "T.L." embroidered on the pocket, which his wife had bought him last Christmas, with a scarf to match, which he knotted round his throat.

Maggie Keggin was in the large old kitchen, sitting before a crackling newly-lit fire, a coffee-mill between her knees, turning the handle. She glanced up with a start as he entered. She looked to have been weeping...

"Good morning, Mrs. Keggin... How are you?"

"Middlin'."

She had lost her brightness, and her lips were tight and turned down bitterly and stubbornly at the corners. Perhaps she objected to Littlejohn's appearance in the kitchen. She blew her nose and wiped her eyes.

"I've got a bit of a cold..."

She gave him a sidelong glance to see if she believed her.

"Sleep well, sir?"

She was expecting something.

"Did you hear anybody up in the house in the night, Mrs. Keggin? I hope nobody was ill..."

"Why should they be? I'm sorry you haven't slept proper. Was your bed not comfortable?"

"Who was up and about, Mrs. Keggin?"

Littlejohn's voice had lost its joviality. He knew Maggie was hiding something.

"It was me... I got up... To close a window that was bangin'."

Her eyes met his in challenge.

"I thought they were all sash windows here; the kind that don't swing in the wind."

"It was a door... The pantry door..."

She put more beans in the mill and started to grind them. The coffee crunched. Littlejohn felt he wanted the sensation again...

"Give me that mill, Maggie. Let me have a try."

He took it between his knees and started to turn.

"The noise I heard was outside... In the old stables, I think. Is there a pony there?"

She looked scared and wrung her old tired hands.

"No... No pony. I heard nothin' there. It was a door. That's what you heard."

"Could it have been one of those funny things that happen in Grenaby at night?"

He had recovered his good humour again. He pulled out the little drawer from the mill and emptied the fine-smelling, ground coffee into the caddy Maggie kept for the purpose.

She was looking at him sternly.

"Don't joke about it. It's true. Grenaby's a queer place and queer things go on here. This house is safe because a saint lives in it, but outside... some nights... I wouldn't stir out. Jimmy Squarefoot's around. That's who was out last night in the garden. Jimmy Squarefoot..."

"Whoever's Jimmy Squarefoot?"

He laughed outright. The name was a joke in itself.

"A man with a pig's head. The *Purr Mooar*, the old folks called him... the great boar. Terrible destructive, he is..."

She had lapsed into Manx brogue in her excitement.

"You needn't believe me, if you don't want. But he was round last night. I've heard him before, and people in the village has been follahed by him. Last night he was right at the door here. Sniffin' and snortin' to get in. I got up to put the bolt on. Perhaps you heard us talkin'? 'Let me in,' he says. 'It's not safe out here.' I said a little prayer to give me strength, and put another bolt on the door..."

"Did he go to the stables, then?"

"I heard him snortin' and shoutin' as he made off. Next, I heard him in the stables. And bang, and he's gone and it's all quiet again..."

"Maggie!"

They both turned. They hadn't, in their excitement, heard the Archdeacon arrive. He was standing at the kitchen door, fully dressed, gaiters and all.

"Maggie! Has Kenneth been here again?"

She started to sob and her thin, sturdy frame shook violently. Tears streamed down her cheeks.

"Come here..."

The parson's voice was quiet and stern. She walked to where he stood like an obedient child. He took her face between his hands and looked sadly in it.

"You know what I said would happen if he came here again..."

She sobbed more loudly.

"Just one more chance, parson, please... *please*. He's not a bad lad. Only a bit wild. If you send for the police, it'll make a criminal of him proper, besides makin' me not able to hold up my head any more."

"Very well. The Inspector is the police. You can make a clean breast of it all to him. And remember this..."

His voice was like thunder.

"...Remember this; the Inspector is our guest, and whilst he's under this roof he'll be told the whole truth and nothing but the truth. I will not allow you to tell him lies. Now... tell him the truth... And you can make us a cup of coffee while you're doing it."

"But it's true about Jimmy Squarefoot, parson. You know it's true..."

"I don't care a hoot about Jimmy Squarefoot, false or true. That's an old wives' tale... Now, tell the Inspector."

She bent her head over the coffee-pot and talked between her sobs and sighs.

"My grandson Kenneth came back to the Island from over in the Spring. He was always wild... He got in bad company. It was the war did it. I think he was runnin' away from somethin' he'd done."

"Go on, Maggie. The Inspector's listening."

"He came here when the parson was out and asked me for his fare back to the mainland. I gave it to him..."

"And since then, he's been back for several more fares, hasn't he? And he's not yet bought himself a boat ticket. Last time he called, I happened to be around and I gave him his fare. I also said if I ever caught him around again, I'd turn him over to the police for vagrancy. I don't mind charity, but I will not have a dear old friend of mine blackmailed and terrorized by a young good-for-nothing at a time in her life when she ought to be enjoying her peace."

"He didn't mean anything wrong, sir. He swore on his oath he'd get the mornin' boat..."

"He did that last time. You'd have thought to hear him, that butter wouldn't melt in his mouth. He's a young scoundrel."

"That he isn't, parson, and don't you be saying it. The war did it to him."

"I won't argue any more with you, Maggie. I'm ashamed. I heard you down in the night at the door, and you gave the Inspector a very disturbed sleep by it when he wants all his wits about him to capture the Deemster's murderer."

She handed round the coffee cups and sniffed, eyeing her master timidly, waiting for the verdict.

Littlejohn sipped the hot, invigorating brew.

"Were you awake during all the disturbances, sir?"

"No... I heard Maggie close her door. I knew she'd been up and what she'd been up for... I fell asleep again, having made up my mind to take it up in the morning. Then I heard you getting up, so I got up as well. What shall we do with this foolish, kindly woman?"

Littlejohn smiled over his cup.

"Let's hope Kenneth gets the boat and bothers her no more. He seems to have slept in the stables, or something, though. There was a lot of noise from that direction in the night."

Maggie turned sharply from the stove where she had started to cook bacon.

"He wasn't over there at all. He went straight for the road. It was after that the noise was in the stables. It must have been the rats upset something. But, I'm very much obliged, Inspector, to you for takin' my part. I'm sure Kenneth will be good in the future. He promised this time, and I know he'll keep it."

Parson Kinrade had been thinking.

"Better get your boots on, Inspector. We'll go and see what's been on in the stables, whilst breakfast's preparing. The grass is too wet for those light travelling slippers. Get your boots on..."

Littlejohn went upstairs and simply changed his slippers for his shoes. Then he joined the vicar and they crossed the rough grass under the old apple trees. A rabbit bounded from under their feet, and a sandy Manx cat with no tail, which had been stalking it, turned in disgust and strolled to the kitchen.

The buildings were dilapidated, but kept in tidy condition for storing garden produce and holding tools and barrows. A magpie flew from perching on the half-open door of the coach-house.

"The bird of ill omen," muttered the parson.

"Like Jimmy Squarefoot, sir?"

"Get along with ye..."

The stables were festooned with cobwebs and the empty stalls held an assortment of implements and garden tackle. Fruit nets, cans of fruit wash, bean poles... Some of the tiles had fallen from the roof and you could see daylight through the holes. An old, rotting horse-collar hung from a peg...

"Nothing here, Inspector..."

They passed to the coach-house, next door. It held sacks of potatoes and fertilizer... Sprawling face downwards, his fingers gripping the cobblestones of the floor, was the body of a man. They knew he was dead before they touched him. His skull had been smashed by a savage blow from behind.

The parson and the Inspector both gasped, but said nothing else. Littlejohn kneeled and examined the body.

"Dead!"

The parson folded his hands before him and sank his beard on his chest.

"Oh, dear! It's the man who called to ask for you last night, Inspector."

"Alcardi? Yes... That's right."

"He must have been terribly afraid of this happening, and came here for your protection... And he found you weren't here, so he fled into the wilderness. Why did he come back, I wonder?"

"I don't know, sir. But there's one thing we must do at once..."

Littlejohn looked at his wrist watch. Eight-thirty.

"We must stop Kenneth from leaving by the morning boat, sir. I don't say he did this, but he was here about the time I heard the noise going on..."

He turned over Alcardi's body. Beneath it lay a small automatic. Littlejohn picked it up in his handkerchief, sniffed at it, and opened the magazine.

"One shot fired. That's what I heard. Alcardi must have tried to protect himself, perhaps missed, and had no time to fire again..."

"This will be an awful blow to Mrs. Keggin, poor woman. The telephone's in the hall, Inspector. Ask for Constable Crellin. He knows young Kenneth Fannin... that's Maggie's grandson... and he'll be able to pick him up on the boat without any fuss. That is, if Kenneth's on it."

Kenneth was aboard the nine o'clock boat for Liverpool. Those already there hardly noticed anything unusual. A plain-clothes man quietly crossed the gangway, looked around, approached an unruly young fellow like a sailor, and asked him to accompany him back to Douglas police station. Fannin made no fuss. They drove him straight down to Grenaby on Littlejohn's instructions, but that did not end the morning's excitement.

A farmer taking his cows to pasture on the country road just above Grenaby, found an empty police-car parked through a gateway off the highway. He reported this to the vicarage at once. It proved to be the car Knell had been using with Littlejohn, and the police from Castletown were sent for to make a search for the missing detective, whose mother told them he hadn't been home all night. Millie Teare, whom they contacted at the village school where she was a teacher, indignantly told them that Mr. Knell was of no interest whatever to her. He had, she said, on the previous evening, taken her to the pictures in Douglas and, just before the show ended, with a brief "Excuse me", had completely disappeared, leaving her to find her way home as best she could and alone, which entailed a four-mile walk up hill all the way from the bus stop at Ballasalla. Her voice changed, however, when she heard Knell was missing. The children in her class were surprised when she burst into tears in the middle of a lesson in vulgar fractions...

They found Knell not far from where Alcardi had fallen, but

the sergeant had been more fortunate. The blow, a glancing one, had simply put him to sleep, and he suddenly appeared before the amazed search party, his face stung all over by the nettles in which he had fallen behind the stables, and a lump on his head like an egg. He was rambling in his speech. "I'll soon be back, Millie," he said. He was rushed to hospital in Douglas where, later, he awoke to find Miss Teare at his bedside, with a large bunch of flowers.

"I won't be long away, Millie," he said. "Millie, my girl... Millie, *my chree*..." And Millie bent and kissed him.

That afternoon, to the horror of the nurses, Knell got up, dressed himself, and deaf to all protests, walked unsteadily from the hospital by the front door.

"I've seen it done regularly on the movies, but never in real life before," said the sister.

After calling at the vicarage at St. Mark's on a small matter of banns, Knell set out to find Littlejohn, to whom he was determined to report for further duty.

"Solve it, or bust," he was heard to say by the kindly constable, who, although off duty, had volunteered to drive him all over the Island, if needs be, in search of the Inspector and the investigation into Deemster Quantrell's death.

7

THE ESCAPADES OF DETECTIVE
KNELL

K enneth Fannin was annoyed with his grandmother when he arrived with his escort at Grenaby vicarage.

"So ye set the police on me, after all... Well, it'll be a comfort to ye to have a grandson who's a jailbird..."

Mrs. Keggin thereupon burst into tears, threw her apron over her head, and stumbled from the room.

"How dare you, Kenneth Fannin, abuse your grandmother in my house, you wicked lad? Speak civil and behave..."

"I haven't done no wrong, parson. All I did was to call and ask the old lady to help me with my passage to Liverpool, where I've got a job offered me on a boat for South America."

Fannin was tall, strongly built, curly haired, and had a tanned square face. He was clean, but needed a shave, and wore a sailor's rig-out, blue jersey and bell-bottomed serge trousers. He carried a cloth cap and a battered fibre suitcase.

The study at the vicarage seemed to have become police head-quarters. A constable guarded the door, the parson sat by the fire, stroking his silver spade-beard nervously, and Littlejohn sat astride a chair at the desk.

"Sit down..."

Fannin started and looked at the Inspector. He'd expected rough handling, now he felt easier. He swaggered to a spare chair and sat down with his legs apart.

"Not that one; this near me, and put down your case and cap..."

"What were you doing round here again last night?"

"I came to ask herself for the fare to Liverpool. I said so..."

"What were you doing at four o'clock? You didn't expect to find your grandmother up and about at that hour, did you?"

"I had to walk from Douglas..."

"It was foolish of you to think of burgling the place, Fannin. That's what you were after, wasn't it? You couldn't have got away from the Island in time..."

Fannin looked truculent. He hadn't been caught red-handed and thought he was safe.

"I never..."

"Don't deny it. Why, if you were honestly seeking help, didn't you ring the door-bell, instead of trying to force open the kitchen window?"

"I swear I never..."

"Don't perjure yourself. Come here..."

Littlejohn led Fannin to the kitchen and out by the door. The housekeeper, still sobbing, sat limp in an armchair, unheeding.

"That's a fresh scar from a small crowbar... a jemmy, isn't it?"

Littlejohn pointed to the joining of the two sashes and the parson who had followed, put on his spectacles and carefully examined the place.

"I saw that when I got up this morning. I heard you in the night. You only stopped when your grandmother came down and bought you off with her savings, didn't you?"

Fannin stood mute and sulky.

"Didn't you?"

Littlejohn gripped Fannin's jersey over the chest and shook him. Fannin's eyes opened wide at the strength of the shock.

"I didn't get in. You've not got anythin' against me. I only wanted to get to the old woman and wake her without rousin' the house..."

"Unless you change your tune and help us, you'll be charged with house-breaking, so you'd better make up your mind, Fannin."

"What do you want?"

"How much did Mrs. Keggin give you?"

"Five pounds..."

"Give me your wallet..."

Sulkily Fannin produced a purse from his trousers pocket. Littlejohn opened it. It held fifteen pounds and some change.

"Take it back to Mrs. Keggin and give her all the notes... Go on... Do as I tell you..."

The procession wound its way back to the kitchen and Fannin put the notes in his grandmother's lap without a word. She looked up at him, laid her hand on the money, but did not speak, and the trio passed on to the study again.

"You know there was a murder committed in the garden at the time you were prowling round here last night?"

Fannin's mouth opened and all his control left him.

"I know nothin' about a murder. I didn't do it. I didn't touch anybody... I swear on the Bible I didn't..."

"Keep the Bible out of this, Fannin, and behave like a man instead of a hysterical female," shouted the parson in his face. The old man was almost beside himself with dismay at the old woman's distress and his own disappointment with Kenneth Fannin.

"You walked from Douglas and got here about four. What time did you leave Douglas?"

"Midnight, about..."

"What were you doing until so late?"

"I went for a drink..."

"Where?"

"*The Eagle and Child* on the quay. The landlord'll tell ye I left just about eleven. I wandered about the town a bit after..."

"It didn't take you four hours to get here, did it?"

"I had a sleep in a field at Kewaigue. I didn't know what time it was when I woke and I didn't know what time I got here, till my grandma told me when she came out. I wasn't clear in me wits after the drink I'd took..."

"You came intending to break in, else why bring a jemmy with you?"

"Only to wake the old woman..."

"Where's the jemmy?"

"It wasn't a proper jemmy. It was a spike I pulled off the top of some iron railings in Ballabeg... I can show you..."

"You needn't bother. We found it in the garden. Lucky for you there's no trace of its being used to brain the poor fellow who's now lying in Castletown mortuary..."

Littlejohn slowly filled his pipe and lit it.

"Did you see or hear anything about here last night when you arrived, Fannin?"

"No..."

"Sure?"

Fannin hesitated.

"No."

"Very well. Constable, take him to the police-station and charge him with suspected murder..."

The parson's eyes opened wide and so did the constable's. Surely, Littlejohn hadn't solved it all already!

Fannin, however, broke down. He shouted and sobbed and begged for mercy.

"I didn't intend to kill him. He scared me. Jumped on me as I crept out of the gate. I hit him with my... my..."

"Your what?"

"My cosh. I had it in my pocket. I dropped it overboard on the boat before they took me."

"Who did you hit? Did you see him?"

86

"A copper. At least, I couldn't see his face, but I saw his car. I could just read POLICE on the sign."

"Where was this?"

"At the gate... Just round the corner."

"The police-car was parked up the road. How did you see that?"

"I passed it on the way out. So I knew I'd hit a copper. That was why I took the boat this mornin' and knew why they came for me."

Littlejohn stood at the window.

"Show me where you met him. Point it out..."

With a dirty forefinger Fannin indicated the spot through the window.

"And what did you do with the body?"

"I was in a panic. He was out cold. I carried it behind the stables and hid it in the bushes."

"The nettle bed, you mean. We found him there."

The vicar looked sharply at Littlejohn.

"Anything more to say, Fannin? Did you see or hear anything else?"

"As I ran up the road, past the car, I heard what sounded like a shot. I thought the copper had come round and was potting at me. Then I went on and dropped into Colby. I walked till the first bus picked me up."

"You heard nothing going on in the garden or the outbuildings when you were trying to get in the vicarage?"

"I thought I heard a horse or something in the stables, but I wasn't scared by that."

"There wasn't any horse there. Lucky you didn't try to steal that as well, otherwise you might not be here to tell the tale. A man was murdered there last night. The constable you laid out has recovered, but is still in hospital. You'll now be taken and charged with violence to an officer, resisting arrest, and house-

87

breaking, and that will keep you occupied for some time. Take him off, constable..."

"And I didn't kill anybody?"

"By good luck, you just missed doing. But don't congratulate yourself. By the way, what have you been doing whilst you've been over here sponging on your grandmother?"

"Nothin' much."

"Well, if you decide to tell us some more, just let the constable know. You'll be our guest for quite a time... All right. Away with him."

The Archdeacon sagged into a chair.

"This is beyond me," he said wearily. "The place must have been alive with people last night and I seem to have slept through most of it. Do you believe that rascal?"

"We'd better hear what Knell has to say when he's fit to talk."

Outside a party of policemen were approaching the vicarage. They had been searching the grounds for clues and had found nothing. The footprints were confused and defaced around the stables and nettle bed and were no use at all. Two other men, knowing that Alcardi had been using an old car and had most likely arrived at Grenaby in it on his last journey, had been hunting for it. They had found it and had called to report.

"We've found the car, Inspector..."

The constable was a heavy, beefy man with a Manx brogue.

"Yes?"

"It was in Joe Henn's summer-house."

Littlejohn could have laughed outright! In the dead of night, somebody had violated Mr. Henn's 'ut, by driving a car into it!

"However came it to be there?"

The constable, red from his efforts, inserted his finger between his helmet and his brow, whereat a trickle of sweat ran down his face and off the tip of his wide chin. He puffed and blew.

"Mr. Henn's making a path past his summer-house into the garden. It's a wide sort of gravelled drive and he's not got a gate for it yet, so it's open to the road, sir. The car must have been driven down it to hide it..."

"In other words, Alcardi may have been followed and was seeking a turn off the road. I wonder if he was running without lights. Was it clear enough for him to see without them?"

"Oh, yes. It was clear and starry with the full moon showin' early in the morning," said the bobby, like an amateur astronomer.

"Then, he must have been chased. I wish we could get hold of Knell and hear his tale... Has anybody inquired about him lately?"

The constable shook his head.

"Not since about ten, sir. He was then said to be sleeping peaceably."

"I'll ring now," said the vicar and went out to the telephone. He was back in two minutes.

"He's got up and walked out," he said. "And this is the last straw. Only forty-eight hours ago, I was getting myself ready to go to Douglas, planning in my mind how to give you a quiet, healthy holiday. Since when..."

He raised his hand and ticked off the fingers.

"Three murders, a policeman laid-out, attempted burglary at my home, a badly damaged detective rises from his bed and walks out of the hospital, and someone violates our friend Henn's pride and joy, his hut, in the dead of night, by driving of all things, a motor-car into it..."

He shook his head.

"I've often wished to take part in a criminal investigation, and when I made a good friend of a famous detective, I was overjoyed. Henceforth, I shall be content with the simple things of life, instead of unleashing every form of crime by my meddling."

"Don't take it hard, sir. These things never seem to come singly. And now, to crown the lot, I see Sergeant Knell, who has arrived in a police car, walking up the drive under his own steam..."

As Knell passed through the gate, he paused, turned to the spot where Kenneth Fannin had laid him out, nodded as though satisfied with the recollection, and strode to the front door, where he loudly rang the bell.

"The tap on the head seems to have made Knell unusually aggressive," said the Archdeacon.

Knell looked a bit pale and dazed, but grimly determined to stick it out.

"I'm glad to see you about, Reggie," said the Archdeacon, and Littlejohn said that went for them all.

"I'm sorry to let you down, sir," replied the sergeant. "But I seemed to be watching two parties at once and only one of them visible. The invisible one knocked me out and the next I knew, I was coming-to in the nettle bed. Then, things went blank again, and when I woke up, I was just getting engaged to Millie Teare..."

The constable standing at the door of the study raised his eyes to heaven. So, Knell was starting rambling again, like he was when they found him earlier in the day! It took the young detective quite a time to convince Littlejohn and the parson, and receive their congratulations. He was shy and confused and his feelings were in a turmoil...

"And what happened last night, Knell? Sit down."

Knell took a seat near the door, like one ready to be off at any moment, his hat on his knee.

"When I left here in the car, sir, I thought I might just go and see my young lady before I put it away. She lives at St. Mark's and it's a bit of a stretch from the 'buses. When I got there, she said she'd like to go to Douglas to the pictures. I couldn't very well say no, sir. So, I ahem... borrowed the car again, intending to take her home after the show and then garage it at Castletown..."

Knell stammered and twisted his hat in his hands.

"Put your hat down, Reggie, and stop fiddling. Get on with your tale..."

The parson was getting impatient.

"It was the last round of the films when we got there... about half-past eight. It was dark, sir, and they'd already started. Then, just before the main feature film, the lights went on so that the girls could go round selling ice-cream. I happened to look behind and who did I see but Alcardi..."

"The Italian?"

"Yes, your reverence; after he called here to see the Inspector, he must have driven back to Douglas instead of over the mountain, and hidden in the dark in the pictures. It was just a bit of luck I saw him. Millie... ahem, my young lady... my fiancée... saw a girl she knew from her own village and was showing her to me... She was out courting with a fellah on the quiet, you see..."

"Get on with it, Reggie. Never mind affairs of heart, now..."

"I'm coming to it, your reverence. I saw this chap on the back row in the darkest spot. He'd his hat over his eyes and his raincoat collar turned up, but I knew him, though I didn't let on I'd recognized him. After that, I kept an eye on him till the end of the show... or nearly the end."

He picked up his hat again and started to knead it with his fingers. It was plain that the emotional part of the story was arriving.

"I was in a bit of a fix, sir. I'd my fiancée on my hands, though at the time, she wasn't engaged to me, if you understand..."

The parson raised his hands in a gesture of resignation.

"When all this is over, Reggie, come to me one or two nights a week, boy, and I'll teach you to express yourself in clear and concise language. It'll do you a lot of good..."

Outside, Joe Henn had appeared and was trying to get through the vicarage gate, from which a constabulary sentinel was struggling to prevent him. Henn was wild-eyed and dishevelled at the violation of his summer-house. They could hear him shouting from where they were, indoors.

"Somebody's parked a car in me 'ut and there's bobbies all over the place. Have *they* put it in, because I'm goin' to make a case out of this. It's shameful. Where's the Inspector. Get that car out of the 'ut..."

The sentinel talked quietly to him, they gesticulated at one another, Henn waved his arms angrily about and ran away, presumably to find some higher authority.

"I said to Miss Teare, 'Excuse me, a minute,' I said. And with that I followed Alcardi, who was leaving before the lights went on again. His car was in the car-park and he went straight to it. My car... the police car, I mean, was there, too, and you can imagine the fix I was in when Alcardi drove off right away. I'd got to follow him, hadn't I? And no way of letting Millie know. There she was, stranded, and might let the last 'bus to Ballasalla go without her. Luckily, she's a girl with some sense, and she caught it without the risk of my not turning up..."

"She'll make an excellent policeman's wife, Reggie. And now get on with Alcardi..."

Knell glanced reproachfully at his tormentor, and the parson waved his hand to speed him on.

"He gave me a rare run for my money. Good job there was plenty of petrol in the tank. We went nearly three times round the Island. He seemed to have gone mad."

Littlejohn removed his pipe.

"He must have been terribly scared of something or someone. First, he called here after Irons warned him. That was presumably to tell me something and obtain police protection. Finding me out, why didn't he go to the police-station, instead of going and hiding in the cinema? After the chase, he came here, even in the small hours, presumably after me, and whoever he feared killed him..."

"But why, as you say, Littlejohn, all this chasing about?"

"I think I have it, parson. He was afraid to go near the official police-stations because he was scared to death that his enemy was on the look-out for him. He came here, therefore, found out I wasn't in, and perhaps decided to hang about and try again..."

Knell indicated that he wished to speak.

"When I left here last night with the car, sir, I came across a car parked in the quiet spot just past Joe Henn's house. I slowed up and the car started off like a shot and tore ahead of me all the way to Ballasalla. I didn't suspect anything at the time..."

He didn't add that his thoughts were entirely on Millie Teare!

"...And when we got to the cross roads, I went on to St. Mark's, and the other car took the Douglas fork. There were a few of us about the cross roads at the time and perhaps if one of the other cars behind followed what we think was Alcardi's car, the Italian thought he was being still chased. At any rate, he ended up hiding in the picture-house..."

"And during this three times round the Island marathon, did Alcardi call anywhere?"

"Yes, sir. He made three calls. Two in Ramsey and one at the airport at Ronaldsway."

"Trying to get off the Island, Knell?"

"Looked like it, sir. The Ramsey calls were, one at a public-house on the quayside, and the other a ship tied up by the custom-house."

"Just a minute, Knell. This round the Island-trip... Did you follow on his heels?"

"Yes, sir. I put my lights out most of the time. There wasn't much about at that hour. He seemed scared to stop. He must have driven on and on, thinking things out and trying one way and another until in desperation, he decided to come back to Grenaby."

"Did you get the impression that someone else was following you and Alcardi, Knell?"

"No, sir. But I'm just beginning to wonder if perhaps some-body had scouts out, looking for Alcardi, and one was posted here at Grenaby, and killed him when he arrived."

"That's passed through my mind. Kenneth Fannin might have

been one of them and when Alcardi fired at him, just brained him, like he tried to do you, Knell."

"You've got the man who hit me, sir?"

"Yes. Unhappily, it's Mrs. Keggin's no-good grandson... He tried to make out he was seeking his grandmother, but we later got his confession to attempted house-breaking. Now, it might be murder."

"God forbid!"

"When Alcardi finally made for here, sir, I followed him rather quietly, knowing where he was making for and letting him have a bit of rope. Suddenly, he vanished in thin air. His lights went off and I couldn't hear his engine or anything..."

"That's right. He side-stepped and hid his car in Mr. Henn's summer-house."

"Did he, now, sir? I took the car up the road, parked it in a gateway and came down here to see where he was. As I came through the garden gate, somebody hit me on the head and I don't recollect another thing till I found myself in the nettle-bed."

"About this night-ride of yours. What route did Alcardi take?"

"Along Douglas promenade and then along the coast road all the way to Ramsey. From there over the mountain road to Douglas and the airport. Then he came to Ramsey again and through Ballaugh and Cronk-y-Voddy to Foxdale and Grenaby."

"And the calls at Ramsey?"

"There was a boat tied-up there. I got the name. The *Jonee Ghorrym*..."

"I know it," interrupted the vicar. "A Ramsey boat. The name, which is Manx, means Blue Judith, the sea-name for mermaid..."

"Alcardi pulled-up on the quay and went aboard. The man on watch and him had words. They got a bit excited. Especially the sailor, who told Alcardi to take himself off. Which Alcardi did... Then, he went to *The Duck's Nest* on the quayside. It's a licensed restaurant and is run by a Frenchman. It does very well with meals in the season and I hear it's a very popular meeting-place among the better-class people and the English residents round Ramsey. Sort of club, it's become."

"And what did Alcardi do there?"

"He knocked at the door and somebody came. He seemed to be asking them to let him in. There was a lot more arguing and then, the man at the door gave Alcardi a push in the chest that nearly sent him flying, and slammed the door. Alcardi ran back to his car and went back to Douglas over the mountain road. As I said, he went to the airport after that."

"Was there anybody at the airport?"

"The control tower was lit up, but the offices were closed. Alcardi then got in the car and back to Douglas and Ramsey again. He tried the boat and *The Duck's Nest* a second time and got the same answers. The last time in Douglas, he went along the harbour. He seemed to be trying to get a ship, but there was only a Dutchman on the old quay and one of the *Ben* boats coasting with coal, and he had no luck there."

"It's obvious he was trying to get off the Island and daren't go on the Steam Packet boat for some reason. Was he afraid of the police, or of someone else? At times, he seems to have got so beside himself that he was prepared to come to me and make some kind of confession... Anything more to report about your night's escapade, Knell? Did you see anybody prowling round here before they knocked you out?"

"No, sir..."

"We have one or two other leads, now. There's the boat at Ramsey and *The Duck's Nest*. And now we can ask Fannin a few more questions about his night's work."

"Did you find the weapon he used on me, sir?"

"He said it was a cosh and he flung it overboard before the police picked him up on the boat."

The telephone interrupted them. It was the Castletown police.

A roadman on the way to repair the surface between Grenaby and Ballabeg on the Castletown road, had come across a police

car parked on the roadside and, on looking inside, discovered a
constable apparently asleep. On investigation, the man was found
to be unconscious from a blow on the head. His hands had been
handcuffed together. It was the officer who had been sent to put
Kenneth Fannin in the cells at Castletown jail. Fannin had been
handcuffed then. He could not have escaped without help and it
seemed that some accomplices had stopped the police car and
freed him. It began to look as if Deemster Quantrell had somehow
fallen upon a well-led gang carrying-on some racket or other, and
had died because of it. And there seemed to be watchers everywhere seeing to it, by death and violence, that none of their party
betrayed its purpose or its head.

8

THE DUCK'S NEST

When the police turned out Alcardi's pockets, they found them empty save for a dirty handkerchief, a packet of cigarettes, matches, and some small change. At the shop he rented in the arcade at Douglas, they discovered little more of use in the case. There seemed to be nothing personal at all, no letters, no money, not even bills. Not a thing, except a dead mouse.

The shop consisted of a single room with a chair, a counter, shelves partly filled with souvenirs for sale. A cheap curtain divided the place, leaving a small private space behind, which Alcardi seemed to have used for a workshop. A bench with a number of etching tools, a press, some bottles of acid, resin, grease, and printer's ink... In the drawers, some new etching-plates and some finished ones of the pictures sold in the shop. There was a new telephone on the sill of a small window which badly needing cleaning. Littlejohn rubbed the glass and gloomily looked out over the untidy back quarters of boarding-house property; in the yard of one a man was peeling a pile of potatoes; next-door a woman was pegging blankets on a line to dry.

Finally, a gas-ring and an enamel wash-stand without water laid on. Beneath the stand, a tin water jug and a little reservoir which received the dirty water from the plug-hole of the wash-basin.

"Funny thing," said Littlejohn. "A telephone, gas laid on, electric light... every convenience in a small space, except running water..."

"That's an easy one, sir," said Knell. "This was once a part of next door, but they've divided it in two. The water's in the sweet shop and they're just divided by a sort of plasterboard partition. I remember seeing them on the job in Spring..."

He rapped the partition with his knuckles just to show that it was flimsy. Somebody started to knock back from the other side...

In one corner, a pile of rubbish, mainly old paper and cardboard. Nearby, a small enamel bin which had once been white but now was rusty round the edges. A pedal raised the badly-fitting lid when you pressed it. Littlejohn tried it with his foot and the lid rose to reveal the receptacle cram-jam full of refuse, mainly paper, cigarette packets, bits of string and scraps of food which might have been the leavings of a packet of sandwiches after somebody's lunch. It was so full that the lid wouldn't shut. On top of the lot lay a dried-up crust of bread and, framed in it, a dead mouse.

Littlejohn eyed the dead animal. It was cold and stiff and looked as though death had come upon it in the middle of a meal.

"Better have the contents turned over and the mouse and the food examined by the analyst... just in case..." he said to Knell. Knell passed on the orders. The constable who carried the bin gingerly to the car outside looked aggrieved.

"Wot next?" he said to the driver, who made clicking noises against his teeth with his tongue.

Littlejohn stood gazing at the telephone, with Knell by his side, waiting for some weighty deduction. The young detective's face had grown long again. He had expected Littlejohn to start on this mine of Alcardi information with a magnifying glass. Knell was a bit at a loss about the whole business. He kept looking in his diary, the title of which, in letters of gold, caught Littlejohn's eye and made him smile to himself. *Policeman's Annual Diary and Guide*. At the front, it contained notes about what to do; a little *vade-mecum* of law and procedure. Knell kept taking a surreptitious peep at it...

"A business of this kind doesn't need a telephone," Littlejohn was saying. "It must have been installed for some other purpose. Perhaps Alcardi got instructions over it... I wonder why he suddenly took fright and bolted after Irons rang him up..."

They locked the place and entered the little police car. The woman in the chocolate shop was peeping through the window watching their movements. Littlejohn took the wheel because Knell still looked groggy; his nerves seemed bad and he squinted a bit when he got excited. They started on the road over which Knell had chased Alcardi the previous night. It was new to Littlejohn, who followed his companion's instructions. Over Onchan Head, Groudle, and along the coast through Laxey to Ramsey.

The sun was shining over Ramsey Bay as they neared the town. In the wide sweep of sunlit blue sea from Maughold Head to the Point of Ayre at the northernmost tip of the Island, boats were anchored, people were strolling along the promenade, and two little steamers were manoeuvring to enter the port.

"Nice, isn't it?" said Knell. "When I was a kid we used to come here on Sunday School trips in wagonettes, and as we topped the hill and Ramsey came in sight, we used to sing a song..."

"Ramsey Town, shining by the sea?" chuckled Littlejohn, remembering Mrs. Keggin's teapot. Knell seemed completely taken aback, as though the Inspector had unfairly stolen his thunder. He grew quiet, remembering this was a murder, not a picnic.

Ramsey reminded Littlejohn of a French seaport. Tall white houses with stretches of whitened gable, lacking only the advertisements for aperitifs to complete the illusion. At a sign from Knell, he turned the car along the small promenade, past a long iron pier, and a pretty little church with balconies facing the sea on its towers. On the right lay the harbour with a swing-bridge, and a long quayside with the river and a lot of pubs, chandlers' and warehouses facing the water. To continue the French atmosphere, railway lines ran the length of the quay.

The tide was in and the smaller boats in the port were rolling in the breeze, which swept along the riverside, whipping up the rubbish.

In the basin, tied-up to a bollard, was a small coaster with a black funnel with a white line about a foot from the top. There was no one on deck. The wind caught the thin wisp of smoke rising from the funnel and teased it about. *Jonee Ghorrym, Ramsey*, in white letters on her stern. She must have been carrying coal from the mainland, for her hatches were off and three sailors were sweeping up the coal dust which blackened her hold.

Suddenly, a small, fat man in shabby naval uniform and an officer's cap tilted over one eye, appeared on the bridge. He leaned over the rail and eyed the men at work, smoking a short pipe. Then he turned his eyes in the direction of the police car, looked hard, and scowled. His face was livid, with a coating of tan, as though constant battling against the elements had strained his heart, and too little exercise on his little bridge had made him too weighty and ponderous for his height. All the same, there was a massive strength about his stocky frame; his blue eyes, set in wrinkles in a round fat face, were shrewd and even menacing. He looked a bad sort with whom to try conclusions.

"That's the *Jonee Ghorrym*... and that's Captain Kewley on the bridge there. She's a coaster. Belongs to a company, I hear, and I think the directors are local men..."

Knell reeled it off like a guide book.

Almost opposite the boat stood a tall, three-storied, narrow house, the fresh paint of which made the surrounding property look cheap and shabby. The adjacent buildings loomed over the trim little place, rising in tiers behind it, with appendages and outbuildings sprouting from them, projecting bay windows built on girders, and chimney stacks looking ready to crash down on the roof below at the next puff of wind. This was *The Duck's Nest*.

A window on each side of the open door, a dark corridor lit by a lantern wired for electric light, and beyond, a staircase. Above the blue door, a sign showing a crude nest with a cruder duck sitting in it. *Duck's Nest Restaurant* (Chez Jules). *Licensed. Choice Food and Wines. Omelettes. Fruits de mer, Poulet Grillé.* It might have been Brittany or the Riviera, judging from the menu in the glass case screwed on the wall.

"How do they make it pay in a place like this...?"

The building next door was empty. FOR SALE. *Apply Burbot and Pallister,* 45a, Parliament Street...

"It seems to do well in the summer. They get a lot of select visitors here. I suppose now they can't go and spend to their hearts' content in France, they come here and pretend they're there..."

Knell had it all off, as though he'd given much thought to it, like an estate agent valuing the place for a mortgage.

There was hardly anybody moving on the quay, except workmen, warehousemen and clerks, going about their daily business.

"Let's go inside..."

It still reminded Littlejohn of the coast of Brittany. The place was obviously a disguised pub, but after the fashion of a French café-restaurant, even to the cards on the walls PERNOD. DUBONNET. BYRRH. COURVOISIER. VICHY-CELESTINS. Over the fireplace of the bar, a large, framed portrait of a magnificent seated old lady. Veuve Clicquot-Ponsardin 1777-1866. Knell looked a bit scared as though expecting a gang of cut-throat apaches to surround him at any moment... or perhaps *les girls* of the establishment!

Instead, nobody bothered.

There were four men in the room, three sitting at a table under the window, a fourth, wearing a raincoat in spite of the weather, stood with them, apparently waiting for an answer to some question or other asked before Littlejohn entered. They all turned in the direction of the newcomers.

The man in the raincoat wore a battered soft hat. He was small and puffy, with a round baby face and blue eyes, a pink complexion, and skin of fine texture, sometimes associated with diabetes or other organic weakness. His hair was sandy. He spotted Littlejohn before the rest, and his eyes travelled to Knell and then back to the Inspector.

His face lit up and he bustled across with outstretched hand.

"Inspector Littlejohn? My name's Colquitt... *Manx Clarion*. How is the case getting along?"

A man with plenty of cheek. He wrung Littlejohn's hand before the Inspector had offered it.

"How do, Knell?" No handshake for Knell.

Colquitt put an arm round Littlejohn's shoulder and led him to the table by the window.

"Three friends of mine. This is the Scotland Yard man I told you about. On the Quantrell murder case..."

The large, red-faced, heavy man, with his dark hair clipped right to his scalp, was obviously the big-wig of the party. The rest waited for him to speak. He wore tweeds and the rolls of flesh of his pink neck folded over the back of his blue soft collar. He had a glass of beer and a fishing hat on the table in front of him.

"This is Dr. Smith..."

"Harborne-Smith..."

The doctor said it without annoyance, just as a man might straighten his tie to put things in order. His voice was thin and high-pitched for one so huge.

"Harborne-Smith... Beg pardon, doctor. A retired colonial who's settled down with us here..."

The doctor brushed it all aside with a wave of the hand, which he then offered to Littlejohn. It was a stiff, muscle-bound grip, more like that of a workman than a physician.

"What brings you to Ramsey...?"

He seemed to say it out of politeness rather than curiosity, and didn't wait for an answer.

"This is Parker... Builds houses... Jerusalem in Manxland's green and pleasant land... Eh?"

The man in the check suit and suede shoes smiled a sickly smile. He was lolling at the table, with his legs crossed and his arm dangling over the back of the chair. He wore a tweed cap to match his suit.

"Delighted, Inspector... How do you like the Isle of Man?" He didn't seem interested in the answer, either, but offered a hand like a fish. A dead fish, cold and lifeless. He was tall and strongly built, too, with lined irregular features and an earthy complexion. His large nose was askew from a badly set break.

The third man introduced himself.

"Tremouille's the name. How are you?"

The journalist took over again.

"Tremouille's a lawyer, aren't you Henry? Manx, in spite of his name. Let's see, wasn't your ancestor a sea captain taken prisoner in the Napoleonic wars, Henry, who stayed on here...? They all come and stay on, Inspector. If you stop here much longer, you'll feel it getting hold of you, and you'll find it hard to go. You'll see..."

The rest ignored the gas-bag. It was evident they'd been disturbed.

"We come here to fix up Parker's building finance..."

The doctor was trying to explain their presence there at that time of the day. What could be more likely than a builder, his financial backer, and a lawyer to fix things up?

Tremouille was dressed in business clothes; black jacket, grey striped trousers, and starched collar with a dove grey tie. He had a round pink face, too, with grey eyes, and a straight sharp nose. His head seemed too large for his body and his thin hair was so plastered to his skull with dressing, that you couldn't make out whether it was grey or fair.

"What'll you have to drink?"

They were all having beer, so Littlejohn ordered the same for himself and Knell. The sergeant, who evidently knew the lawyer and the reporter, was a bit shy. It also said something about not drinking on duty in the Hints for Beginners section of his *Policeman's Diary*.

"Amy..."

The doctor shouted in thin oboe tones.

They were all smoking; the doctor a short pipe, the rest cigarettes. The air in the room was like a fog. Spirals of smoke clung round the electric lights and seemed to strike the window and recoil like springs.

"Amy...! Where the hell's that girl?"

Amy entered without haste. In fact, you would have said she was being deliberately slow. Her eyes were red and swollen. She might have been having a little weep somewhere. The three men at the table glanced hard at her. She seemed crushed into apathy. Tall, dark, with a long anaemic face and a flat chest, she wasn't the type men look at twice. And yet... some might have done. There was a strange attraction about the large eyes with their heavy lids and unhealthy, almost smoky settings. The type the French call *les yeux fatales*. Some might have found a morbid fascination in looking at her and wondering what she was thinking. She wore a black dress and a white apron and lace cap. She came and stood by the table without speaking. Littlejohn and Knell drew up chairs and formed a second row at the table which was too small to hold six. Littlejohn watched the long pale hands of the girl clench and unclench as she stood waiting.

"Where've you been, Amy?"

The doctor slipped his hand round her haunches. She angrily shook him off and he first looked surprised and then smiled to himself. Evidently a bit of a lady killer...

"Same again, Amy... Six..."

The girl turned without a word and her eyes sought those of Littlejohn and held them for an intense moment. Then she left the room.

"What's bitten Amy?"

The reporter looked quite surprised.

"Her boy must have walked out on her..."

Parker didn't seem inclined to be sociable. It was evident that the police had interrupted their business and he was anxious to see the last of them.

"Are you any nearer finding out who's doing all the killings?"

Tremouille's voice was dry and cultured. He smiled politely as he asked the question, baring his even, white teeth. He lit a cigarette from the stub of the last one.

"No, sir. Not a bit nearer."

Littlejohn was filling his pipe, so Knell did the same.

"What brings you to Ramsey?"

You could feel that the four men had become suddenly interested in the answer. They seemed to grow tense without showing it.

"The latest victim, an Italian called Alcardi, had connections here. In fact, he came here the night he died... We thought we'd have a look round..."

The doctor turned his prominent eyes on Littlejohn and looked at him in silence for a minute, expecting a fuller explanation. Littlejohn seemed interested in lighting the tobacco evenly.

"We heard about Alcardi. A pity. Quite an epidemic of killings. Have you any leads here?"

"No. This place... And the boat opposite... Alcardi called at them both on his last night and got short shrift. He seemed to be trying to get help or to contact somebody and must have been unlucky. Who owns this place?"

The doctor shuffled in his seat.

"Where's that beer? What's the matter with that girl...? You were asking about this place. It's a company. The manager-cum-chef started it and some of us put money in it. It does well in the season; and out of season, quite a lot of people from all over the Island come. The food's A.I. Morin's a damn' good cook."

"Is that the Jules on the sign outside?"

"Yes. It sounds French. I don't quite know where he comes from. He might be French... or Greek... He came after the war."

"Where is he? I'd like a word with him."

"We'll tell Amy to bring him when she comes back."

"No. I want a private talk with him..."

They all looked hard at Littlejohn, as though, having accepted their hospitality, he was being a bit ungracious keeping them in the dark about Jules.

Amy was back with a tray of beers. She stared hard at Littlejohn again when she thought the rest weren't looking.

"The Inspector wants a word with Jules. Where is he?"

"In the kitchen, getting ready for dinner..."

She spoke in a dull, flat voice.

"I'd like to see him..."

The doctor didn't give her a chance. He went to the door and shouted down the passage.

"Jules! You're wanted..."

Then he sat at the table again.

"Good health, Inspector... Good health, Knell... It *is* Knell, isn't it? I saw it in the paper that you were helping..."

"Yes, sir. Good health, gentlemen..."

Jules was there before they heard him. He wore a white chef's cap and jacket and had a tea-cloth tied round his waist. Medium build, slim, long legged, with a long, very narrow face and high cheek bones. His black hair was shaggy and hung over his collar, and side whiskers reached to the middle of his ears. Sallow complexion with dark, red-rimmed eyes. There was a scar down his left cheek, which might have been due to a razor slash.

"You wanted to see me?"

He spoke with a trace of an accent, but there was self-conscious slang in his speech. He was anxious to speak fluently and over-did it.

"This is Inspector Littlejohn from Scotland Yard... You know where that is, Jules?"

The doctor was being a bit patronizing.

"Of course, I know. It's the London cops isn't it? I once worked in London. Howdy, Inspector..."

"Hullo, Jules. Have you a private office? I'd like a word or two with you."

Jules bared his yellow teeth and shrugged.

"A little word on the side, eh? Come with me, then..."

The dining-room, next door, was empty. About a dozen tables laid, with bright cutlery, glass, and napkins folded like mitres. There was a good carpet on the floor, the tables for four, and the chairs were in light oak. The lighting was a bit overdone... Globes suspended from the ceiling with a green band dividing them in two.

"We can talk here..."

"Do you know a man called Alcardi...? An Italian...?"

Jules rubbed his hands on his tea-cloth, took a cigarette from a battered packet in his hip pocket, lit it vulgarly, and blew out a spray of smoke.

"Alcardi? Yes, I know Alcardi... Or did. He's dead now...? O.K?"

"Yes. Did he call here last night after midnight?"

The chef's eyes began to flicker. He would have liked to deny it, but he didn't know how much the Inspector knew.

"Yes. He called. He wanted a bed for the night. I told him we were full up..."

"You take in boarders?"

"We have three rooms. They were full. I told Alcardi nothing doing, eh?"

"Did he ask for anyone?"

"Eh? Ask for anyone? No. Just a room. He argued. I chucked him out. That's all."

It seemed to tally with Knell's story, but there was something fishy about Jules's tale. He wasn't telling it all.

"Nothing more, Jules? You're sure?"

"Sure, I'm sure."

"Very well... Let's go."

"That's all? O.K?"

"Yes... O.K..."

Amy was hanging round the door as Littlejohn went back to the bar. Jules returned to his kitchen and you could hear him rattling pans and whistling. The four men and Knell were still in their places.

"All right, Inspector?"

The doctor seemed to be waiting for an account of what had gone on.

"Yes, thanks. We'd better be going. Glad to meet you all, and thanks for the drinks..."

It was clear that Amy wanted to say something to Littlejohn. She kept fixing him with her eyes, but one or another of the four men at the table kept her in view. She scribbled on the pad of checks which hung on a cord from her waist, and handed one to Littlejohn.

"What are you doing, Amy? The drinks were on me... I'll pay the bill..."

Littlejohn held the slip of paper in his fingers. Amy had torn off two. Her eyes held his again. He was standing with his back to the table and quickly separating the two bills, kept one in his palm, and passed the other for five shillings as he turned to the doctor.

"If you insist, doctor. Thank you. Good day, gentlemen..."

"Good day. If time hangs heavily, Inspector, you're always welcome here. Come again..."

The doctor waved a fat hand.

At the door Littlejohn read the note in the palm of his hand.

Meet me at Curpheys drapers parliament street half hour.

He put it in his pocket.

From the funnel of the *Jonee Ghorrym* a thick trail of black smoke was blowing over the harbour. Captain Kewley was on the bridge, smoking, his eye on *The Duck's Nest*. He turned his back on the detectives when they appeared.

"What now, sir?"

"I'm going on the bridge there to have a word with the captain. Whilst I'm there, go down below, Knell, and look at the crew's quarters... don't miss anything..."

Captain Kewley turned sharply as they crossed the gangway.

"Hi! No strangers aboard. Keep off."

"I want you, captain. Police."

"Better look sharp. We're due out..."

Littlejohn climbed the iron ladder to the bridge. He could hear Kewley shouting down at Knell.

"Hi... Nobody allowed below... Here... Do you hear? Nobody..."

"A word with you, Captain Kewley."

"Well?"

The captain removed his pipe and spat over the side. He stood like a rock on his bridge, his jaw set, wheezing from his efforts and shouting.

"I'm captain o' this ship. I won't have anybody makin' free of 'er. What are you after?"

"Do you know a man called Alcardi?"

"No. Why should I?"

"He came here last night and asked the man on watch for something. Who was on watch?"

"I know all about it. It was reported. He wanted a passage across. Walker was on duty. He told him, nothing doing. We don't carry passengers. The Eyetalian started to argue. Walker told him to be off, or he'd chuck 'im off. Quite right, too. And now, I've got to get down."

He was uneasy about Knell and what Knell was doing. That was obvious. Littlejohn's bulk barred the way.

"Let me pass... I've got to get below. We're getting steam up. Are you going to...?"

He was too late. From where they stood they could see Knell coming from below. He was shepherding two figures before him like a couple of sheep. As they came into the light, Littlejohn felt like raising a cheer. How Knell had done it, he didn't know, but there they were; handcuffed together, too. A bonny pair. Irons and Fannin!

9

THE REPENTANT FORGER

The *Jonee Ghorrym* didn't sail that day. Instead, the captain and his two disreputable passengers were taken over to the police-station, situated in the picturesque court-house building.

"Fannin and Irons were drinking tea in the fo'c'sle and were so surprised to see me, that I had the handcuffs on them before they quite gathered what was going on..."

Knell was modest about his share in the capture. A true Manxman, he hated a fuss.

As the party made its way to the lock-up, Littlejohn could see the quartet in the window of *The Duck's Nest* watching them curiously, and Tremouille followed them quickly to the court-house.

"I'm the advocate for the shipping company," he said explaining his appearance. Littlejohn left them with the Ramsey police whilst he went to find Curphey's shop and keep his date with Amy, the waitress.

Curphey's was an old-fashioned place, almost a Victorian survival, which dealt mainly in feminine matters. You could get carpets and curtains there, but women's dress materials, camisoles, corsets, underwear and tapes were their staple bread-

and-butter lines and the arrival of a man in their midst caused a
mild panic.

The Misses Curphey eyed the Inspector up and down and one
of them snatched a plastic artificial bust from a stand and
concealed it under the counter. Then she looked around in alarm.
There was far too much allure to hide away from this nice man...

"Do you happen to know Amy, the waitress at *The Duck's Nest*
on the quayside, madam?"

Littlejohn removed his hat, ignored the merchandise, and
spoke to the blushing little woman on the other side of the
counter.

Miss Caroline Curphey was a small, timid, grey-haired lady,
very good at doing a profitable business with members of her
own sex, but nonplussed by the invasion of a man in this store of
feminine intimacy. She felt she might be being mistaken for a
matrimonial agent... or worse. Although the name painted on the
shop window belied it, Miss Maude Curphey, her sister, had been
married once to a man named Hake, who travelled in buttons and
tapes. They preferred to forget it, however, for he had, early in
their married life, fled on the "Sunday midnight" with their money
and jewellery. Miss Maude was, therefore, regarded as the sophis-
ticated one of the firm; the one who had been "through it" and
knew it all.

"Do we know Amy of *The Duck's Nest*, Maude?"

Maude was chubby, grey, and very gay, in spite of the blows of
fate, and she played the organ at a Methodist chapel.

"Yes... Why?" Maude eyed Littlejohn archly. Caroline had
thoughts of adventurers and naughty men who ruined innocent
girls and fled overseas; but Maude hadn't. "Wasn't he nice, Carrie?"
she said when the Inspector had finished and gone.

When Maude Curphey heard what Littlejohn had to say and
he had proved his bona fides by showing her the café check, she
assumed a conspiratorial look, said she pitied Amy, and took
him in their private room at the back of the lock-up shop, where

they daily brought from home their cat, dog and canary and kept the gas-ring and cash safe. The bird started to chirp, but the two animals, fat and contented, slept through the whole adventure.

"Wait here for her..." And with that Miss Maude retired to the shop.

"Police," she said to Carrie, with her lips only.

"Eh?" framed Carrie's mouth, soundlessly.

"P-O-L-I-C-E... Pohleece..."

Carrie gave a little screech and covered her mouth with her hand.

The bell on the door clanged and Amy entered. One minute she had been peering in the shop window and furtively looking up and down the street; the next second she was in. Maude passed her to Carrie, and Carrie whisked her into the room behind.

"Hullo, Amy. You wanted to see me?"

The girl started and turned paler.

"You gave me a fright. Yes... I can't spare long. They'll wonder where I am..."

"Who will?"

"Jules and the customers..."

She was still in her cap and apron and had evidently just run from the café as she was. She was singularly lacking in feminine charm, with her long face, greasy hair, flat bust, and angular body. And yet, she might have attracted people in trouble, because she was obviously troubled herself. The sort who fully understood the dirty tricks fate can play...

"I said I was coming over to get some new serviettes we ordered. I'll be missed if I'm long away."

Even now, she seemed uncertain whether to talk or not.

"What is it, Amy? You in trouble?"

"It's about Mr. Alcardi... Joe... The one who was killed last night."

She did not weep or show any signs of grief. She was numb

and taut with emotion, but there was a sort of unbeaten dignity about her.

"He wanted to see you, sir. Joe, I mean."

"How did you know?"

"He told me. Last night, he came to *The Duck's Nest* after midnight. He telephoned from Douglas about nine o'clock to say he must see me. About eleven, he said he'd be here, but to wait till he got here. He said he'd knock at the front door. I was to slip out from the side door in the alley and meet him. It was a bit awkward, but I said I'd a headache and went to bed at eleven. Then I sneaked down and waited as he wanted..."

The bell rang in the shop and you could hear customers coming in. In the harbour one of the incoming boats blew a blast on her siren.

"He was very late. The quay was nearly dark and while Joe was arguing at the front door with Jules, pretending he wanted a bed for the night, I slipped in the car on the offside and waited. He came back. We couldn't sit there talking, so Joe drove round the Island on the T.T. course while he told me things and then he brought me back to Ramsey and I sneaked back to my room..."

"Nobody saw you?"

"No. I was lucky. Joe was terribly frightened. He wanted to get off the Island."

"Your name is Amy... what?"

"Amy Green. I came over from Liverpool for the season. Joe Alcardi used to come to *The Duck's Nest* to see Jules. We got friendly."

"He was your lover?"

"Yes... He had a wife somewhere in London. He lived there till he was interned in the war. So we couldn't get married. He was a good sort. He took a shop in Douglas, but he couldn't make a living selling souvenirs and his sketches. He was a good artist..."

"So I gather. Especially where banknotes were concerned..."

She didn't seem surprised.

"He told me you were on to him about the notes. He was a clever engraver. It was his trade. I don't mind what you know now. He's dead and past harming. He wanted to tell you everything, but he couldn't find you. You were out when he called. He said unless he found you before they found him, his life wasn't worth much... He was being watched..."

"*They... Who's they?*"

"I don't know."

"Suppose you sit down and begin at the beginning..."

"I daren't. I've got to get back."

Littlejohn went in the shop and spoke to Miss Maude.

"Ring up *The Duck's Nest*, if you don't mind, madam, and argue a bit with them about the serviettes they want. Tell them Amy's here and you have been trying to sell her some that aren't quite so cheap as those ordered. Tell them anything, but don't let them suspect she's talking here with me. You understand?"

Maude nodded enthusiastically. Her mouth was full of pins, and the lady she'd been measuring for some intimate article had to wait in discomfort.

"Now, Amy, begin at the beginning."

The girl was still bemused, speaking in a flat, monotonous voice.

"He said I was the only friend he'd got left. He wanted me to tell you if anything happened to him, he wasn't a murderer. He didn't know."

"Didn't know what?"

"He got mixed up with something shady. He'd have gone bankrupt in his shop and then, one day, a man called Irons, who'd lent him money to start with and who was always pestering him, said he knew how Joe could come by some easy money. They were smuggling watches, nylons and liquor in. The sales were easy in the season with all the visitors. Irons had the jewellery and watches, Joe and some others dealt with the liquor, and Captain Kewley brought them in. The *Jonee Ghorrym* got them, Joe said, from contacts in Dublin and at English ports where she went. There was quite a syndicate working it. The *Jonee* would meet a boat that put off from the Island and unload, and then the boat would row in at the Llen shore..."

Miss Maude's head appeared round the door to indicate that all was right from her angle. Amy didn't seem to notice it.

"Joe got in their clutches proper. He used to go out with the boat and then deliver the nylons and other things in his car. He got fed-up, though, and said he wanted to break away but they wouldn't let him. So he started a little business on his own."

"Banknotes?"

"Yes. Somebody said how easy it would be here in the season to pass off faked notes. He engraved some plates and a pal on the mainland got the paper. He didn't do many. Irons found out. He saw one of the plates Joe had left lying around when he called. Irons said his orders were that Joe was to stop it. The banks were too clever and if Joe got caught, he'd bring down the smuggling gang. Irons told Joe they didn't trust him once he got in the hands of the police. The truth was, Joe was honest at bottom and it was only his doing so bad in the shop made him turn to something not straight."

"Irons was passing-on orders from a third party?"

"So Joe said. Irons was the mouthpiece of a gang. I'll bet Dr. Smith... Harborne-Smith, he calls himself, is head of it. He's chairman of the *Jonee Ghorrym* Company. He's always around..."

"What about the other two; the builder fellow, and the lawyer?"

"They're directors, too, but Dr. Smith seems to lend money to Mr. Parker, the builder, and they meet at our place to settle-up. Mr. Tremouille comes there when they have to sign papers."

"*The Duck's Nest* seems to be Smith's headquarters..."

"That's it."

"Now, Amy, what about the murder Alcardi talked of?"

"He told me that Irons rang him up to say that Deemster Quantrell was on his track and on the track of the smuggling too.

He'd been snooping around the Lhen and the *Jonee Ghorrym*. From what Joe said, the Deemster was by way of being a bit of an amateur detective. It was his hobby."

"Irons rang up Joe to say that Deemster Quantrell had got a batch of Joe's dud notes and some smuggled stuff from the *Jonee*. It was the morning of the Castletown court and Joe said that Irons told him the Deemster had it all in his bag. They'd got to get it..."

"But why choose the court-house of all places?"

"The Deemster always travelled down in company. They couldn't risk holding him up, if that's what you mean."

"Why use Alcardi for the dirty work?"

Amy sighed.

"Joe had been a crook in Italy, and he had all the crook's ways of moving quietly and without fuss. They called him 'The Shadow' in the camp when he was interned. If anything was wanted, Joe was always the one to get it. He stole food, and when the men in the camp wanted silver and such to make souvenirs to sell, he'd get it for them by breaking in the locked rooms of the boarding houses where they were billeted... the rooms where all the owners' property was locked up. He said Irons and his party must have got to know somehow and that was, so to speak, their reason for getting him to join up with them."

"Go on with his visit to Castletown, then..."

"I must be going. Jules will wonder..."

"Hurry, then."

She started to gabble.

"Irons went to see Joe. It was the day before the Deemster died. They couldn't steal the bag in which the judge carried the evidence he was going to give to the police because he took it with him in the courtroom. So it was arranged that he should be drugged in his room where he dined alone. The only way to do so was to drug his cough mixture, which everybody knew he took. When he was in court, Joe was to sneak in and put some dope from a bottle into the mixture, which His Honour always had in his coat pocket. Then, when the dope acted after lunch, Joe was to go in, take the stuff from the bag, and bring it away."

"It all sounds very stupid to me. But go on..."

"It was stupid, sir. Joe admitted it, but it was a trick to frame him with the Deemster's death. He wanted to tell you, but he got killed before he could do it. Irons sent the bottle of dope round by a sailor who was in the smuggling racket with them. A man called Fannin. It was all planned. They'd got a key to the private door from somewhere. Joe let himself in, put the drug in the bottle which was where Irons said it would be, and went out. He was to go back, but when he got there, His Honour was dead..."

"So...?"

"Joe thought he'd given him too much dope. But later it got out that His Honour had been given poison... Joe was sure nobody saw him. He'd thrown away the little bottle..."

"After emptying what was left of it in his little rubbish bin... He wasn't much of a criminal... He was too neglectful of detail. Well?"

"When it got out the Deemster was dead, they all took fright. Irons was packing his bag ready to get away from the Island, but you called and told him you'd see he didn't get away. He rang up Joe to tell him that you were on his track. Joe panicked and bolted, but then thought he'd better make a clean breast of it and tried to get hold of you. When he couldn't find you, he tried to get a passage on the *Jonee* to the mainland, but they wouldn't take him. Fannin panicked, too, when he got to know that the stuff he brought to Joe was what killed the Deemster. He got himself mixed up with the police some way..."

"Who told you that? Joe was dead by then..."

"He came to *The Duck's Nest* and I heard him and Smith talking. He said on the way to jail in the police car, he was handcuffed, but hit the bobby in the car over the head with his cuffs, stunned him, got the key and got away. He made for the *Jonee* and Captain Kewley took him and Irons aboard to get them to Eire out of the way."

"Alcardi brought you back to Ramsey, and then left you?"

"Yes. He said he couldn't wait any longer. He'd have to wake you up. He said he'd only be safe in jail. He was sure whoever was at the bottom of it all, the leader, wouldn't let him rest till he was out of the way. Can I go now?"

"One more thing, Did Alcardi say anything about a boy scout who was killed? You've heard about that?"

"I heard about it and so had Joe, but he didn't know the boy had been killed till the news got out."

"Had he any idea who they were working for?"

"He said he knew how to find out. He wouldn't tell me, but he said he would tell you. He was sure that Irons and Fannin were only in the gang like himself. The organizer, the brains, were in the background."

"And you think this Harborne-Smith may be in the know?"

"I'm sure he's something to do with it."

"Very well, Amy. You can go. If you find out anything more, ring me up at Grenaby parsonage, not at the police-station. It might be better for you to go home to Liverpool. We'll see later..."

He saw Miss Maude again and she agreed to take Amy back to *The Duck's Nest* and finish the so-called argument about the price of the table napkins, just to prevent Jules being suspicious about Amy's errand.

At the police-station, Captain Kewley, Irons and Fannin were still there. They had been provided with cups of tea by the policeman in charge, but until Littlejohn returned, they were not to be set free. They had signed statements under the eye of lawyer Tremouille, who had now gone back to the office he kept in Ramsey, as well as his main one in Douglas.

Littlejohn read the statements. He had made up his mind to make no reference to the smuggling. It might, as yet, be dangerous to Amy.

Captain Kewley's testimony was to the effect that he had simply agreed to carry the pair as passengers and they had paid their fares. He did not know they were flying from the police and, as he had met them before and believed them respectable, he agreed to take them over.

It was all right for a tale. Superficially it held water. Kewley had a wife and family in Ramsey and wasn't likely to bolt and lose all he had; command, home and respectability. It was safe to let him take his cargo to Eire. He'd come back if he were sure they didn't suspect him of the smuggling game. After all, quite a lot of decent mariners did it. They regarded the Revenue as their natural enemy.

Captain Kewley had lost none of his assurance. He was smoking his pipe and glaring at the police. He gave Littlejohn a particularly dirty look.

"How much longer? The *Jonee Ghorrym's* under steam and ready for off. There'll be a row about this. I acted honest in my dealin's with these two. You can't say I didn't. You can't hold me..."

"No..."

Littlejohn laid down his statement and puffed his pipe.

"No... Let him go, officer. He'll be on call when he returns to port. Right, Captain Kewley. You're free. But don't try any tricks. See you come back."

The captain spat in the fire.

"What do you mean? My living's here; I'm not one to run out on my responsibilities. I've done nothing wrong and I've told lawyer Tremouille to take a note of all this and be ready to take proceedings for unrightful detention. I know the law..."

"I'm sure you do. You'd better think it over when you're on the high seas and have time for thought. Bon voyage, captain."

"To 'ell with you..."

Captain Kewley stamped from the police-station and back to his ship without so much as a look back.

"What about us, Inspector? I was only trying to get away for my health. Can I go with the *Jonee Ghorrym?* I can get to the south of France if I fly from Dublin..."

Irons was fawning and begging in turns.

"I told you, Mr. Irons, you were staying here till I said you could go. You've forgotten that, and tried to slip away. I want a long talk with you..."

"But I told you all I know... I didn't withhold anything, sir."

"We'll try again and see if you can't remember something else. Meanwhile, Fannin will be detained in custody on a charge of house-breaking. And this time Fannin, don't try rough stuff on the police. Did anyone help you when you broke away before?"

Littlejohn was determined to tell none of them what he had learned from Amy.

"No. The man who took me in the car was a bit free and easy. He gave me a cigarette and as he lit it, I got my hands up... I'm sorry, sir. I was scared..."

He still looked scared. All his truculence had gone, his face was dirty and his hair unkempt. His eyes were red rimmed from anxiety and loss of sleep.

"Put him in the cells, officer. You'll get your reward for repaying the kindness of the constable at Castletown so generously, Fannin... And now, Mr. Irons, we'll have our little talk."

They led Fannin off and Irons licked his lips and backed away.

"Sit down, Mr. Irons..."

Littlejohn started to fill his pipe.

"Now... Let's begin at the beginning, Mr. Irons. When did you meet the late Mr. Alcardi?"

"I didn't kill him. I've got an alibi. Captain Kewley knows I was aboard the *Jonee Ghorrym* all night. You can't pin it on me."

The contemptible rhinoceros saving his own skin! Littlejohn looked at the gross body, the slobbering lips, the uneasy eyes... This wretch couldn't kill anybody! He was too scared of being killed first, or else being found out.

"Nobody's trying to pin it on you, Mr. Irons. But Alcardi's wasn't the only murder. There are others. When did you first meet Alcardi?"

"When he was interned in the camp. I used to go up there. I sold them mattresses and things."

"And what did Alcardi sell *you*?"

"He was good with his hands. He made souvenirs and sketches and asked me to sell some for him in the shop."

"You got friendly? So friendly that you trusted him enough to make him a partner in dirty work you had in hand?"

"There was nothing like that, Mr. Littlejohn. I swear..."

"We don't want any more oaths. Yours are like pie-crusts. You introduced Alcardi to your smuggling friends..."

Irons showed a bit of spirit for the first time. His servile manner vanished and his eyes flashed.

"What has Fannin been saying? He's a liar. You can't believe a word he says. He's only trying to save his own skin..."

"All the same, it's true you and Fannin were in the smuggling trade. You roped in Alcardi. But the Italian was on a racket of his own. He was making little etchings of banknotes and making money for himself. He did it so amateurishly that he looked like bringing the police limelight on the lot of you. So you warned him off. The banks suddenly stopped being worried about the dud notes..."

"It's a lie. I hadn't nothing to do with banknotes..."

"But you had with smuggling... Now don't deny it, Mr. Irons. We know all about it. But you were all taken for a ride. To put it mildly, the watches, liquor, nylons *and* banknotes were all small fry. The big game was that somebody duped you into murdering Deemster Quantrell..."

Irons was on his feet, waving his stumpy arms, clinging to Littlejohn, frothing at the mouth.

"I had nothing to do with it. I never went near the court the day the Deemster died. You can't say I did. I got an alibi..."

Littlejohn flung him off.

"Who was it told you that the Deemster was carrying round evidence which would put the lot of you behind bars for a long stretch? Who suggested that the ex-crook, Alcardi, who could move around like a cat, should dope the Deemster's cough mixture and, having put him to sleep, enable you to get back the evidence? Who gave you the bottle of so-called dope, which turned out to be prussic acid, to put in the bottle? And you sent the bottle by Fannin to Alcardi with instructions..."

"It's all lies! I never..."

"We know all about it. No use denying it. And when you heard the Deemster was dead and Scotland Yard was on the job, you panicked. You warned Alcardi, sent him scuttering round for his life, tried to get away yourself, and took Fannin with you. You didn't think of murder, I know, but it *was* murder and that terrified you..."

Irons was seeking a way out. He looked around as if contemplating a breakaway, licked his thick lips, ran his finger round the edge of his dirty soft collar, and sank in a chair.

"We was terrified... That's right. We didn't know it was murder. We was tricked. Everybody does a little smuggling. I could tell you of well-known respectable men on the Island who..."

"We don't want to know. We want your story. Who put you up to the trick that ended in the death of Deemster Quantrell?"

Irons was still terrified.

"I don't know. I swear, I don't know."

"Don't be silly. Who gave you the bottle of poison and told you to send Alcardi?"

"I was told over the telephone and I don't know who it was. The smuggling was run by a syndicate, but we never knew who was at the top. He did all the arranging by telephone or else by letter which was always to be burned. He told me over the telephone. Yes... over the telephone."

The relieved look Littlejohn had seen before came into Irons' face as he concocted his tale.

"What about the poison?"

"It came by post... The bottle in a little box. That was all."

"And you, of course, burned the box and the wrapping?"

"Yes."

"I don't believe you! You know who gave the orders. Well, you can cool off in jail till you make up your mind to tell a correct tale. You'll be charged with smuggling, passing forged notes, and we'll also hold you on suspicion of murder. That's enough for the time being."

"No bail?"

"No bail."

Irons looked relieved.

"I wish I could get you bail, Mr. Irons. You might start a mad career round the Island like Alcardi did, with someone's revenge keeping you on the move. What did Alcardi say when you rang him up and warned him I was after him?"

"He said he was getting out..."

"Like the rest of you? Except that he was going to tell me things to save his neck from the rope. He had an idea of turning King's Evidence and somebody evidently knew it. Who did you tell he was on the run?"

"Nobody..."

"Very well. The police will take another statement from you. You can have your lawyer if you like."

"I don't want no lawyer. I won't have a lawyer. They're all twisters. The lawyers is out to get somebody because their Deemster was killed. Well, I didn't kill him and I ain't going to take the rap. I'm goin' to defend myself and what I have to say will be said in court, not to you, Mr. Inspector. Where's the cell...?"

This was a new Irons. He seemed flushed with fresh confidence. Something in the course of the conversation had changed his outlook.

"Very well. Lock him up. He'll be charged before the magistrates to-morrow..."

"When's the next General Gaol Delivery?"

The dealer, his fingers in the armholes of his waistcoat, was now truculent.

"Three weeks," said the sergeant in charge.

"Might as well make myself comfortable till then..."

And they led Irons off, looking very pleased with himself.

"Let's get back to Grenaby," said Littlejohn to Knell. "I've had quite enough for one day..."

As they passed the quay, the *Jonee Ghorrym* had cast off and was making for the open sea under full steam.

10

THE SECOND DEEMSTER

P arson Kinrade greeted Littlejohn like a long lost sheep when he turned up at Grenaby late in the afternoon.

"I'd given you up, Inspector. It's good to put a sight on you again. I thought you'd got murdered yourself."

They took tea as Littlejohn told the Archdeacon of his day's work. Mr. Kinrade knew nothing of the background of the players in the day's drama. Irons, Harborne-Smith and his builder pal, Amy and Alcardi, they meant little to him. They were, for the most part, birds of passage, on the Island because of the low rate of income tax, or else to reap the harvest of the holiday season and then go with their pockets full.

"The only one I know is Tremouille. He's a good lawyer and, though his name seems to belie it, a good Manxman. Clever advocate, too, who practises at Ramsey as well as Douglas. He's well in the succession for the bench."

Maggie Keggin came and went with the tea things, sniffing and sighing from her private grief at the disreputable conduct of her grandson.

"I'll never get over it..."

"Don't you worry, Maggie. There's a home here for you, as always, till all this blows over. It'll be all right, won't it, Inspector?"

"Of course. If what I believe's true, he'll not get more than twelve months, and then he can start again."

"Twelve months' prison!"

Mrs. Keggin moaned, threw her apron over her head, and rushed from the room, feeling her way like somebody playing blind-man's-buff.

"Poor old darling. All the rest of her children and grandchildren are so good. This one's the black sheep..."

The parson kept hemming and hawing as if he had something on his mind. At length he spoke about it.

"I ought to go to Peel before dark comes on. I was wondering... Would you like to come along? I've to talk to the second Deemster about to-morrow's funeral. There are arrangements to be made and the formalities..."

Littlejohn smiled and lit his pipe.

"Were you thinking we might go in the police car?"

The parson stroked his beard.

"Well... yes. Looney's tumbril's a bit rough after the car you're driving around in."

"All right, parson. We'll take Knell down to Castletown and then go on from there. That do?"

The evening was setting in, and the sun was going down over the moorland in the direction of Peel with the promise of another good day to-morrow. A farm tractor rattled past the vicarage gate on its way home, and the parson's hens, which had a predilection for roosting in the trees instead of the hencoops, were flying up one by one into the branches, falling down as their weight bent the boughs, and then launching themselves up again.

"Stupid things!" said Archdeacon Kinrade, as they watched them through the window.

Difficult to believe the strange things going on not far away! A gang of smugglers, a dead counterfeiter, a murdered Deemster lying ready for burial to-morrow, an unknown murderer skulking around, perhaps under their very noses, and a lot of fat hens incessantly jumping into trees and falling out again till, finally, luck favoured them with a good balance and they slept...

"Could it be...?"

The parson changed the subject.

"Yes?"

"Could it be that you're barking up the wrong tree about this smuggling and forged notes? Might there not be some other reason, Inspector? Something more subtle, more evil, more complicated and human than simply a plot to shut Quantrell's mouth against the petty criminals...?"

Littlejohn gave the parson an admiring smile.

"You ought to have been a detective, sir."

"I can smell out evil, as I've told you before. These little men... Irons, Fannin, Alcardi... They're the small fry, the supers of the drama, the walkers-on. The main characters haven't yet come on the stage. You agree?"

"With every word. We're as far away from the solution as ever. We've cast the net to-day, and caught a lot of little fish. But they might serve as bait for the big ones in time. Shall we go?"

Knell had been feeding in the kitchen with Maggie Keggin, who knew his old mother. He had been trying to comfort her in her trouble and anxiety about Kenneth, and Maggie had been weeping and keening about it. Knell looked ready for a good cry himself. He wasn't very steady emotionally after his knock on the head and the sudden change in Millie Teare's behaviour... He was anxious to get a night off and see Millie. Hitherto, Knell had not been a very sentimental chap, but now,... Whereas, once he had thought of Millie as a good-looking girl whom a man would be proud to have walking out with him, a sensible one who would help him save his money, keep his house clean, cook well, and bring up the children nicely, now, he felt a sudden madness in his blood. He didn't care if he spent *all* his money on her, which was a change of face for a thrifty Manxman. Tears pricked the back of his eyes as he thought of her teaching a lot of kids at school. He once thought poetry effeminate. Now, all the Manx ballads of his childhood, the lovely lines of their own poet, T. E. Brown, came back to mind about Millie Teare. He kept muttering them under his breath and looking furtively round lest he be overheard and misunderstood.

> *Woman, a word with you!*
> *Round-ribbed, large-flanked,*
> *Broad-shouldered (God be thanked!)*
> *Face fair and free,*
> *And pleasant for a man to see...*

Knell wished he could meet the Deemster's murderer face to face, perhaps trying to carry off or kill Millie Teare. He made a loud clicking noise with his tongue against his teeth to signify his own fist contacting the point of the murderer's jaw.

"Yessir!"

Littlejohn told Knell what they were going to do, that he could have a night off after a gruelling day, that he had been a great help, that he had better look after himself and Miss Teare more carefully than on the previous night, and that he might give the Inspector's kind regards to Millie. Knell, blushing, smiling, stammering, springing to attention, trying to drive the car, and thinking of the bliss to come, almost uprooted the gatepost of the vicarage on his way out.

The Castletown police had spent a very busy twenty-four hours. Nobody could help them about the duplicate key to the Deemster's quarters in the castle. How they'd sneaked the original key from the police-station was a mystery.

"It might not have been that key," said Littlejohn quietly, and they all looked surprised and waited for him to say more, but he remained quietly smoking his pipe and watching a coal boat manœuvre her way past the small swing-bridge into the basin, on the high tide. Two swans were swimming gracefully on the Silver-burn, which entered the sea there...

"We've checked all the regulars who were in or about the castle the day the Deemster died, sir," said the sergeant in charge. "Advocates and court officials, litigants, witnesses, the press, the police, and the locals who were spectators. There were one or two visitors there, as well, but we've been lucky, although we didn't know their names; they came by a motor-coach which left before the lunch recess. The court-house seems to have been empty more or less from the time they adjourned till the time they found His Honour dead. There was just a policeman tidying up the court-room, one looking after Deemster Quantrell, and the custodian of the castle in his quarters with his family. The rest cleared out and went for a meal. One or the other could give alibis. I can't think of any that might have come back..."

"That seems to be a proper job attended to... Thanks for it. At least it clears the decks..."

Littlejohn was still watching the swans and the coaster. In his mind's eye, he could see, at the same time, the knots of gowned advocates leaving the court, the witnesses and parties to cases shuffling out, a bit discontented at having to wait until afternoon, the police officers tidying up, the press chatting together, the castle slowly emptying... And then, the Deemster, all alone, drinking his cough mixture...

But before that... Long before...

"What time did you say the boy scouts arrived?"

"Just on eleven, sir..."

"And the Deemster... What time would he get here in the morning?"

"Around ten, sir..."

Between ten and eleven, then, Alcardi had entered by the main gate...

"Did anybody see Alcardi enter the castle between ten and eleven?"

"No, sir. We've checked all the comings and goings. But the man on the gate went for a walk round at about eleven... or just before. Alcardi or anybody else could have got over the turnstiles. There was nobody about..."

"Not even in the police-station...?"

"Well... It was court day and we were all a bit busy, sir."

Alcardi had got in about eleven, then. And someone had, as likely as not, followed him, watched from the dark interior of the coach for the Italian's return through the private door from the Deemster's room... Young Mounsey had arrived and butted in... opened the door of the coach and seen someone... someone he knew! Just as Alcardi was expected back from his mission, which whoever had planned it was carefully supervising, unknown to the Italian.

"The boy scouts... I mean the whole troop... Did they get to know many people on the Island?"

The attendant policemen looked at the brooding Inspector in astonishment. Knell thrilled with satisfaction. This was it! The investigation had started now, good and proper. Just like the real Sherlock Holmes. He held his breath waiting for Littlejohn to pronounce judgment and tell them whose name to put in the warrant for arrest.

"Yes, sir. The troop young Mounsey was with were here as kind of guests. They'd won some sort of first prize for smartness at a jamboree in Lancashire, and were being honoured by the Commissioner for the Island. They'd been on conducted visits to the Museum, the House of Keys, the castles, the Laxey Wheel, and what not... They had several feeds as well and been entertained at them by Island notables. There was a kind of reception for them the first Saturday they came... a meal, a concert, and then they did their drills and such... They'd meet... or, at least, see and know, most of the nobs of the Island... saving your presence, Mr. Kinrade..."

The sergeant coughed behind his hand as he remembered the Archdeacon, seated by the desk, taking it all in silently.

"Don't mind me, Cregeen. Tell us who they were likely to see."

Sergeant Cregeen coughed again.

"Well... Most of the notables... The Governor, the Deemsters, Members of the Legislative Council and the Keys... some of the police... the Mayor of Douglas and the councillors... oh, lots of people..."

Cregeen dried up at the thought of the multitude who might be involved. If they'd got to screen all that lot, they were going to have their work cut out...

"Thank you, sergeant... You ready, sir?"

Knell's disappointment was profound. His face fell.

"Are you going to St. Mark's, Knell, because we'll drop you on the way?" said the parson. The local policemen smirked at Knell, who blushed and fled to start the car.

They left Knell at the door of a whitewashed cottage where the Teare family lived in the village of St. Mark's, riding high and clear over the inland plain, and then turned to Ballamodda and through the old mining village of Foxdale. The parson pointed out the great mass of South Barrule rising between them and the setting sun, with the hills which sheltered Peel beyond.

"This murder's a nuisance, Littlejohn. We ought to be enjoying the hills and the sunset, instead of chasing evil all over the Island. But I've got to see the other Deemster. The funeral's to-morrow... At the family vault at St. Luke's church, near where the Quantrells live. The vicar of Braddan will read the service in English and I shall read it afterwards in Manx. That's what Quantrell wanted. It reminds me of the old days when Quantrell and I used to read the laws together every July from Tynwald Hill... He'd read them in English and I'd read them in Manx... side by side, with the crowds listening and silent, the sun shining, and a little wind blowing from the sea and making the flags fly..."

They turned at St. John's to the Peel Road.

"Straight over and then left at the first turn... The house is called Gat-y-Whing... the Narrow Lane. The Deemster's called Milrey... Finloe Milrey. He deals with the North of the Island at Ramsey, as well as sitting in Douglas. Now, he's set to become first Deemster, and High Bailiff Cosnahan will follow him as second. As likely as not, Tremouille will be the new High Bailiff..."

"You seem to have it all arranged, parson..."

"One can always make a good guess. Both Cosnahan and Tremouille are very good men and rank high at the Manx bar... Here we are..."

Gat-y-Whing, Deemster Milrey's home, was old, turreted and dark, and surrounded by gloomy trees and untended bushes.

"His wife died last year and he's taken it hard. He's got a bit careless about the place. If Julia had been alive, it wouldn't have been like this..."

The woodwork needed a coat of paint, but the lawns and flower-beds were tidy. It just looked too big to keep up properly on a judge's salary. The Archdeacon tugged at a chain hanging by the front door, which was set in a square porch. Inside, a dog barked.

"Good evenin', sir... Will ye please to come in...?"

An old Manx woman dressed in black showed them into a large, cosy room, lined from floor to ceiling on three walls with books of all shapes and sizes. There were books on the floor and lying horizontally on top of others on the shelves. A large fire of logs crackled and sputtered on the hearth and an oil lamp with a large green shade cast a bright circle of light on a table littered with papers and more books, between the door and the great fire-place. At the table sat a grey-haired man, whose bright dark eyes sparkled to greet them as they stood in the doorway. He rose and extended his hand...

Deemster Milrey was very short and slim; you would almost have said he was dainty. He moved on small light feet and the hand he extended was white and well cared-for. He wore a black velvet smoking jacket and was smoking a pipe. But what you noticed first was the fine troubled face, the broad, high forehead, the delicate, arched nose, the trim grey pointed beard. He was the greatest of the living Manx scholars and it was said that had he remained at Cambridge, instead of returning to his native isle, he would have gone very far...

The forthright Archdeacon told Littlejohn as much as he introduced them. Milrey waved a deprecating hand.

"I couldn't settle elsewhere than here..."

Littlejohn suddenly remembered the quartet in *The Duck's Nest* at Ramsey. The little, chubby, carrotty journalist had said the same. You'll find it getting hold of you and you'll find it hard to go. You'll see...

They drew up chairs by the fire, the Deemster produced cigars and whisky.

"It's time you two met..."

"Not another murder, I hope..."

Littlejohn smiled to himself in the half-light. It was obvious that the Archdeacon had been making an excuse for bringing him over to Gat-y-Whing to meet Milrey. Hitherto, the old man hadn't so much as mentioned to-morrow's funeral. He didn't blame the parson for wanting to call on the Deemster. Here was real comfort, grace and culture. The log fire, the books, the air of scholarship and good taste, the soft glow of the lamp. Not a thing that struck a wrong note. And yet... the sad, unhappy face of the owner of it all. On a side-table stood a photograph in a silver frame of a sweet, grey-haired, middle-aged woman, standing smiling at the square-framed outer door they had just entered...

"No... Not another, Finloe. We've had enough already. But the Inspector's investigations could never be complete without a word from you. That's why I've brought him."

Littlejohn could make out in the dim periphery of the reading-lamp in which they were sitting, the grey head of the Deemster cocked inquisitively.

"You know all about the crimes, sir?" the Inspector said.

"More or less. The Island's a small place and news travels fast. You were in Ramsey to-day..."

Deemster Milrey laughed.

"We have a Manx word, *Cooish*, which has no proper English equivalent. The French *causerie* is near it. It means a chat, in which the affairs of the day are slowly retailed and turned over, passing from group to group, and being gravely considered. You, my dear Littlejohn, are the main topic of every Manx *cooish* at present and at every fireside and in every pub and sewing-class at this moment, the subject is 'the Inspector from over the water' and his doings... There was a chapel 'tay', or tea-party, this afternoon at which Mrs. Karran, my housekeeper, attended. Mrs. Cain, the post, was present it seems, and the news came over the wire from one of the banks in Ramsey where Mrs. Cain's eldest girl works. Subsequently, of course, there was a little *cooish* between Mrs. Karran and me..."

Deemster Milrey lifted his glass to his lips.

"So, you know it all, sir?"

"Well, perhaps not quite. You arrested three men, including the captain of the *Jonee Ghorrym*, who was later released."

The Archdeacon was struggling to keep calm, but there was a rasp in his voice.

"What was the use of our coming all this way if you know it all...?"

"Don't get annoyed, Caesar. It was just my joke..."

"Tell him then, Littlejohn..."

Littlejohn felt like an undergraduate taking his *viva* before two professors. He didn't quite know where to begin.

"*Three days ago, about eleven o'clock, an Italian named Alcardi carried out orders to drug Deemster Quantrell's cough-mixture in order to put His Honour to sleep and enable Alcardi later to steal incriminating evidence which the Deemster carried on his person...*"

"But who was this Alcardi? And who gave the orders?"

The ash from his cigar fell on Milrey's silk lapel, and he dusted it off with a fussy gesture.

The bottle by Fannin, the orders through Irons, the mysterious key to the Deemster's private quarters...

"Have you a key to that door, Finloe?"

The Archdeacon said it casually as he flicked the end of his cigar and took a drink from his glass. He looked half asleep. There was a pause.

"Yes. I carry it on my key-ring. I do go to Castletown to sit now and then... Why?"

"Nothing... I just wondered. Excuse the interruption..."

"*Alcardi found he had been tricked. It wasn't dope they sent in the little bottle, but prussic acid... He was terrified when he found out. He realized that he was serving ruthless men and that his own life wasn't worth the candle if he didn't watch out. He made up his mind to turn informer and tried to find me. He was not successful. So...*"

"How did you find out all this? Not by deduction?"

"No, your Honour. Alcardi had a mistress in Ramsey; a girl called Amy, a waitress at a place called *The Duck's Nest*. He told her everything in terror before he was killed. She told me."

"I see... And then?"

"*Someone was waiting to see that Alcardi did the job. A Mr. X. X hid in the old coach which stands in the passage just by the private door in the castle. A boy scout inquisitively opened the door and, I think, recognized X. It would not have done, when the murder was discovered, for little Mounsey, the scout, to prattle about the contents of that black coach at that particular time. X drew the boy inside and left him dead...*"

"But what had Quantrell *done* to deserve such a fate?"

The forged bank notes, the smuggled nylons and watches, the goings-on aboard the *Jonee Ghorrym*...

"All of which *we* don't believe were the real cause of the crimes. There was some deeper evil, Finloe... ,"

In the darkened room with the firelight flickering and the three of them sitting in the shadows, the parson's voice seemed to come from another world and denounce the everyday one outside.

"So you have three murders on your hands, with, as yet, no motive and no clue as to who was behind them?"

"That is so, sir."

The parson filled up his glass with a finger of whisky and a noisy splash of soda.

"That's where you come in, Finloe. We thought you might help."

Deemster Milrey jerked upright.

"*I* might help? How can *I* help?"

Littlejohn sat back in his chair. The parson had taken the initiative from his hands and was evidently following out some plan he had hatched on his own.

"You were Quantrell's closest friend. He spent a lot of time with you. Did he never mention his amateur detection? Did he never tell you his suspicions about dirty work going on anywhere? Didn't he mention the forged notes, the smuggling, the *Jonee Ghorrym*...?"

Deemster Milrey helped himself to more whisky, signalled to Littlejohn that he would like to fill up his glass, and then stretched his slippered feet to the fire.

"Yes... But that was, as you say, mere child's play. Unless, of course, it involved somebody of note on the Island, somebody who could not dare have a scandal round his name..."

"That may be so, sir..."

The Deemster raised his hand to indicate he hadn't finished. It was a habit of his in court.

"What I have been reminded of in the course of your story,

Inspector, is a strange remark of Martin Quantrell's made to me a month or so ago..."

He paused to thrust on more logs and stir the fire with a huge wrought-iron poker like a trident. The flames leapt and lit up his face.

"Apropos some cases of robbery with violence we had before us in Ramsey, he said 'The Carrasdhoo Men are back. I know it.' "

"Merciful heavens!"

Littlejohn waited. It was beginning to savour of gothic horrors and he feared to break the spell.

"You've never heard of them, Littlejohn?"

The parson couldn't wait for Littlejohn to ask.

"No, sir."

> *"The Carrasdhoo men were a fearful race,*
> *A band of borderers none might trace;*
> *Whose band or lineage no one knew*
> *In the wild lone isle wherein they grew;*
> *But in the empire of old M'Lear*
> *None could in vice with them compare."*

The Deemster recited it in a soft, cultured voice.

The parson was annoyed.

"Rubbish! That was simply imagination... Esther Nelson made it up for a ballad, that's all..."

"There was truth in it. They operated between Ramsey and Jurby and their headquarters were a tavern near the Curragh..."

"You're bemusing Littlejohn. The empire of M'Lear's another name for the Isle of Man, and the Curragh's the fen country north-west of Ramsey. The whole thing's a fable."

> *"For the Ullymar bogs have a hideous slime,*
> *And the Ullymar bogs wear the hue of crime!"*

The Deemster kept on...

"I tell you, it's moonshine..."

"And I tell you..."

The Manx scholars were losing their tempers with one another. Littlejohn sat back and laughed. And that brought them to earth.

"I'm sorry, Inspector. I'm a poor host. Fill up your glass. This parson and I never see eye to eye on Manx lore. He's always on the prowl for the pagan and profane..."

"You shouldn't bait me, Finloe... But did Martin say that?"

"He did. Probably speaking figuratively, as he used to do. But he meant there was some revival of evil down Ramsey way. I can't say more."

"It's all most exasperating. Why couldn't Martin have taken somebody into his confidence? Then we wouldn't have had all this trouble."

"Unfortunately the Carrasdhoo legend has been borne out in his case..."

"What do you mean?"

> *"I rede ye beware of the Curragh glen!*
> *For he that will dare it, comes not again;*
> *In whispers his fate is told..."*

"Stop it!"

"Very well, Caesar. We'll change the subject. Is there anything you care to ask me, Inspector? Anything that you may have come across which puzzles you?"

"Do you know anything about *The Duck's Nest* at Ramsey, sir?"

The Deemster seemed surprised and said he didn't, but he would find out anything he could.

"Or about a party which seem to make it their headquarters: a Dr. Harborne-Smith, a builder called Parker, and the lawyer, Tremouille..."

"Tremouille? He's quite above board. He practises at the Manx bar... For the rest, I've heard of them casually, but I'll ask more discreetly and let you know..."

The party broke up very shortly after that, Milrey saw them to the door, and bade them good night. They left him still standing on the threshold, apparently deep in thought.

"Poor Finloe... He misses his wife... Was he any help...?"

Littlejohn hadn't the heart to say anything but yes to Parson Kinrade. The old man was so anxious to co-operate. All his own business for to-morrow's funeral had been done in a word or two. The rest had been an effort to further the investigation.

Littlejohn spoke to his wife by telephone again. It refreshed him and cleared his mind to speak to Letty, but once in bed his depression returned.

He kept thinking of Deemster Milrey in his old house, alone with his memories and his gloomy thoughts. The Carrasdhoo Men and the bogs of Ullymar... And he dreamed of the journalist with red hair and the baby face. "You'll find it getting hold of you and you'll find it hard to go... You'll see..."

11

THE EMPTY DESK

"Caghlaa obbyr aash," muttered Mrs. Keggin to herself as she put plates of Manx kippers in front of Littlejohn and the parson for breakfast.

She seemed better for a good night's rest and was now taking the misfortunes of herself and her unruly grandson with peasant stoicism.

"What are you chattering about...? And don't speak Manx in front of a man who doesn't know it. It's rude, Maggie..."

The parson forked a mouthful of kipper and small bones into his mouth and shook a finger in protest.

"Change of work is rest, then, if you want it that way. This burying will be like a holiday for you both... You and your crimes. No good comes of it..."

"And what's that you're carrying about with you, Maggie?"

"A piece of luck-herb for the Inspector's button-hole. It's ter'ble good to bring good luck and to keep off the butcheraghey and evil eye..."

She stuck a small sprig of St. John's Wort in Littlejohn's coat and left the room in confusion.

"Let her be, Littlejohn... It's just to show she's overlooked what you did to Kenneth. Butcheraghey, by the way, is witchcraft. Quite a lot in these parts still believe in it..."

Littlejohn quietly enjoyed his food. He'd something to say to the parson and he wondered how best to put it.

"I'll be leaving you for a day or two, sir," he said at last. "I've got to get to work in Ramsey. There's something going on at *The Duck's Nest* that needs investigating. I hope you don't mind..."

"I've been expecting it..."

The parson laid down his knife and fork.

"It's too much of a holiday for you staying here, isn't it? The whole Island, in fact, isn't conducive to hard work. *Traa dy Liooar*, they say... Time enough. Always putting off what should be done to-day till to-morrow. It gets you... Am I right?"

Over and over again; the same thing. "You'll find it getting hold of you. You'll see..." as the red-headed reporter had said.

"Yes. It's quite true. I'll have to take a hold of myself and see the job through. Then I can enjoy the rest of my stay with you."

"Are you going to stay at *The Duck's Nest*...? Silly name!"

"They do take one or two in, but I doubt if I'll be welcome there. I can try."

"Let me book you in, if I can. I'll not give the name... I'll just say I want a room for a friend from over..."

The parson went to the telephone right away and came back smiling.

"That's done..."

The car with the Archdeacon and Littlejohn met the Deemster's cortège at Ballagarry, his home, and the long procession of vehicles started for the church of St. Luke, where the Quantrell family vault was waiting for them. There were no women present in accordance with an old custom of the Isle. A brief family service had been held in the house and they had then bidden good-bye to the last of the Quantrells.

The long file of cars wound its way through a tunnel of autumn-tinted trees, slowly climbing uphill, until finally they reached the open where the small stone church of St. Luke, surrounded by a graveyard, was visible. Behind, the sunlit background of Injebreck and the hills which form the backbone of the Isle of Man, framed the scene like a giant backcloth, with Snaefell mountain towering in their midst. High white clouds passing quickly on the wind cast great shadows over the hills...

They were removing the coffin from the hearse and six young law students were shouldering it ready to bear it along The Rough Road—Raad Garroo—which skirts the churchyard and leads to the ruin of Keeill Abban, the former chapel. Littlejohn remained in the road, watching the proceedings, whilst the Archdeacon adjusted his gown and joined the vicar of Braddan at the graveside. The throng included the Lieutenant-Governor of the Island, his officers, members of the upper and lower Houses of Parliament—the Legislative Counsellors and the Keys—the surviving Deemster and the law officers, members of the bar, and innumerable other officials and notables. Young Lamprey was well to the front by the graveside and at his elbow, Tremouille, the advocate, who, it turned out, was the lawyer of the Quantrell family. Somehow, Littlejohn got the impression that, standing, as he did between Tremouille and Deemster Milrey, Lamprey was held in their custody...

"Are you Inspector Littlejohn...?"

Most of those present had eyed Littlejohn with curious or friendly interest, but, so far, nobody had addressed him except in brief greeting. The man at his elbow was small and elderly, with a wrinkled pink face and watery blue eyes. He wore a black suit, which, owing to his increased paunch since it was bought, missed meeting at the buttons by several inches and looked pinched and crumpled at the waist. He carried a bowler hat and his thin white hair fluttered in the breeze.

"I thought you'd like to know... ahem... that the mouse and the bread... ahem... you sent for examination... ahem... contained poison... ahem..."

He looked sadly up at Littlejohn as if disappointed to have to tell him this. After every phrase, he cleared his throat as though he had difficulty in speaking at all.

"My name is Godfrey... Dr. Godfrey... They asked me to... ahem... examine the ahem... I gather you, ahem... *thought* they might contain... ahem, ahem... prussic acid...you were quite right...ahem...Enough to kill a man or two even on the bread... ahem... which might have been used for bait to kill the... ahem... the mouse. Excuse me... ahem... You'll get my official report. Got to ahem..."

He hurried to the graveside, without another word, clearing his throat loudly above the noise of intoning.

Littlejohn forgot the ceremony.

X, the brain behind the crime, had tricked Alcardi into murder, but, it seemed, had followed on the heels of the Italian to see the job was properly done and, perhaps for some other purpose after the Deemster died. X had hidden in the coach, then slipped up after Alcardi had left His Honour's room. As he returned through the private door, did he hear footsteps and hide in the dark coach? Enter little Willie Mounsey, who made straight for the coach to confirm what his pals and the custodian wouldn't believe was there? Willie opened the door...

X had wanted to be sure the Deemster was dead and sure that Alcardi should take the blame for it. How would he lay the trail to the Italian? By placing the newspaper cuttings and the dud notes in the Deemster's pocket? Sooner or later, the police would find them, make inquiries, and, perhaps, deduce that the Deemster with his flair for detection, was on the track of the counterfeiter... But how to bring in Alcardi if nobody had seen the slippery Italian around on the day of the crime?

Littlejohn saw himself and Knell the first time they visited Douglas and Ballagarry together. Lamprey ringing up Alcardi ostentatiously from an outside telephone box as the police passed by. Then, Irons telephoning Alcardi and getting him on the run.

X, whoever he might be, had worked it all out, enmeshed Alcardi in the web of murder, set the pointers in his direction, fooled the police into thinking they'd solved the crime by finding Alcardi guilty. And then, X had slipped up. They'd got Alcardi so much on the run that he'd panicked and tried to get to Littlejohn to confess his share and try to excuse himself by saying he'd been deceived in the contents of the bottle. Perhaps after hearing the Deemster was dead, Alcardi had tried the contents of the bottle as mouse-bait with terrifying results...

It fitted after a fashion.

X had kept Alcardi under surveillance. He might have followed him himself, or kept a man posted at Grenaby to see that the Italian didn't get near the vicarage...

Yes; Fannin had been sent there as scout because he knew the place and, as he waited, Fannin had tried house-breaking to kill time and, being unsuccessful, had wakened his grandmother and extorted more money from her. Then, when somebody arrived in the dark, he'd hit him hard, as instructed. But he'd got the wrong man, Knell. So, X watching others doing his dirty work, had needed to intervene when Alcardi arrived. Fannin thought he'd killed Knell and was mistaken. But X made sure about Alcardi, especially when the terrified Italian drew a gun and fired at him.

It would have been all right had it worked to plan. But it didn't by a long way. Alcardi was never seen in the castle. The police had never had a chance of interviewing him. The trail was laid right to him and his counterfeiting, with the Deemster on his track, and then... Alcardi wasn't expected to turn informer. They hadn't thought of that, or of the Italian's temperament.

Fannin, ordered to keep Alcardi in sight, loses him in Douglas and gets drunk. So X has to take over and do the trailing himself. Fannin, fuddled, combines house-breaking and cadging with his watching for Alcardi and then hits the wrong man and not hard enough. Otherwise, as likely as not, the Italian would have appeared guilty of murder and silenced in the garden at Grenaby, would have been unable to tell his tale to the police.

The main slip-up by X was that he didn't know of Amy at *The Duck's Nest* being Alcardi's girl and that, cast-off by his confederates at *The Duck's Nest*, by Irons, and by the *Jonee Ghorrym* lot, he told Amy the whole story, either to clear his conscience or else to put the police on the right track...

So, all the dud notes, the smuggling, the Deemster's amateur detection were red herrings. There was some deeper motive, as he and the parson suspected...

The procession was leaving the graveside and Littlejohn made for the car to join the Archdeacon again. An elderly, rheumaticky man, evidently dressed in his best suit of black and wearing an old billycock, raised a large hand to indicate that he had something for the Inspector. It was Crellin, the Quantrell's gardener. He held a note in his fingers.

"Inspector... Herself gave me a note for ye..."

If you care to be present when the Will is read and the desk opened, I shall be pleased to see you after the funeral.

Lucy Quantrell.

He joined the Archdeacon, told him of the message and together they followed the family cars to Ballagarry. Tremouille looked hard at them as they entered. Littlejohn showed him the note.

"Bit odd..."

Tremouille smiled sourly and bared his even white teeth. At close quarters his face looked old and lined. His thin hair, so close-plastered to his head, was grey, his eyes pouched, his thin lips tight.

"I suppose it's all right..."

Lamprey had already helped himself to a drink and was offering one to the lawyer. He frowned as he saw Littlejohn.

"I say... This is hardly the time for police..."

"We're here at the special request of your aunt..."

"Oh, very well. I didn't mean you, Archdeacon. You're always welcome..."

With this final cut at the Inspector he turned on his heel.

The blinds had been raised and in the drawing-room a small knot of relatives had gathered. Two old men, the Deemster's cousins; three old ladies, his aunts; and a tall, stooping very old man with a fine scholarly face and a shock of white hair. He carried a stick and turned his sightless eyes on Littlejohn. He was introduced as the Deemster's father, Juan Quantrell. The Deemster's widow hardly ever left the old man's side. They were like a pair of dignified and bereaved strangers among a lot of fussing outsiders.

The old man did not mention the murder or the death of his son. Instead, he allowed the Archdeacon to lead him aside and they spoke together quietly.

Tremouille entered accompanied by the surviving Deemster. They both looked upset and made for Mrs. Quantrell. She indicated the Inspector and the three of them approached him. Tremouille cleared his throat. All eyes turned to the little gathering round Littlejohn.

"I think you ought to know, Inspector, that the desk has been unlocked and the private papers removed..."

He looked at the Deemster to give him his cue.

The quiet, cultured voice took up the story.

"I've been saying... I was with Quantrell about a week ago and he opened his desk to refer to his diary. It was chock-a-bloc with papers... In every pigeon-hole... Now, with the exception of knick-knacks, printed matter and the manuscript of his book, it's empty. The diary, even, has gone... I can't understand it... He kept the key himself and it hasn't been broken open... The drawers seem to have been cleared of all but printed matter... I just can't understand it..."

"I can..."

They all looked at Littlejohn.

"I beg your pardon..."

Tremouille's voice was harsh, as though Littlejohn might be having a joke.

"I can quite understand it all. But first, you have the Will?"

"Of course. That was kept in my safe."

"Suppose you read it, then, and we deal with the other later. The relatives and servants are waiting..."

Tremouille's look was almost one of hatred. He didn't like being told what to do by anyone.

The Will seemed fair enough. The Deemster's father had sufficient money of his own and was simply left mementoes. You couldn't tell what the old man was thinking. His firm face and sightless eyes reflected none of his thoughts. His fingers shook as he gripped his cane and he rested his chin on his hands.

The servants were to have their legacies...

The rest was all for Mrs. Quantrell, absolutely. The dead man said he knew he could leave to her his family commitments, the allowances to the elderly relatives, the charities they had supported... All his belongings except those already bequeathed, were hers as well.

And that was all...

There was a pause as though everyone expected a lot more.

Littlejohn stared hard at Jeremy Lamprey. His face bore the astonished look of one who had been completely thrust out against his wishes.

Then, everyone started to talk at once. The elderly ladies, it seemed, had for long been dependent on the Deemster's bounty. They did not ask outright what they were now to do, but started to make small talk with Mrs. Quantrell in the pathetic hope of reassurance. "He has left everything for me to attend to and it will be just as before..."

"But..."

One of the male cousins could not contain himself, in spite of the circumstances and the recent tragedy.

"But I understood that he wasn't a rich man. Just his pay as Deemster and a few insurances. Not enough to keep things up as when he was alive, even if the government give you a nice pension, Lucy..."

"Really! You seem to forget yourself, Charles..."

The Archdeacon put a hand on the shoulder of the importunate cousin.

"That's all right, Mr. Kinrade. My husband was wealthier than we all thought. There's quite enough to see me through with all he wished..."

The eyes of the relatives sparkled with curiosity and those of the old men with greed as well.

"Oh... If that's the case..."

The three old ladies were pathetically pleased and wept with relief and gratitude. One by one they put on their outdoor things and crept away. Only Tremouille, Deemster Milrey, Lamprey and the Archdeacon remained with Littlejohn and the late Deemster's wife and father.

"Now, sir. What's all this about your knowing that the desk had been opened?"

Tremouille said it like a policeman interviewing a malefactor.

"That can wait, sir, until a more suitable time. We must be going now..."

"I insist that you tell us at once. This is a serious matter and, as the deceased's lawyer, I must press for your explanation."

"Don't you think you'd better, Inspector?"

Deemster Milrey's soft voice broke in more diplomatically.

"No, sir. I'd like a word alone with Mrs. Quantrell, if she doesn't mind..."

"This is preposterous!"

"Please, Henry..."

Tremouille shrugged his shoulders.

"Very well, if that's the way you want it. But I don't like it, and I must say, I take great exception to the Inspector's high-handed way of doing things. If he knows anything about the desk, we've a right to know, surely..."

The Deemster, the advocate and Lamprey left the room, Lamprey hesitantly, but obviously intent on seeking more drink if he had to go. Littlejohn followed them and closed the door, before Juan Quantrell and the Archdeacon had reached it.

"Will you two please stay. I want you both to hear this..."

They stood in a group on the hearthrug.

"Mrs. Quantrell, has the Deemster ever spoken about losing or missing his keys of late?"

"Not to my recollection. Why?"

She looked puzzled by the question.

"Please think if you remember anything associated with keys..."

She smiled a thin smile.

"I can think of a lot of things... mere trifles. He insisted on carrying them in the side pocket of his trousers and was always wearing holes in the linings. Yes... I do remember a silly incident quite recently... It was really a joke I made about them, and he got quite annoyed..."

"What was it, Mrs. Quantrell?"

"Quite silly, really. He went to a dinner a little over a week ago... The Medical Society, I think. He was a guest... Next morning, he couldn't find his keys. They turned-up in the side pocket of his dinner jacket. He said he was absolutely sure he'd put them on his dressing-table the night before when he undressed. I was asleep when he got home and I just said he must have taken too much wine and forgotten what he was doing, and also that I was pleased he'd put them in his jacket pocket instead of wearing out his trousers... He was quite annoyed with me. First, for suggesting he might be a bit tipsy, and secondly for doubting his lucidity in putting them on the dressing-table over night..."

"Do you occupy the same room, madam?"

"Yes. The Deemster had a dressing-room just off it..."

"With a separate door to the landing?"

"Yes..."

"It was kept locked?"

"Of course not. Why? We trust everyone here."

"The keys... Would they be put on the dressing-table of his dressing-room, or yours..."

"The Deemster's... Why?"

"I'm afraid someone must have borrowed them and taken impressions. I suspected that, before you mentioned this incident. They were taken from the dressing-table and whoever did it was either absent-minded or in a hurry and put them back in the pocket of the jacket..."

The rest of them looked thunderstruck and Mrs. Quantrell spoke what was on all their minds.

"But who...?"

"Was Mr. Lamprey here at the time?"

"Yes, but Jeremy wouldn't. . ."

"I must ask him, to be sure of it. Could I see him alone?"

"Of course, but I can't think he would do such a thing..."

"Who else, madam? The servants? They are old and faithful retainers, judging from the Deemster's remarks in his Will... I know it is rather a grave accusation about your nephew, but I fear we must settle it at once..."

Even the Archdeacon cast a look of reproach at Littlejohn as the three of them left the room. Lamprey was not long in appearing. He had been drinking and his face was flushed.

"You want me?" he said insolently.

In reply, Littlejohn took him by the collar and shook him. It was an unusual sort of behaviour for the Inspector, but he was sure of his man this time. Lamprey's response was hysterical. He bent in rage and bit Littlejohn's thumb on his lapel. The Inspector released him and slapped him across the face with the back of his hand. Then he raised his other hand and did the same on the other cheek.

"Now, you little swine!"

Littlejohn hit him in cold blood, thinking of the contribution Lamprey had made in the wrecking of the very home which had given him shelter and of the very man and his wife who had treated him almost like their own son.

Lamprey felt his burning cheeks with the palms of his hands as though trying to find out if they were still in their places. He recoiled a step and, like a small boy after a hiding, pointed a sagging finger at Littlejohn and snivelled.

"I'll make you pay for this. You wait till I tell the local police. It's not allowed, beating witnesses or torturing to make them talk... I'm going to tell the Deemster and Tremouille..."

He made for the door, but Littlejohn was there first. He seized Lamprey by the scruff of the neck, carried him across the room and flung him in a chair.

"*Let me alone...*"

"What do you think the Deemster and the courts will have to say to *you?* The man who provided the murderer with the key to enter his own uncle's private room and kill him..."

Lamprey's jaw fell and his eyes opened like small round saucers. The goat-nostrils dilated. There was guilt written all over him.

"You took them from his dressing-table, made impressions of them, and supplied whoever ordered you to do it with the means to kill Deemster Quantrell... Don't deny it. I know all about it."

"You can't prove it. You're trying to trick me."

"I can prove it just as easily as if I'd been present when you did it. Now tell me who gave you the orders and tell me fast. Otherwise I'll arrest you as an accessory to your uncle's murder."

Lamprey put his head in his hands and started to weep. Loud, noisy bellowing, like a child trying to get its own way and mighty sorry for itself.

"I couldn't help myself. I had to do it. But I didn't know they wanted them for that. They said they wanted them to get papers from his desk here and in the court."

"Who are *they?*"

"It was Alcardi. He told me he had orders to make keys of the private chambers at the Castle and of my uncle's desk. I was to get them. I said I wouldn't and then..."

"Then?"

"Promise you'll not use it against me. It has nothing to do with my uncle's affairs. It was my own business."

"I'll promise nothing and you'd better tell me if you don't want to spend the night and many others in jail."

"I met Alcardi through buying painting materials. I ran up a bill I couldn't pay. He told me how to make some cash. He'd got some counterfeit banknotes. If I'd pass off twenty of them, I could have ten... I fell for it. When they wanted the keys, he said we were in it together and if I didn't, I was for it..."

"How much did they give you for the keys?"

Lamprey looked amazed at the knowledge.

"Twenty-five... Real notes..."

He whispered it. Like Judas.

"What happened?"

"He left them one night in his dressing-room. I made impressions. It was a big bunch of keys and I'd to make about eight impressions to be sure to get the right ones..."

He sounded affronted at his uncle for carrying so many!

Littlejohn stood with his back to Lamprey, looking through the window as he listened to the sorry tale of treachery. A charabanc passed full of hilarious holidaymakers. They were wearing paper caps and waving rattles and flags. On the cap of one laughing woman you could see KISS ME in large letters...

"Go on. What did Alcardi say he wanted them for?"

"My uncle had got some proof about the fake banknotes and they wanted to search his desks and papers. They said if I didn't produce the keys, I'd be in for it with the rest if my uncle caught up with them."

"Who else besides Alcardi was in this?"

"I don't know. I got my contacts through Alcardi. He made the keys. He was good at it. I never knew who ran the racket really."

"Who gave Alcardi his orders?"

"Irons, the antique man. I hear you've got him. He had it coming to him. He was a swine."

"I wouldn't call the pan black if I were you, Lamprey. How did Irons get his orders?"

"Alcardi said it was over the 'phone. Nobody knew who ran the show."

"Indeed! It must have been the invisible man! You all tell the same tale, but one or another of you is going to tell me... and quickly. Have you anything more to say?"

"No..."

"When I first called to see your aunt and you were eavesdropping outside the door there, did you telephone anybody from here before I brought you in again?"

"I don't get you..."

"Don't tell me that. Who did you telephone, and who told you to go outside ostentatiously, and make a show of telephoning Alcardi, just to get us to trace the call and put us on his track?"

Lamprey looked as if he couldn't believe his ears.

"Who told you I did it?... It was Irons! I might have known. Very well. He's told on me. I'll tell on him. I was told to keep Irons informed about what went on if you came. I did tell him and he told me to contact Alcardi from the callbox and say it looked as if the cops were on to the forged banknote racket..."

"I thought so. Very well. Is that all? What else are you involved in?"

"Nothing. I swear it. What are you going to do?"

"It's what *you're* going to do. Do you, or do I tell your aunt all this... and in front of the rest of them...?"

Lamprey almost fell on his knees.

"Not that! I couldn't stand it. All of them to know...! Don't make me do it..."

He started to bellow again in an infantile way.

Littlejohn took him roughly by the arm and towed him into the next room.

"What are you doing, Littlejohn? What have you done to him?"

Tremouille moved swiftly to the door to meet them.

"Lamprey wishes to tell his aunt that it was he who supplied the keys to the desk and the private chambers in the castle..."

The whole sorry tale came out. Even to where, in the absence of his aunt on the business of her husband's burial, someone unknown, with the help of the duplicate keys, had entered Balla-garry, rifled the desk and stolen the papers.

They were all dumbfounded.

"What am I going to do...?"

Lamprey wept again, thinking of himself turned out of doors and flung into the world on his own. Littlejohn provided the answer.

"You're coming with me to jail for the time being on a charge of uttering forged banknotes and you will not be allowed bail, because I shall also have you held for complicity in the murder of Deemster Quantrell. I think, if you ask him, Deemster Milrey will tell you I'm within my rights..."

"You can't do that. I suffer from asthma and my kidneys are diseased. It would kill me..."

"You'll receive any medical attention you need in jail. Get your things and come along."

There seemed nothing anyone could say about it and Lamprey, with his bad chest and kidney trouble, was taken and lodged in the town lock-up until further notice.

12

MR. IRONS EATS HIS SUPPER

Littlejohn and Knell had arranged to meet in Douglas after the funeral, but the sergeant had his morning's work to do and he set about it with a will.

Find all you can about the *Jonee Ghorrym*, Littlejohn had said. There was plenty. Enough to make Knell's eyes open wide and fill him with a frenzy to tell it all to his chief. He couldn't write fast enough in his little book as he perused the register of shipping and then the register of companies.

She hadn't been named the *Jonee Ghorrym* to start with. When she was launched at Birkenhead in 1920, her name had been the *Glen Auldyn*. A Ramsey company had owned her then and Knell, taking down the original list of shareholders, found later he had to cross them all off, because they'd parted with her long ago. The first master had been Ebeneezer Teare. Knell wondered if he were any relation of Millie...

Then, the company had gone into liquidation in 1938. The ship had changed hands and name. The *Jonee Ghorrym* had been bought by the Jonee Ghorrym Company Ltd., with a capital of £30,000. Her tonnage was 400, her length 140 feet, breadth 23, speed 10. Knell took it all down religiously. Then, the shareholders. There had been quite a few changes, but the one which Knell marked with little pencil crosses seemed significant.

300 shares of £100 each, fully paid. And in 1944, Martin Quantrell had owned 30 of them. Then the list for 1945 showed *inter alia*, 20 shares in the name of Lawrence J. Parker; 40 owned by S. Harborne-Smith; 30 by Martin Quantrell; 10 by H. J. Tremouille; 5 by J. H. Kewley; and the rest divided among ten others. Dividend, 11¼%.

In 1946, the Deemster's name disappeared and instead, that of J. Lamprey appeared! Dividend 10%, bonus 7%. Things were looking up!

The 1951 return showed a shuffle in shares. All the odds and ends of holdings vanished and instead the list read:

- Harborne-Smith......80
- Parker......................80
- Tremouille.................80
- Kewley.....................30
- Lamprey...................30

The Ramsey *Duck's Nest* gang held the lot between them, with the exception of Lamprey, whose holding hadn't increased. The dividend was the same.

Knell scratched his head. He was in deep waters and wanted someone to help him out. And he thought of the very man. Walter Teare, Millie's brother, Knell's brother-in-law elect! Walter was a chartered accountant who did a lot of shipping work. He happened to be in when Knell arrived at his office in Athol Street, Douglas.

"Mr. Teare in?"

The little girl in the outer office eyed Knell up and down. She was drinking a cup of tea and drained it before she took action.

"Who shall I say?"

"Sergeant Knell. . ."

He almost said 'of Scotland Yard' and just stopped in time.

Walter Teare was a brisk young man with a large dark handlebar moustache, a survival of his fighter days in the R.A.F. He was six feet two and broad with it. He slapped Knell on the back just to show he was welcome to the family and to the office.

"Come in, Reg. Cup of tea? You're just in time..."

"I'm just on a job for Scotland Yard..."

"Yes. Millie told me. Congratulations, old man. Though I says it as shouldn't, Millie's one in a thousand. My loss is your gain, old chap. Guess I'll have to get married myself when Millie goes. Got to have somebody to cook my morning rasher, eh? Well? What can I do for you? Get weaving, Reggie..."

Knell managed to get a word in and then started in full spate. He didn't stop talking until absence of entries in his book dried him up.

"Strictly confidential, Walter."

"Sure, sure. Now let's get this straight. What are you after, Reggie? Finance or facts?"

Knell didn't quite know.

"What does all the chopping and changing mean, Walter?"

Mr. Teare looked over Knell's spidery writing, scribbled things on a pad, browsed over them, consulted books of reference from a book-case... He massaged his large moustache and then went and stood and looked through the window for a long time. Suddenly he turned and spoke gravely, giving Knell a bit of a shock.

"Lamprey was obviously a nominee for the Deemster. I know Lamprey. He's a little slug, who hasn't got a bean. Always on the cadge. Inference; Quantrell was made Deemster in 1946. It's not the thing for a Deemster to hold interests in companies he might be called upon to rule for or against in court. Quantrell disposed of his holding. Lamprey took them over, but I suppose His Honour kept a hold over Lamprey... Sort of a beneficial interest. We've no way of knowing, short of going through the Deemster's papers... Of course, he may have *given* them to Lamprey in trust, or something... In 1951, the three Ramsey shareholders held control and Kewley, that's the captain of the boat, was cut in more heavily..."

Walter Teare sat down again, closely examined the data, stroked his moustache and thumped the table.

"Captain Kewley... Now he's not a native Manxman at all. I believe his forebears were Manx but he came from Liverpool, married a Manx girl, and settled here. Kewley got five shares when he took over the *Jonee Ghorrym* in 1945. Perhaps they had to do that to tempt him..."

"Why?"

"Because she might be termed an unlucky ship. Ben Teare was washed from his own bridge and drowned in 1945... I remember it well enough. The year I came back home from the R.A.F. He was no relation, but anything happening to a Teare... Well... You know how it is, Reggie? When Ben Teare was lost, we felt it was one of us, just like you'll do after you join the family... Get me?"

Knell said he did. He wrote it down the better to explain it to Littlejohn when he reported later.

Duck's Nest lot own all shares, except 30, held by Lamprey.

Captain washed overboard in storm, 1945. Kewley took command.

"Wait a minute. Let's see..."

Teare was telephoning to another pal who was in the know.

"Say, Sandy... Any changes in the holdings in the Jonee Ghorrym Company lately... I'll hang on... No, I'm not buying. Just curious..."

There was a pause.

"Yes... That's right, Sandy... Who bought. . .? Smith? Spell it. Harborne-Smith... Right... I'll stand you a drink when I see you... By the way, don't forget the thirtieth... Bring Tiny along... Gercher... S'long..."

"The Deemster... or Lamprey, sold out six months ago. Chap called Harborne-Smith, same as in your book, bought 'em."

"How much for?"

"Search me! Private company, private deal..."

"How could I get to know, Walter?"

"Ask the Deemster's bank. He might have got a cheque, or something..."

"They wouldn't tell, would they?"

"That's your headache, Reggie..."

The sight of Littlejohn arriving with Lamprey for the lock-up, drove his own eager affairs from Knell's mind until the prisoner had been charged, found a lodging, and his lawyer sent for. Then, Knell told his tale, breathlessly, mixing the deductions of his brother-in-law to-be in with the information, and tapping his notebook with his pencil like a professional accountant.

"Good! Excellent, Knell! Now for the bank."

"But they won't tell you..."

"They'll tell Mrs. Quantrell..."

First, Mrs. Quantrell; then the bank.

"Yes," came the energetic voice of Mr. Kerruish. "Yes... Mrs. Quantrell says we can divulge the item. Hold on..."

A cheque had been paid in in March...£15,000... payable to Jeremy Lamprey, endorsed over to Mr. Quantrell... Later the full sum invested in War Loan... Cheque drawn by S. Harborne-Smith..."

"Thank you, sir..."

Littlejohn whistled.

"Knell. The thirty £100 shares, worth originally say £3,000, changed hands for £15,000... More than five times their nominal value... Bought by Harborne-Smith. Well, well... No wonder the Deemster said he'd provided for his wife! That would go a long way towards it. Let's have another word with Lamprey..."

Lamprey was in his cell, sitting miserably on the solitary chair. They'd tried to make him comfortable. There was even a cushion on the hard seat. He gave Littlejohn a nasty look.

"I'll make you pay for this after I've seen my lawyer. You'll see.

This will just about kill me. My asthma isn't so good and I can't even bear to think what my inflamed kidneys will be like after a night in that bed if I don't get out on bail..."

"You held some shares in the Jonee Ghorrym Company until March this year..."

"What if I did? You can't hold that against me. I've a right to do what I like with my own money, haven't I? And who are you to start nosing in my finances...?"

He made a quick note in a little diary he took from his pocket. He seemed to be piling up an indictment against Littlejohn.

"But it wasn't your money. It belonged to the Deemster."

"That's just where you're wrong! It did not. Put that in your pipe and smoke it."

"It wasn't your own."

"You can't make me talk about my private affairs..."

"It wasn't your own. When you sold out, Deemster Quantrell got the money and invested it..."

"You seem to know all about it. Why ask me...?"

He sniffed, his goat-like nostrils twitching. Littlejohn took hold of the lapels of Lamprey's coat, gently this time, but it was enough.

"Here... Leave me alone... You can't rough-house me... I'll tell my lawyer..."

"Whose nominee were you for the shares? The Deemster obviously couldn't be a shareholder after his judicial appointment. Were you *his* nominee...?"

"Let me go. He gave them to my aunt and I was *her* nominee. Now are you satisfied?"

"How was the sale transaction brought about?"

"I got an offer..."

"*You* did. A good one, wasn't it?"

"All coasters are raking-in the money now."

"Not to that extent. Harborne-Smith made you the offer?"

"Yes. I knew the other shareholders. I asked for bids."

"And got £500 for a £100 share..."

"What of it? They're worth it..."

"What do they pay?"

"I don't know..."

"Come, come. You drew the dividends..."

"Leave me alone... I'm not saying any more. I got the bid, I took it, and that's enough for you."

"They must have wanted them badly."

"I'm saying no more. I've told you too much as it is after the way you've treated me. And you bullied that out of me. I'll tell Tremouille when he arrives. It's against the law..."

"Very well."

Lamprey was making a fuss of coughing and wheezing as they left. He spat in his handkerchief and carefully inspected the result.

"I expect I'll be spitting blood before morning... And my back's started to ache. It's my kidneys..."

Irons and Fannin had also been brought to Douglas jail. Fannin was quite different from Lamprey. He was busy working out a football pool when Littlejohn entered his cell.

"Might as well try my luck. It's money that counts. I'll bet Irons is getting different grub from me. He can pay. I haven't a bean. If I win a packet I'll make somebody wish they hadn't been born..."

"Now, Fannin... You help us and we'll help you. I want to know who told you to keep an eye on Alcardi the night you were last down at Grenaby vicarage. You were told he was trying to contact me there or elsewhere. Instead, you got drunk and lost him. Then you made your way to Grenaby and kept watch. To occupy your time, you tried to break in and blackmailed your old grand-mother. Then, mistaking Sergeant Knell for Alcardi, you hit him..."

Fannin was on his feet. He'd forgotten his football pools and his putative fortune.

"Irons has been talking, has he? The dirty double-crosser! He said he'd see me right."

"Were you told to hit Alcardi hard enough to kill him?"

"I said I wouldn't. I might be what you call bad, but I'm not a killer. I know how to use a cosh so's not to go all the way... Irons said if I quietened Alcardi, they'd see to the rest and take him away and stop him from talking."

"Who's *they*?"

"Irons and his mob. I only know Irons. I got all my orders from him."

"Including the bottle of so-called dope you took to Alcardi?"

"So, he's told you that tale, too... All right. Anything more you want to know? I'll talk, if you'll see me right and give me protection."

"Protection from whom?"

Fannin looked a bit sick.

"You saw what they did to the Deemster and Alcardi..."

"*They*, again. Who?"

"Irons and his pals..."

"Did you ever sail in the *Jonee Ghorrym*?"

"Quite a bit when they wanted an extra hand."

"Where to?"

"Whitehaven, Liverpool, Dublin... And once to St. Malo and a place called Quiberon, south of St. Malo."

"What did you carry?"

"Coal, timber, bricks... General cargo."

"And from France... Quiberon? St. Malo?"

"That was a trip from mainland ports to France for produce... Spring vegetables, early fruit, potatoes, and such.

"And contraband?"

"Don't ask me. They wouldn't tell me. That's the truth."

"Very well, Fannin. I'll see what I can do for you, if you'll keep straight in future. Did you like Captain Kewley?"

"A surly devil, but if you work, you don't come up much against him."

Fannin was right. Irons was eating steak puddings in his cell for his late lunch. He raised his sad eyes as Littlejohn entered. His lips were slobbering and his jaws rotating.

"A bit o' lunch, sir. Nothing left now but to eat, sir. And then I put on more weight and my breathing suffers."

He was trying the heartbreak trick, sorry for himself.

"How long am I goin' to be here? I'll have to get to the south, you know. Another winter here and it'll be my last, sir. You'll bear that in mind?"

"You and Lamprey ought to start a private sanatorium, Mr. Irons. You with your breathing and Lamprey with his asthma and his bad kidneys. You're a pair."

Irons stopped eating.

"Lamprey? Is he *in*, too?"

"Yes. *And* Fannin. They've told me quite a lot. It seems, according to them, that you're the cause of all their misfortunes, Mr. Irons. You've a lot to answer for."

Irons breathed heavily. He broke a square of bread, mopped up the gravy with it, and chewed it absent-mindedly.

"What have they told you?"

"Mostly about the way you treated poor Alcardi. The bottle of poison... The trail you laid for us to follow to him... The instructions you gave to Fannin to follow him and slug him, and then you'd see to the rest when he was laid out. Were you going to slit his throat?"

Irons picked the bread from his teeth with his tongue.

"Now, now, Mr. Littlejohn. Come, come. I'm no murderer, sir. I am too sensitive to value yooman life so lightly. I have my principles, sir, though the police may not think it. And as for killing pore Mister Alcardi. I told Fannin to knock him out and I was going to take him away in the *Jonee Ghorrym* for a break over the water. You found me and Fannin, you know, and we intended to have Joe with us. But Joe was dead. I don't know who killed Joe, I do assure you. It was none of my doing. I was trying to help him. He wouldn't be helped. So I told Ken to *make* him be helped.

Instead, the fool got drunk and coshed a policeman. What can one do with such...? After finding the big mistake we'd made with Alcardi putting him in a panic and getting him scared stiff, it was up to me to do my best. If he'd come to you, sir, you'd have seen him swing. I couldn't let him do it, sir. It was against my better nature..."

Irons shrugged his shoulders. Irons the philanthropist! He forked more steak pudding in his mouth.

"Who's *we*, Mr. Irons?"

"I don't know. I get all my orders through post, Mr. Littlejohn. I little thought where they was goin' to lead to once I had started on the downward path to destruction. I only know they'd got me and pore Joe in their grip because, as you know, I got innocently involved in the dud note racket. I was in it before I knew. They said they'd see I got a stretch for it if I didn't act as their mouthpiece..."

"Rubbish! You know as well as I do that you simply committed a minor crime in passing the notes. You're not so simple, Irons, as to take a murder rap out of fear of a few years in jail..."

Irons spoke with his mouth full.

"It was more than that! My life wasn't safe. You seen what they did to Alcardi and the Deemster..."

"And the little boy... Go on..."

"The Deemster was on their tracks for something. I don't know what..."

"And Lamprey. Who did Alcardi make the keys for? Did you *tell* him?"

"Yes. I got it over the 'phone, sir."

"And someone had the desk key delivered to him. How was it sent and who got it?"

"Alcardi made the keys; two for the room in the castle and one for the desk at the Deemster's house..."

"Why two for the castle...?"

Littlejohn knew now that his theory about X following Alcardi was right, but he wanted to know if Irons knew it as well.

Irons licked his lips. He was sitting on a small chair which his huge, flabby body completely enveloped. It made him look to be sitting suspended in mid-air without support.

"I don't know..."

Fear was creeping in the fat man's eyes now. Littlejohn could see it, the bulging whites, the winking lids, and the tongue for ever busy moistening the thick lips.

"Who had the second key and who rifled the Deemster's desk...?"

"I don't know..."

"How did you pass on the keys then?"

"I want to think it over... I want to get it clear in my mind."

"Don't be stupid, Mr. Irons. Lamprey stole the keys and made impressions; Alcardi made the new keys and gave them to you; who did you pass them on to?"

"I—I was told to leave them hanging on a nail in the porch of my shop when I left for the night. In the morning they had gone..."

"And you didn't wait to see who collected them?"

Irons shrugged his shoulders. He had recovered his confidence and was now mopping up the congealed gravy on his plate with the last of the bread and eating it.

"I knew better than do that..."

All right for a tale! Irons knew more than he'd say, but he was scared to death by the fate of others.

"Very well. You'd better think up a better tale, Mr. Irons, for when I come to-morrow..."

But there was no to-morrow for Mr. Irons. He died that night in his cell. It was gluttony that caused it. Irons wanted fish and chips for his supper; he said he couldn't sleep on an empty stomach and would pay for his food. He also didn't like the prison tea; it made him retch...

A constable, complaining at the indignity of it, went to the restaurant round the corner, where, before a large brass range, they fried fish and chips, and came away with a liberal helping of each and a large jug of coffee. As he did so, the Jubilee clock struck ten. Mr. Irons consumed his meal and drank the coffee and then started to die. At first, they thought his greedy eating had made him sick, but soon realized that it was more than that. When the doctor arrived, it was too late. Irons had given himself a heart attack through vomiting, an operation which he provoked by sticking his fingers down his throat.

There was enough arsenic in the coffee to kill half a dozen men.

The constable said he had merely put the jug down on the counter, till they'd wrapped up the fish and chips. He hadn't kept an eye on it; he was talking to the owner of the restaurant. The shop had been packed with holidaymakers buying alfresco suppers... They'd all dispersed, they were strangers on holiday, and it was going to be a terrible job to find them again. They traced one or two of the occupants of the restaurant who lived in the vicinity, but they weren't much help. One old woman, who'd called for her son's supper, did recollect something vaguely. A man standing at the policeman's elbow eating his meal from the newspaper which held it.

"I jest reckerlect 'im. Eatin' his chips from the paper over the top of the perliceman's jug. There wasn't much room... Packed like 'errings, we was..."

"What did he look like, this man?"

"Smallish. Didn't see 'is face proper, but 'e was puttin' 'is fish an' chips in his mouth under 'is moustache... I remember the moustache... and his cap... a dark one. Wore an overcoat, too. A bit too big for 'im, was the coat. Sort of clung over the backs of 'is 'ands as he eat his supper..."

13

NIGHT AT THE DUCK'S NEST

Morin was amazed when Littlejohn claimed his room for the night. At first, he said they were full-up, but the Inspector reminded him that Archdeacon Kinrade had already bespoken it.

"I didn't know it was for you. I thought it was for another churchman; a priest or maybe a bishop..."

Dusk was falling and the promenade lights were on. There had been a gale warning over the wireless and small ships were putting into Ramsey Bay for shelter. Two local coasters, tied-up in the harbour, were getting up steam and the wind blew the black smoke from their funnels all over the place. Behind the town, the silhouette of North Barrule grew gradually darker and the Albert Tower on the hill at the back seemed more ominous and larger as the day failed. The navigation lights of the harbour shone fitfully and the lighthouse at the Point of Ayre flashed rhythmically. The town was quiet. All the shops were closed; only the glow from the half-deserted cafés on the seafront and in Parliament Street showed between the street-lamps. The first house of the cinema was ending and a thin string of people emerged from the swing doors and melted away in various directions. The pubs facing the harbour were lit-up and active. Drunken shouts could be heard and in one, somebody was singing in a passionate tenor, slightly off pitch...

Then rises like a vision, shining bright in nature's glee,

My own dear Ellan Vannin, with its green hills by the sea.

The piano was out of tune, too, and the singer and the instrument had catches in their voices.

At *The Duck's Nest*, things were warming up. One of the rooms was reserved for a private party to celebrate an old man's eightieth birthday and guests in evening dress were arriving in cars. Littlejohn, his bag safely in his room, was sitting in the bar with the back of his chair to the wall under the portrait of the widow Clicquot-Ponsardin. Before he sat down, he looked casually at the back of the picture. There was a label on it.

Matelas Frères. Negotiants en Vins. Quiberon (Morbihan).

"You're a native of Quiberon, Jules?"

Morin, who had brought in the beer, because Amy was looking after the private party with the aid of a hired waiter, paused and eyed Littlejohn with his bright, crafty look. He shrugged his shoulders, raising the beer mugs he was holding as well.

"Maybe..."

He was puzzled about how the Inspector knew it.

"Excuse me... A party going on... High jinks, eh?"

He hurried away to his kitchen. The cuckoo clock in the hall shouted eight times.

There were one or two people drinking in the room by now. Holidaymakers, by the looks of them, seeking a bit of light and high-life in the quiet town. Suddenly, the door opened and Colquitt, the reporter from the *Clarion* entered. He'd already had a drink or two and was flushed and talkative.

"Hello, Inspector. What brings you here? You're not one of the party, are you?"

"No. I'm just here for a day or so. Making routine inquiries about Alcardi and his connections with Ramsey. I thought I'd better stay over instead of travelling."

"Where are you staying?"

"Here..."

Colquitt looked surprised. He raised his eyebrows.

"Lucky, aren't you? Morin's a bit choosey, you know... What'll it be? Beer?"

He rang the bell and this time, Amy entered. She was dressed in her best uniform for the party. Black frock, starched apron and cap. And she'd had her lank hair waved. Her cheeks were rouged and she'd been using lipstick. She must also have been wearing one of the Misses Curphey's plastic devices, for she was no longer flat-chested... Colquitt noticed it. She looked quite attractive and he passed his arm round her waist and started to caress her flanks. She bridled.

"Leave me *alone*..."

Her eyes held those of Littlejohn for a minute and she smiled slightly.

"You think because I'm not invited to the party, I'm nobody. But you'll see... A double whisky for me and a pint of bitter for the Inspector..."

Colquitt sat by Littlejohn.

"Still enjoying yourself, eh? Like the Island? It gets you, doesn't it? Blunts your liking for work. You'll see..."

He *said you'll see* to everything, as though quite sure of the future.

"I'm here reporting on the party. It's old man Parker's. He's eighty... Father of Parker, the builder you met the other day. He's old and had a stroke a few years since, which made him bad on his feet and took the use of his arms a bit. He sits there like a waxwork most of the time, but he was determined to celebrate his four-score... His friends and some of the nobs of Ramsey are coming..."

Amy was back with the drinks.

"Put it down to me, Amy. I'll pay at the end. I'll be here some time watching the party. Taking notes ready to print 'em... The power of the press... what?"

He drank half his whisky at a gulp.

"You're looking quite pretty, Amy. Why aren't you always like that? Has Jules been makin' a pass at you?"

She tossed her head and flounced to the door.

"...Old Parker, by the way, is still the tyrant, in spite of his age. Owns the contractors' business and won't let his son, Lawrence, even have a share. Lawrence works for a wage! Can you beat it? Every day the old man's nearly carried to his desk at the office and sits there like a mummy, glaring, muttering orders, complaining about what's spent... and Lawrence does the work. No wonder Lawrence is bitter. The workmen hate him. The firm can't keep workmen. Lawrence follows them round seeing they do the job properly. No workman worth his salt's going to stand for that. Here's health!"

He drank another large mouthful of his whisky and soda.

Littlejohn found himself thinking of the morose, middle-aged Parker, dominated by the will of a helpless old man. Parker, who followed his workmen round seeing they made a proper job of it. Parker who was one who controlled the *Jonee Ghorrym*... Parker who might have followed Alcardi, seeing that *he* did the job properly, too...

Through the glass panels of the bar door, you could see people entering for the party. They were bringing in old Parker, now. A small, red-faced wisp of a fellow, with a mop of white hair, and malicious eyes set in a skull which was almost that of a dead man already. He wore a dinner suit and shuffled along with his son on one side and a plain, fat woman with hennaed hair and a lot of sparkling jewellery, on the other. The woman wore an evening gown which showed a lot of bosom and fat flabby arms. You couldn't hear what she said, but she seemed to be shouting orders to her husband on the other side of the shuffling man. The old paralytic kept grinning malevolently at her in approval. Between them they were leading Lawrence a dance...

"What did I tell you..."

Colquitt rang the bell for more drinks.

"My turn, sir..."

"Not at all, Inspector. My guest... Hello, Silas! You waiting-on to-night? Same again, Silas..."

A man like an ostler took the orders. He wore a waistcoat with sleeves, a green apron, and a soiled white collar and white stock. A jockey gone to seed...

"Silas is the handyman. A warned-off jockey... Hullo, here comes the Count de Tremouille. Just look out for his wife. She's the belle of the Island..."

Tremouille had shed his funeral weeds and was in full evening dress. Well-groomed and ruddy, he looked like a visitor from an embassy ball. He wore a monocle on a black cord over his white vest. He was followed by a tall, striking woman with dark hair and eyes and a beautifully moulded face. The broad brow, fine features, delicate arched nose were spoiled by the sensual, unhappy lips. She wore a pale green evening gown with a bodice like a tulip, from which her exquisite shoulders and neck emerged as from a flower itself. She seemed to be nagging Tremouille about some cocktails.

"I'll see what I can do, Daphne... But they're short-handed, it seems..."

She deprived her husband of all the dignity his clothes imparted. He almost ran to find somebody to give them drinks. Silas entered without ceremony.

"Eh?"

"Champagne cocktails, Silas..."

"Wot? I'll have to get the boss to see to those. We're short-handed an' I don't know a champagne cocktail from a shandy-gaff..."

He hurried out to find Jules.

Tremouille waved a hand in the direction of Littlejohn and Colquitt. His wife nodded to the reporter and looked hard at Littlejohn. They seemed quite out of place in the room... Like a conjurer and his partner ready to go on the stage. Jules entered. He wore his chef's cap and white clothes, this time without the tea towel.

"Come in my room, sir. I'm mixing some drinks there..."

Colquitt put his feet on a vacant chair and puffed cigarette smoke vertically to the ceiling.

"Just like 'em to turn up in that rig-out. Her father was consul to some tinpot South American republic and she's never got over it. Tremouille met her somewhere on the mainland. She's a lot younger than he is. He dotes on her. Better if he'd married the girl he wanted. By the way, did you know he was keen on Deemster Quantrell's wife when they were young. She chose the better man, even if he was much older... Another drink? Hurry up... I'll just order another..."

He left the room a bit unsteadily and returned with a cocktail glass.

"Champagne cocktails at old man Parker's expense. Good old Parker! Worth a packet, but keeps his son on a wage! Bet Lawrence wishes he'd drop dead after this little flutter. Where were we...?"

He sipped his drink, his little finger in the air above the glass.

"Tremouille... yes. I was saying he wanted the Deemster's wife. He never forgave Quantrell for that. Or for getting the Deemster-ship before him. Every time the prize has been there, Tremouille has been baulked by Quantrell's getting there first."

"Yet, he's the Quantrell's lawyer?"

"Oh... That... Just like Quantrell. Never bore any ill-will. Besides, it helped Tremouille to keep in touch with his old love. Not that she'd look twice at him. But when he sits back and thinks of the dance this lovely he's got leads him, he must curse his luck. Lovely woman but runs him in debt and treats him like a dog. I'll bet Tremouille hasn't got a bean, except what he makes in practice. And that won't be much. Now, I guess, he'll be High Bailiff or something when they fill the vacancies... and from that to Deemster. That'll give him a regular income, if nothing else. He does so want to be some-body, too. Look at the way he dresses. You'd think he was the Count of Monte Cristo... And he can't even afford a proper holiday; stays with his wife's relatives on the mainland every summer..."

Colquitt had certainly got it in for Tremouille. He seemed to be going out of his way to caricature the guests at Parker's dinner. A lot of frustrated, penniless spongers, to hear him talk...

"I'd better be seeing to a list of guests. Got to get it in the paper next time we go to press. Get a few guineas in Liverpool, too. I'm correspondent here for some mainland papers. Another drink, first... Why, look who's blown in..."

It was Harborne-Smith, bulging from his evening clothes, fat, pink and jovial, with a girl half his age on his arm. They were laughing and talking as they passed the glass door on their way to the bar Jules had improvised outside, for a drink.

"You'd think he owned all Ramsey. Instead of which, he's a remittance-man, sent here out of the way of his family. I once met a man who knew him when he was in practice on the mainland. He had to go abroad. No confidence. Specialist in unsuccessful operations. Finally gave it up and the family gave him an income to get him out of their hair... Expect you think I'm a mine of infor-mation. Trust the press for getting the news... Let me get you one of the old man's cocktails. They're good..."

"I think I'll turn in, sir. I've a full day to-morrow..."

"Can you give me a line for the paper? Any clues? Suspects? Likely arrests?"

"So far, nothing, sir."

"Not even a slant on anything?"

"Nothing..."

"What about the men you arrested...? Irons, Fannin and Kewley? Did you get anything from them?"

"Not so far... I'll be talking to them later. Perhaps they know something that will help..."

"Perhaps they do... Good luck..."

Colquitt looked at his watch and Littlejohn did the same. Nine o'clock. Somewhere at the back, you could hear a wireless giving the Greenwich time signal. Outside, the wind was still rising, but they were casting off the ropes of one of the tramp ships. There was a lot of shouting and steam hissed from the safety-valve.

"I'd better get my information and be off. I've another function to report before I finish. See you later, Inspector. You won't want to leave the Island when the time comes. It gets you. You'll see..."

He hurried out and you could hear him greeting people in the lobby. In the other room they seemed to have started the meal. Amy and the hired man, a broken-down flat-footed waiter in a shabby tail-coat, were carrying in the dishes.

Tremouille, Parker, Harborne-Smith... A pretty trio, if what Colquitt said was true. Malevolent little blighter, with his tongue loosened by drink.

"Forgive me, but are you the Scotland Yard man over on the murder case?"

It came from a tall, well-built young man with a large handlebar moustache, sitting with a good-looking fair girl near the window. Hitherto they had sat drinking beer in companionable silence. They seemed on good terms and thoroughly to enjoy each other's company without any fussing. They wore tweeds and Littlejohn remembered seeing them getting out of a little sports car now parked on the quayside.

"Yes, sir. How did you know?"

They all laughed. After Colquitt's chatter all the Island must know!

"I've been wanting to meet you, sir. My name's Teare. Walter Teare. I think I can claim an introduction because I'm the brother of Millie Teare who's engaged to your assistant... or that's what he says he is... Reggie Knell."

"A very good fellow who's been a great help. Please tell your sister that. It'll perhaps get him a good mark."

"I will. Will you have a drink, sir?"

"No thanks, I've had more than enough. May I buy one for you?"

"I'm the same. Had enough. We've to drive home to St. Mark's yet. Sorry... This is Miss Barbara Quine, my fiancée... and you're the first to know it. We've just got engaged this very evening..."

"Then we *must* have a drink. I believe there are some champagne cocktails going. They're the very thing for a celebration of this kind."

Littlejohn crossed to the little room Jules used for his office, now a temporary cocktail bar. In the large room across the passage, the one in which he'd interviewed Morin the first time he called, he could see about forty people in the middle of a meal. A lot of white shirts, bare backs, bare arms, permanently waved hair. Knives and forks hard at it, hands raising glasses... And in the midst of it all, old man Parker, propped in his chair, doing the honours, with his son's wife cutting up his pheasant into small pieces... *The Duck's Nest* gang, as Knell had called them. The *Jonee Ghorrym* lot, perhaps faintly uneasy at the presence of Scotland Yard on the Island, with a smuggling charge in the offing. And Captain Ebeneezer Teare washed from the bridge of his own ship... what of that?

There was nobody about, but there were half a dozen champagne cocktails standing on the little sideboard. Littlejohn took three of them with him.

"The very best of luck to you both..."

Barbara Quine was a nice girl who worked in the government office and who was still a bit 'dazed at the whirlwind wooing of Walter Teare. Compared with that of Knell, who'd been at it over seven years, it seemed a record!

"It's very nice of you, Inspector. There's something I wanted to tell you. I intended telling Reggie to-morrow, but if I tell you... It's just that Reggie was in my office this morning, inquiring about the *Jonee Ghorrym* set-up. The shareholdings, the captains and what-have you. Well, over lunch, I chanced to mention the thing casually to another friend, a marine assessor, and he said that Deemster Quantrell had been on the same tack a couple of months ago. He asked my friend, a chap called Mylchreest, all about the *Jonee*, especially about the loss of the master, Teare, some years ago. Teare was washed off his bridge in a storm. The Deemster was trying to find out the names of any members of the crew at the time. They all seemed to get scattered, though. They don't carry a large crew and it happened in 1945. There was an inquiry but none of them seems to have seen what happened really. I thought you might like to know..."

"I certainly would... Thanks very much. It may help."

The girl thought she ought to say something to show the Inspector was welcome in their company.

"I see you got caught up with Trevor Colquitt... He's a bit of a bore and cheeky chappie when he's had a drink or two."

"Yes. He seemed to be pumping me for copy and also giving me thumbnail sketches... and not too flattering at that... of his Ramsey friends."

"He's a bit bitter and malicious, Inspector. You should have seen the last report he gave on our dramatic show. I'm a member of one in Douglas. It was a scorcher. And really, everybody said the play was quite good. Seeing that Colquitt was once a good amateur actor himself, you'd have thought he'd have a bit of sympathy for others, wouldn't you?"

"Yes; it would seem so. He was a bit of an actor, then?"

"Yes. In his young days, about ten years or so ago..."

She spoke with the ruthless cruelty of youth. She was twenty-one and Colquitt was about forty-one or two! In his young days...

"...He was quite up to professional standard. In fact, a touring company that came for the winter wanted him to join-up with them."

"The hero, was he?"

"No. Character parts. Like Churdles Ash in *The Farmer's Wife* and the old parson in a Brontë play. You know the sort I mean. A master of makeup. You wouldn't have known him. He met his wife on the stage. She was a member of the same stock company who wanted him to join them. Lucky he didn't. The war came and put them out of business. But he married one of the girls and she stayed on here for a while. Then, two years later, when the company came back, Rosemary... that was her stage name, her real one was Ivy... Rosemary bolted with one of the men in the troupe and left Trevor in the lurch. So, I guess that's made him bitter."

Walter Teare massaged his moustache.

"Really, old girl, once you get going you're quite a little chatter-box, aren't you? You never talk so fast to me..."

"You never let me get a word in edgeways, Wally. It must be the champagne cocktail..."

Littlejohn was just thinking of leaving them to their own company when Silas came to bring him to the telephone. He looked at his watch. Ten fifteen.

He bade the happy couple good night and went to get his message. It was the Douglas police with the news about Irons. He'd just died after eating his supper. All the signs were of arsenic poisoning. The chemist was busy now on the coffee and the police were out in their numbers questioning everyone and trying to trace who'd been there when the coffee was bought in the fish-and-chip shop...

Littlejohn sighed. He might have known it. But somebody had a nerve to take the war right into the police-station where, he'd hoped, both Irons and Fannin would have full protection.

"See that nothing happens to Fannin and Lamprey. Don't let them have food from outside, and no visitors. No, not even a lawyer, unless someone's there with them..."

He telephoned to his wife in the Fens. Everything seemed all right in the vast parsonage, except that it was blowing a gale and some slates had fallen in the courtyard. Oh, and the Canon had been liverish. He said it was the water...

He felt like another drink and ordered one from Silas. The party was over. There had been a few speeches and old Parker had been hoisted to his feet and replied in words nobody could hear except those at his elbows. It had been voted a good party and everybody had gone home in good spirits, including the host. Littlejohn retired after his drink, and undressed leisurely. There were three rooms on his landing, then three steps up, and three more rooms where Jules and the staff slept. He knew Jules's room was the one at the end of the passage. He'd seen him coming and going there as he took up his bag.

On each side, the rooms seemed to be occupied by two married parties of old Parker's guests. They took a long time settling and then, just as all was quiet, Littlejohn remembered he'd left his pipe on the mantelpiece of the bar. He slid out of bed and slipped on his dressing-gown. The pipe was there and he recovered it by the light of the dying fire without even putting on the lights.

As he returned softly up the stairs in his travelling slippers, the door of Jules's room opened noiselessly and he saw Amy, the waitress, enter furtively, half-clad, and as quietly close it.

14

THE AFFAIRS OF THE JONEE
GHORRYM

"Commissaire Luc? Bonjour, mon brave! Comment-ça-va?"
Littlejohn spoke to his old friend Luc, of the Paris
Police Judiciaire, in good French. They had, during the War, when
Luc was in London, worked well together.

The line from Ramsey police-station to the Quai des Orfèvres
was so clear that they might have been speaking across the street.
By the time they had finished, Luc had amiably promised to do
many things, including a visit to London in the following Spring.
The next step was to get a picture of Jules Morin across to Paris as
soon as possible. If it left by the morning 'plane to Manchester,
the local police there would see it safely aboard the afternoon
flight from Ringway to Le Bourget, and it would be at its destina-
tion that night. The point was, the photograph.

One of the constables at Ramsey had a bright thought. Last
Christmas, Morin had made a monster cake, iced and ornamented, for a banquet, and the local newspaper had taken his
photograph standing in chef's attire beside his masterpiece. The
local police saw to it that the photograph of cake and cook was on
the way in half an hour.

Amy had appeared as usual at breakfast, wearing her apron

and cap, with no suggestion of leaving for safety on the mainland, as Littlejohn had suggested. She seemed to have thought it all out and now insisted on seeing the thing through. It was the least she could do in duty to the dead Alcardi, she said. Littlejohn did not argue with her. He'd seen quite enough the night before and as soon as his meal was over he took the Ballure Road in search of Parker's office.

Lawrence Parker was pottering about his builder's yard... or rather, his father's... seeing that the workmen did their jobs properly. Men were busy there, sorting out timber, loading bricks and tiles on lorries, sawing-up wood, mixing mortar in a noisy mill. Parker seemed to be here there and everywhere, questioning the men, urging them on. For the most part, they ignored him, knowing he couldn't sack them without asking the old man.

Just beyond the gates of the large yard, stood a brick office with wide windows and through one of them, you could see old Parker, already on the job before nine-thirty, sitting in his chair, his bowler hat on his head and a rug over his knees, motionless, the only signs of his continued survival, his eyes, overlooking the yard and all that went on in it. Now and then, an elderly typist approached him, ostensibly to ask if he wanted anything.

Lawrence Parker wasn't pleased to see Littlejohn.

"We're busy," he said. "You're interrupting the work. If you want to talk to me, why don't you come to *The Duck's Nest* at one o'clock when I have my lunch?"

He still wore tweeds and a cloth cap. In spite of the time he spent in the open, his face was pale, almost the colour of parchment. He was a chain-smoker and lit one cigarette from the stub of another. For one so tall and heavily built, the small cigarettes looked out of place. He had a nervous twitch of the eyelids, as though from gazing at a bright light, and his fingers were never still.

"This is urgent, sir. I've no time to wait."

"What is it, then?"

"You're a director of the company which owns the *Jonee Ghorrym*?"

"Yes. What of it?"

"You know we arrested Captain Kewley yesterday for carrying passengers forbidden to leave the Island? He was later released."

"Yes, I know. A bit high-handed, I thought it."

"You think helping criminals to escape from justice is high-handed?"

"What proof had you that he knew they were fleeing from you?"

"Fannin was on his way to jail, escaped, and later turned up on your boat. Irons had been told not to leave. Irons, by the way, died last night..."

"What?"

Parker screwed up one side of his features in an astonished grimace. The sign that he was shaken was mainly in his eyes, which opened wide and their lids stopped flickering for a brief spell. He fumbled in the pocket of his coat for another cigarette which he lit from one half-smoked.

"Irons was murdered last night."

"I didn't know that. How did it happen?"

"He was poisoned in jail... Somebody poisoned his coffee."

Parker was angry.

"What the hell are the police doing? Since you came here there have been nothing but murders going on. The Deemster, that scout, Alcardi... And now Irons. Where's it all going to end? It's time you showed results. This sort of thing..."

"If you and your friends would help a bit, we might get on much quicker, The *Jonee Ghorrym* seems to have become the centre of gravity in these crimes."

"What do you mean by that? I've nothing to do with it. Nor have any of my friends."

"You know, of course, that the *Jonee* has been engaging in smuggling."

"That's a lie! It's slander. You'd better tell Tremouille that, and see what happens."

"Alcardi, Irons and Fannin were all in it and, if smuggling was going on, the directors should know something about it. At any rate, the Customs people have been told and you'll have to answer to them on that count."

"I've nothing more to say. You can deal with our lawyer. You can't talk like that about a properly run company, police or no police. I'll. . ."

The middle-aged woman from the office was crossing the yard, gingerly picking her way between piles of slates, stones and timber, like a cat on a rainy day.

"Mr. Parker wants to know what's going on, Mr. Lawrence."

"Tell him... Tell him..."

He glanced in the direction of the office. The old man was still looking through the window, his hat on his head, his eyes peering intently at the group outside.

"He says to come in and see him..."

With an angry gesture, Lawrence Parker turned on his heel and left Littlejohn without a word. He entered the office and you could see him appear before his father at the window, like a small boy called to the headmaster's study. Parker, senior, remained motionless, only his mouth moving. His son's arms flailed as he gesticulated and tried to explain or excuse what was going on.

"I think you'd better come inside, too, sir. He wants you."

The woman had not left with Mr. Lawrence, but remained standing, waiting for Littlejohn to jump at the boss's orders. A dark, faded, baggy little woman, who looked scared to death of displeasing anyone. Life to her was one long apology. If she got the sack from Parker's, she'd probably have difficulty getting work elsewhere...

The Inspector followed her. The room where the old man held court was hot and stuffy. A fire burned in the grate and there was an electric radiator near his chair.

"Here he comes. He can tell you himself. He says they've been smuggling on the *Jonee*. It's a lie!"

"Be quiet and let me deal with this."

Old Humphrey Parker spoke slowly, hardly moving his lips and flecks of foam appeared at the corners of his mouth, as though it strained him to talk. The tone was slurred and monotonous; the eyes were cold and cruel.

"What do you want?"

"In the first place, I've called to ask your son, who's a director of the company which owns the *Jonee Ghorrym*, why they tried yesterday to take passengers wanted by the police, and to warn him that the Customs people are instituting inquiries about smuggling activities aboard her."

Humphrey Parker sat immobile. His slumped figure, with the black, out-of-date hat crowning the lot, might have made a good illustration for a Dickens novel. Scrooge, Dombey, Squeers, Quilp... Any old reprobate due for reform. Except for the eyes. There was nothing comic about them, nor any character. They moved, taking all in, but they were dead; dead to compassion, the gentler things of the world around, even the details of what was going on. All they contained was malevolence.

"You'd better talk to me. He only holds the shares in the company on my behalf. My son's no good at business. He only achieves bankruptcy... He does as I tell him, here and everywhere else."

Littlejohn looked from father to son and back again. Lawrence Parker was biting his lips and taking out another cigarette.

"That's all he can do. Smoke!"

It was incredible! A man in his late forties, completely dominated by his father. Why didn't he pack up, defy the old man, salvage his pride, and launch out for himself?

The Inspector caught Humphrey's malicious glance, and he was aware the old man knew what he was thinking.

"What do you want?"

"That's all for the present..."

Littlejohn had more important work to do than wasting time with a mad old man and his nitwit son.

"I may be back, sir, when I've got a little more information..."

"Information?"

He said it slowly, with difficulty, syllable by syllable.

"About the *Jonee Ghorrym* and what happened to Captain Teare, the night he died on his own bridge. Good day."

He left them at that and as he turned through the gate, he saw that the old man had roused himself. They were helping him out of his chair... His hat was still on his head...

Harborne-Smith lived on the Lezayre Road in a bungalow built on colonial lines, with palm trees in the garden. He was sitting in a bath-robe on the verandah enjoying the warm morning sun.

"Morning. Drink?"

He indicated the bottle, syphon and glass at his elbow. He was starting early on his whisky. The type who, in the colonies he'd left, would disgust his compatriots by his slipshod habits.

"Did you know that Irons was murdered last night, sir?"

"Yes. Tremouille 'phoned me. Funny business. You'd have thought the police would have..."

He waved his glass about and fixed his bloodshot blue eyes on the Inspector's face, his lips twisted in mockery.

"Also, sir, the Customs people are making inquiries about contraband on the *Jonee Ghorrym*..."

Harborne-Smith gulped at his whisky.

"No good, Inspector. They'll not nail us for that, you know."

"You're a director, I believe, Dr. Smith..."

"Harborne-Smith, please. Too many simple Smiths. Got to have a sign of distinction, you know. Yes. I'm a director. I'd know if any queer stuff was going on. Who told you the tale about smuggling?"

"Alcardi... Irons... Fannin..."

"Alcardi? He was dead before you caught up with him."

He paused. It was obvious he wished he hadn't said it.

"Yes? How did you know he didn't see me before he died, doctor?"

"Somebody told me... Jules, I think."

"You were a director when Captain Teare was drowned?"

"Yes. It was accidental and the court ruled it that way. No sense in frying old fish, Inspector. It'll lead you nowhere."

"And all the crew at that time have left?"

"They're always changing. Sailors are that way."

"Not if she's a good ship."

"The *Jonee's* all right. Sure you won't have a drink...?"

"We'll have to find out, sir..."

Inside the house, someone was moving about. A door opened and closed and the scent of bath-salts wafted on a hot blast through the open French window beside which the doctor was sitting. A girl in a dressing-gown entered the room behind, shook out her dark hair and was making for the window when suddenly she spotted Littlejohn. She disappeared as quickly. Harborne-Smith's blue, codfish eyes sought those of Littlejohn and his mouth twisted.

"My housekeeper..."

"Do you still practice, doctor?"

"No. Why?"

"Do you keep a stock of drugs?"

"No. I'm not registered here and I don't propose to get registered. Why?"

"The Deemster died of prussic acid and Irons of arsenic. They're a bit difficult to get..."

It didn't shake Harborne-Smith at all. He was too indolent even to jump up in temper. Instead, he looked amused.

"You don't think I..."

"No. But you associate with company formerly frequented by Irons and Alcardi... And Alcardi murdered the Deemster."

"Who says he did?"

"We know."

"Well, the poison didn't come from me. I don't keep poisons around. All I want is a quiet life, not murders or suicides... I can't help you..."

Littlejohn made his way back to town to see Tremouille. A motley crew, he thought. Parker, tied to his father's apron strings and afraid of something. Harborne-Smith, sowing his wild oats like mad on his remittance money. Tremouille, a good lawyer, but living above his means with an embittered wife he obviously was mad about...

Knell was waiting with the car at the police-station. He looked relieved to see Littlejohn.

"All right at *The Duck's Nest* last night, sir?"

He looked as if he might have expected them to fish the Inspector from the harbour with his throat cut.

"Yes, thanks, Knell. The next thing is to find Mr. Tremouille, if he's in Ramsey to-day..."

"That's easy, sir. I saw him going in his office as I drove in. Just off Parliament Street."

Tremouille looked to be suffering from a hangover when they ushered Littlejohn into his office. His eyes were baggy and dull and the lines in the dark-shaded sockets were deeper than ever.

"Still in Ramsey, Inspector?"

The room was shabby. An old desk, old chairs upholstered in worn horsehair, dusty dog-eared law volumes on the mantelpiece and window-sills, more of them on shelves on each side of the fireplace, and a carpet which had seen better days. The room obviously hadn't been decorated since the tenant took over. The office was a cheap, second-rate one. Opposite, a greengrocer's shop, with somebody playing the piano in the living quarters above it. A tinkling, badly played tune, over and over again.

I'm singin' in the rain...

The bottom halves of the windows were covered by gauze

screens. *Lander and Tremouille, Advocates.* Lander had been dead for years.

"You've heard that Irons died last night, sir?"

"Yes. That was a bad business. Somebody was slow..."

He stood before the fire, his hands in his pockets, rocking on his heels. His shoes were old and well-cleaned and his suit, though neat and tidy, was threadbare; shiny at the elbows and the bottoms of the trousers frayed.

"I don't agree, sir. Irons insisted on having his supper brought to his cell. Fish and chips and coffee. The constable who was good enough to pander to his gluttony and bring in the stuff, wasn't to know that someone was going to put arsenic in the jug."

Tremouille looked nettled. He was used to deference from the police. Here was one back-answering him. His face grew thin and pinched.

"Don't try to excuse them. The police haven't been too bright by any means on the Quantrell case. It's time we had results instead of more murders..."

Littlejohn slowly lit his pipe.

"Mr. Tremouille... If we'd had a little more help from you and one or two others, things wouldn't have been quite so complicated. For example, why did the *Jonee Ghorrym*, the controlling company of which has you on its board, try to smuggle a couple of men wanted by the police, off the island? That wasted us a lot of time. There is also a smuggling charge in connection with her in the hands of the Customs people. If you and your friends would kindly assist and let us get on with the case, instead of having us chasing all over the Island after red herrings, we might now be showing the results for which you seem so anxious..."

"Look here. I won't stand your insinuations. What Captain Kewley does when in command of his ship is no affair of mine or my co-directors. We don't run her, even if we own her. And I resent your remarks about obstruction. I didn't like the way you carried on at Ballagarry yesterday. After all, the Deemster had only just been buried. You might have spared the widow the ordeal of. . ."

"Everything was done at her request. You've seen Lamprey?"

"Yes. Why have you resisted bail? He's not likely to run away."

"Isn't he? That's not the reason, though. I resisted bail because I'm having no more meetings of plotters like the late Irons, Fannin, and the lamented Alcardi. This case has been complicated enough so far. I'm going to keep the parties under our eye from now on..."

"We'll see. Habeas corpus runs in the Island, too, you know."

"I'm well aware of it. But I really called to ask if it would be possible to see the log of the *Jonee Ghorrym* for 1945, sir."

Tremouille's eyes narrowed. He brushed back his sleek hair.

"What has that to do with it? How can the log of a ship help you with the case in hand?"

"I'm sorry, Mr. Tremouille, but I'm not prepared to argue the pros and cons of the matter. Can you or can't you, tell me where I can find the log?"

"I think I can, but I'm not at liberty to hand it over. There'll have to be a directors' meeting first. I've no power to produce it to you nor has any other director without a meeting to agree..."

"I think you're being deliberately obstructive, sir. I'm not asking to take it away from the office where it's kept. I want to see certain entries..."

"I've told you, Littlejohn, I'm a lawyer and my conduct must be strictly correct. A court order or the permission of the board is what I need and even then I'm not sure I can lay my hands on the book."

"Very well, sir. Kindly call your meeting and call it soon. Your board is composed of local men. I suggest to-day will be a good time. I'll telephone to-morrow..."

"I can't manage before to-morrow. I've to be in court in an hour. I'll let you know..."

"In that case I shall have to speak to Deemster Milrey..."

"That won't help. He'll order it to be produced in court and that will take a week. I'll see what I can do in a day or two..."

"Don't bother. I'll have to take the long way round. But please don't talk to me in future about the speed of the investigation, sir. Or about results. I think you know a lot more than you tell me about the murder of the Deemster, the affairs of Irons and Alcardi, and the whole set-up of the *Jonee Ghorrym*, and I intend to find it all out. Good morning. . ."

"Here... Come back..."

But Littlejohn was in the street. Above, the piano was still tinkling away...

Singin' in the rain; yes, singin' in the rain...

"Let's drive back to Grenaby, Knell. I'll come back to *The Duck's Nest* for my bag later. I've not finished there..."

The Archdeacon was snoozing in the hot morning sun in his neglected garden when they drew up. It was like another world. Great clouds casting shadows over the hills and, in the distance, the moors were on fire.

"Glad to see you back, Inspector. You, too, Reggie. How are you getting along? Any nearer a solution?"

"No, sir..."

He told the parson all that had happened since they last met.

"And now, I want your help, sir. Do you know where I can find the widow of Captain Teare who was lost on the *Jonee Ghorrym* in the Spring of 1945?"

"Yes. She married again. She's getting on now, too. Turned sixty..."

And Archdeacon Kinrade was eighty-three!

"She and her husband are farming near Cregneish... that's in the South, almost opposite Calf Island. Did you want to see her? We could make it in half an hour..."

"We? Would you like to come along, parson?"

"Sure I'll come... But after we've had our lunch..."

Cronkbreck Farm consists of eighty stony acres at the very

south of the Isle of Man. Littlejohn and the other two drove over the moor and dropped down a narrow mountain road to Port St. Mary, and then took the steep road to Cregneish. Cronkbreck was in sight of the sea beating itself against the steep rocky coast, with Calf Island, isolated and wild, beyond the treacherous Sound.

Mrs. Teare had, after her husband's death, married Arnold Maddrell, and they were happy and, in spite of the stony ground, moderately prosperous. She was making butter in the dairy when the party arrived. The sight of the Archdeacon smoothed the way and she took them to her best room, cold and damp from lack of fires and from the salt air. The place was full of knick-knacks. A large sideboard, an ancient piano, a suite upholstered in red plush, and what seemed to be hundreds of family portraits, singly and in groups, all of them looking either surprised or agonized at the ordeal of 'being took'. It spoke well for the generous spirit of Arnold Maddrell, that he allowed a large, framed portrait of Mrs. Maddrell's 'first', the late Captain Teare, to dominate the room from over the fireplace. Bearded heavily, with a stern glance and an old-fashioned captain's cap and reefer jacket, he seemed to stare out of countenance the many relatives the former Mrs. Teare had acquired through marriage.

"We've come to have a word with you about Ebeneezer, Mrs. Maddrell," said the parson after he had introduced his companions. Mrs. Maddrell had known Knell's family back to about the fourth generation from Reggie, and felt at home with him. She was a bit shy about Littlejohn. She insisted on giving them tea and her home-made soda cakes.

"Good job we haven't a lot of places like this to call on," said Mr. Kinrade as they waited for the kettle to boil. "They get insulted if you won't take a bite with them. Very hospitable. After a round of calls, you get quite blown-up with tea and soda buns..."

"You remember the spring Ben was lost, Mrs. Maddrell? The Inspector wants to talk to you about him and the time he died..."

Could she ever forget it! Mrs. Maddrell told them in a voice full of lamentation of her last good-bye to Ebeneezer Teare, of the night of the storm, of their bringing the news he'd been washed overboard. She made up her mind after that, never to marry a sailor again. And she'd kept her word. Maddrell was good to her. She was very comfortable. But she'd rather have been farming inland, where you couldn't see the cruel sea...

"Did your late husband ever talk to you about his trips and his ship, Mrs. Maddrell?"

"Yes... I don't remember much about it now. Time passes, doesn't it? It passes, and we forget..."

She looked up at the stern countenance of her 'first' and nodded at it, just to reassure Captain Teare that she hadn't forgotten him, though she couldn't recollect much of what he'd said and done.

"He kept a little diary. My first husband was a bit of a scholar. He was powerful good with the pen..."

"You still have the diary?"

"Of course. I wouldn't part with it for all the money in the world. Maddrell once went to sea before he took to farmin'. Sometimes in winter, when we sit by the fire with the wind howlin' round the house, I read parts of the diary to Arnold. He likes it better than made-up stories from the library. Says it's real good. Not that I'd be one to judge, but Arnold has done a fair bit of readin' in his time..."

"Could we see the diary, Mrs. Maddrell?"

"I'll get it..."

A Manx cat entered carrying a kitten by the scruff of the neck, laid it at Littlejohn's feet, and started to rub round his legs. He picked her up, stroked her, and she settled in the crook of his arm and started to purr.

"Here it is, sir..."

It was a large heavy book with stiff backs marked *Diary* on a label in front. It had been well-thumbed, presumably for the delectation of the absent and generous-hearted Arnold Maddrell. The pages were filled with writing, under date headings, in a bold, rather boyish hand. On the fly-leaf, in another script, someone had written a jingle.

> *Captain Teare it is my name,*
> *Master Mariner is my station,*
> *I live at Douglas, Isle of Man,*
> *And Heaven's my destination.*

Littlejohn turned to the entries for 1945.

Knell, who had been munching soda cakes incessantly, now took out his black notebook and pencil.

"I'll take down, sir, if you like to call it out..."

Mrs. Maddrell, overawed by the might of the law, remained silent, glancing up at the portrait over the fire now and then, as if calling on the late Teare to bear witness.

"Could we borrow this, Mrs. Maddrell, if you don't mind? I'd like to go properly into it. You see, we're interested in the *Jonee Ghorrym* and..."

She threw up her hands at the mention of the name.

"She's a bad ship, that one. Somebody's put the Eye on her. My husband... my first, I mean, would never have a wrong word said against her, but I always knew no good would come from her. They should never have changed her name for one thing and *Jonee Ghorrym* isn't a lucky name, either. My first husband used to laugh at me. Said I was superstitious and a Manx witch, but I do have the Sight now and then, and I was certain sure about that *Jonee*... Yes. You can take the book, but I'd like it back for the winter. Maddrell's that fond of having it read to him on winter nights..."

"Of course, Mrs. Maddrell. You can have it back to-morrow..."

They left her to her work. As they crossed the yard, Arnold Maddrell entered the gate. A tall, powerful man, with clear blue eyes and a sinewy frame. He shook hands all round with a grip of iron. They told him why they'd called.

"Aw... A great scholar was the late Captain Teare and taught my missus a lot while they was together. Herself reads beautiful out of that diary. Makes me want the sea again, but then the missus wouldn't hear of it. A great man with the pen was the late Captain and my missus is so good at readin' what he wrote..."

His clear eyes shone with admiration. He was ready for a good gossip in praise of his wife and her 'first', but they had to leave him. They saw him take off his cap and then lift the latch of the kitchen door, as though in awe of the woman who'd consented to take him as 'second' after such a paragon of a 'first'.

Knell took it all down as they sat in the vicar's study later.

First, in neat sequence, the crew of the *Jonee Ghorrym* at the time the Captain was lost.

Ebeneezer Teare, Master, Douglas. John Vondy, Kirk Bride, Mate. Peter Skillicorn, Douglas, Engineer. Thomas Killip, Laxey, First Hand. Fred Moore, Onchan, Deck Hand. John Kermode, Douglas, Deck Hand. Philip Moore, Onchan, Deck Hand. Arthur Costain, Douglas, Stoker.

February 14th, 1945. We leave for Quiberon to-morrow. Ballast to Barry, steam coal Barry to Quiberon. Early vegetables etc. English port (London?)

I do not like the Brittany trip since cousin Andrew's ship lost with all hands on Glenands. Navigation hard and dangerous.

There followed various other entries. This was evidently a diary which Captain Teare left at home when he sailed; he must have relied on the log of the *Jonee Ghorrym* as his sea record.

March 24th, 1945. The Company have arranged another Quiberon trip. I do not like them, there is something about them I do not understand. We must be undercutting freights to obtain steam-coal cargoes for Quiberon. Our competitors on the mainland have faster, better ships. One of the directors, Mr. Parker, sails with us to Quiberon on a business trip. No change in crew, but Vondy, who dislikes the Parkers, complained about Mr. Law. Parker coming. If this Brittany business persists, must think of obtaining another ship. Vondy talks of doing the same.

Interesting to note that I can make myself understood by talking Manx to the Bretons. Manx and Breton having much in common as languages...

April 26th. After coastal trade Island and Mainland, the Brittany trip again. Told the directors I did not like it. They said it was profitable and they did not wish to seek a fresh master. I said I would reconsider. Not much chance of a new command at present, so I must go. Sailing to-morrow for coal at Barry. Have had to take on new deck hand temporarily. Fred Moore, after drinking at Friendship Inn, Ramsey, walked out and fell in harbour. In hospital and unable to sail. Weather stormy and we look like having a good blow...

New hand: Jack Gordon, Liverpool, resident in Ramsey at present.

There were plenty of other interesting entries before the last one on April 26th, 1945, but the ones Knell had copied were sufficient for their purposes at the time.

After reading through the diary again, Littlejohn decided to return it at once, in view of its value to Mrs. Maddrell. He found her at tea with her husband. She asked them to join them again, which they did. In the course of conversation, she gave them further surprising information.

"Himself," she said, indicating Arnold Maddrell, "Himself said to tell you poor Deemster Quantrell was terrible interested in the diary, too. Him being a bit of a sailor, for a hobby, like. I forgot to tell you when you came before."

"What did the Deemster want, Sarah?" asked the Archdeacon, after she had shyly reminded him that when she had been one of his parishioners long ago, he had called her by her Christian name.

"Aw, he just came an' asked if the Captain left a diary. When I said, yes, and brought it out, he read it very eager, like. He came at eleven, started to read an' take notes, had his dinner with us and stopped along, makin' more notes, till tea. I thought he was goin' to print them, or somethin'... But the poor man died..."

Yes, the poor man had died, and as likely as not, the diary was partly to blame. For Deemster Quantrell had obviously been along the exact road Littlejohn was following and had met his death because of what he found on the way.

15

ECCLESIASTICAL GRAPEVINE

T he Inspector and the Archdeacon talked far into the night. When their voices ceased, momentarily, a complete hush descended, broken only by the wind in the trees outside, the tick of the case clock in the hall, and the tinkle of embers falling on the hearth.

"For an amateur detective, the Deemster didn't do so badly. He seems to have travelled as far as we have done along the road to solving some crime or other. But what could it be?"

Littlejohn filled his pipe and lit it.

"As far as I can see, sir, it was smuggling and then murder..."

"Murder? But who got himself killed?"

"Let's try to start right at the beginning... The Deemster held shares in the *Jonee Ghorrym*. When he was made a judge, he turned them over to his nephew as nominee. His dividends were paid, the boat sailed and was kept busy. He didn't bother his head much about her. Until it came time for him to retire and he started to arrange his finances. Like many such men, he wanted to take his money out of risky industrials and invest it, let's say, in government stock. He sold his shipping shares and was amazed to find eager buyers. To keep the shares in their own hands, the directors of the company were prepared to pay Mr. Quantrell five hundred pounds for a hundred pound-share..."

"Which made the Deemster suspicious. He was a man with his wits about him and must have wondered at the price..."

"And at the eagerness of certain people to acquire his holding. I think they must have outbid one another to get them. It was the first false step the gang made..."

"The gang. You mean the *Duck's Nest* lot?"

"Probably. It started the Deemster on their trail. Most likely he thought of smuggling. He looked into the records of the *Jonee Ghorrym* and then finding her former captain, Teare, was lost at sea, began to investigate that event, as well. My theory is, Teare was suspicious about the goings-on at Quiberon and kept his eyes open. On his last, ill-fated voyage, he must have discovered the extensive smuggling racket and caused trouble. He had to be eliminated..."

"You mean, they cast him overboard?"

"Yes. And I think the Deemster got so far... in suspicions, at least. He mentioned his suspicions to someone..."

"Who?"

"Well... We know he mentioned The Carrasdhoo Men to Deemster Milrey. That was significant... They were smugglers or wreckers, weren't they?"

"Yes... Mythical, though, I think."

"That may be. But didn't we hear that Mr. Quantrell had been making trips on his own to the Curraghs and The Lhen. I've been looking at the map. The bogs of Ullymar were mentioned. They were supposed to be near Jurby... not far from The Lhen and the Curraghs. Quantrell had been round there, probably watching the *Jonee Ghorrym* and had found out something. In other words, he knew of the smuggling and probably the story of Captain Teare's death, too. And as likely as not, he knew who was concerned in it. He made the mistake of telling someone. That sealed his fate. They'd got to kill him. There was no question of buying or threatening to keep him quiet. They tried twice to murder him and succeeded the third time."

"And who are *they*? Do you know?"

"No, sir. There's still a lot to do. For example, we want to see someone who was aboard the *Jonee Ghorrym* the night the captain was lost. Was the body ever recovered?"

"No..."

"So, nobody could say whether or not there was foul play. Knell has looked up the report of the inquiry into Teare's death. He was seen to go on deck. There was a howling gale blowing. He was never seen again. Vondy, the mate, was asleep in his cabin; the man on watch, Killip, saw nothing. In other words, it was only assumed that Teare was washed from his ship. The inquiry closed inconclusively, but, as the mate and crew were all local men of repute, nobody was suspected. Jack Gordon, a temporary hand, left ship at Quiberon and didn't return. We must find some of that crew and get them to tell the tale of that night again. It's going to be a big job..."

The parson knocked out his pipe.

"Maybe I can help. By the side of the entries copied by Knell, is the parish of each member of the crew. To-morrow, I'll ring up the vicar of each of those parishes at the time and see what he knows. There were three hands from Douglas as well as the master. That might be a bit of a handful, but we'll get over it. Douglas, Bride, Laxey and Onchan. I'll get the ecclesiastical grapevine, shall we call it, going first thing to-morrow. You've no idea the amount of information we parsons can exchange when it's necessary. Better than any inquiry agency..."

"We're both in for a busy day to-morrow..."

Next morning, in the middle of his breakfast in bed, Littlejohn was roused by a telephone call. Maggie Keggin came up with the news. Her face expressed distaste.

"It's from Paris..."

Littlejohn had a feeling that had he been telephoning to the devil in hell, Mrs. Keggin wouldn't have approved less. She handed him the receiver between finger and thumb as though it might be contaminated by the foreign city where, she thought, evil kept headquarters.

"Have you been up all night, Luc?"

They had certainly made a thorough job of the inquiry.

Jules Morin had been known in Quiberon as Charles Cosans, ex-Communist. Member of the underground during the war, twice captured by the Vichy police, twice escaped. Born, Vannes. Age 37. Fingerprints and official dossier following by mail. Convicted 1944/5 for black market and currency offences. Light sentences on account of wartime record. Thought to be a member of a widespread band of operators in black market. Vanished from Quiberon, May 4th, 1945. Not seen since...

May 4th, 1945. The date the *Jonee Ghorrym* left Quiberon on Captain Teare's last trip!

Littlejohn filled his pipe at the door of the vicarage and enjoyed the peace of the place and the view of the hills as he waited for Knell to arrive with the car. No more skating about on the surface. Now they'd got their teeth in something. Archdeacon Kinrade stumped down the stairs on his way to breakfast. He refused to eat in bed.

"You look like a giant refreshed, Littlejohn..."

"I feel it, too, sir."

His account of what had happened in Paris so inspired the parson, that he insisted on ringing up his clerical colleagues, two of whom he roused from bed, before he took his food. Littlejohn had to barge in and ask if he could first make his own calls to arrange his day's work.

First, to Deemster Milrey's home at Gat-y-Whing. His Honour had already set out for Ramsey where he was that day, holding court.

Then, to Mrs. Quantrell, whom the Inspector wished to see

about her husband's activities just before his death. Knell and Littlejohn set out for Ballagarry at once.

"I had intended leaving the Island and going to stay with friends on the mainland for a time, but I can't go yet with Jeremy in jail. It distressed me very much..." she said when the pair of them arrived.

They were preparing to close the house. The room in which Mrs. Quantrell had received them when first they called, was now sheeted and cold. She invited them into a small morning room with a view across the valley to the east. A fire was burning and she had had a table laid for coffee, which she invited them to take with her. Knell seated himself on the edge of a chair and opened his black book.

"I'm terribly worried about Jeremy... I knew he mixed with bad companions in London... An artistic crowd of poor repute. But I'd no idea that over here he did the same. I can't understand it. Please don't think, Inspector, I'm blaming you. He has done a terrible thing, if what you say is right. But I must stand by him. He has nobody else, now."

"His people are dead?"

"Yes. His father died when Jeremy was a small child. My sister brought up the boy, but he had too much of his own way and he had inherited some of his father's wildness..."

She seemed in a hurry to pass over the account of Lamprey's childhood. Knell's eyebrows rose and his pencil trembled. Wildness in connection with the Quantrells was unheard of!

"We did what we could for him... Jeremy, I mean. He came to us a lot. He never had a proper job. He was a freelance artist and didn't make much money."

"Did you know about your husband's interest in a ship called the *Jonee Ghorrym* from Ramsey, madam?"

"Yes. Very well. He bought the shares years ago, at par. They fell considerably just before the war, but rose later to phenomenal heights..."

"When he became a judge, he transferred his holding to Mr. Lamprey?"

"No; to me. But as I wasn't much of a business woman and my husband liked to take a practical interest in his local investments, we thought it would be something for Jeremy to do if they went in his name as my nominee."

"And he actively interested himself in the affairs of this little shipping company?"

"Very much so. My husband was quite pleased at first that it should have found Jeremy some useful interest. He went a lot to Ramsey on the shipping affair when he was over here..."

"You said 'at first'. Why?"

"Later, my husband wasn't so sure. Jeremy got in bad company again. The directors were drinking men and used to gather at a place called *The Duck's Nest* at Ramsey. One or two of them had poor reputations and Jeremy got drinking too much with them. Also, my husband rather suspected the *Jonee* was doing a bit of smuggling. He told me in confidence and asked Jeremy outright. Jeremy denied it and my husband said he intended to look into things when he had time. Then, in view of his retirement, he decided to sell the shipping holdings and take out annuities. An amazing thing happened. Several people wanted the shares and were prepared to pay well for them. The directors said *they* wanted them. There was some trouble, I remember my husband telling me. Something about the directors refusing to accept transfers of shares to persons they didn't want connected with them. My husband, as a lawyer, soon put them right there. They couldn't refuse, he told them. And then they offered him five hundred pounds for each one hundred pound share! He accepted and I must say it has made my financial position very much easier..."

"Do you remember who bought them, madam?"

"Yes. Dr. Smith, of Ramsey, one of the directors."

"Did the Deemster pursue his inquiries about the ship?"

"Yes. But he didn't tell me the results. He said when all was clear to him, he'd tell me."

"Did he ever talk to Mr. Lamprey about this investigation?"

"He did. One day, after one of his trips alone, he took Jeremy in his study and they had a terrible quarrel. It seems, my husband said, that as our nominee, Jeremy had abused our confidence by countenancing what he said were irregularities on the *Jonee*. That was a fortnight before the Deemster died... I never quite knew what it was all about."

"Your husband was very upset?"

"Terribly. He kept his own counsel, except that he went to talk to the second Deemster, Mr. Milrey, about it. Perhaps he could tell you more."

"Thank you, madam. I'll try him, then..."

They called at the local jail on their way to Ramsey. The police were still investigating the death of Irons without much success. They had searched Douglas for the man described by the old woman as small and wearing an oversized overcoat.

"I'll tell you what you might try," said Littlejohn. "There was a man on the boat when I crossed who answers to the description. He was in Castletown one day and spoke to me. He'd come in a charabanc... Let me see... McHarrie's Tours, I think it had on the back..."

"That's right, sir," said the sergeant-in-charge. "There is a firm of that name."

"They might remember him. No harm in trying. Perhaps they picked him up with a party at one of the boarding-houses. It was a trip to Rushen Castle..."

"We'll try it, sir."

Lamprey was in his cell complaining about the cold.

"This'll be the death of me. My old kidney trouble's back. And no wonder. The bedclothes are damp and the food's uneatable..."

"You're not in Park Lane now, Mr. Lamprey. You're in jail and very nicely looked after for a criminal..."

"I'll make you pay for this. Tremouille's watching my interests and when this is aired, there'll be a real scandal. I wouldn't like to be in your shoes."

His nose was red and he looked to have spent a sleepless night. He was sitting hunched on his bed, half-dressed, with a blanket draped round him like a dressing-gown.

"You knew, of course, that smuggling was going on the *Jonee Ghorrym?*"

"I knew nothing of the kind. Who told you that tale?"

"Never mind. Your uncle told you shortly before his death, didn't he?"

"You don't mean to say my aunt's turned against me and blown the gaff on all my uncle said..."

He paused as if he'd said too much.

"All your uncle said... Including the murder of Captain Teare on the night he brought Jules of *The Duck's Nest* across from Quiberon to Ramsey."

Lamprey's complexion turned from excited pink to yellow.

"I'd nothing to do with that. Whatever my uncle found out had nothing to do with me. I wasn't connected with the company then... It was only a theory of my uncle's..."

"A theory which he'd backed up by facts later."

"I don't know anything about it. He got mad with me because I'd got the shares. As if I could do anything. I wasn't even on the board. All I did was..."

"Was what?"

"Nothing. I want a doctor. I'm not well. It's the treatment I'm getting. I couldn't help it, if my uncle tried to play detective and landed himself in trouble."

"You knew all about the smuggling and your friends told you if you didn't do as they wished and get them the keys, you were in trouble yourself. . .?"

"I didn't know they wanted them so they could kill him. They said they wanted the proofs he'd got in his papers."

"Who are *they?*"

"It was Irons asked me for the keys. The directors of the company knew about the smuggling, but there was somebody else at the back of it. I don't know who it was... Can't I have a doctor? This is killing me... If they don't let me out quick, I'll commit suicide. I swear I will..."

"Better get Lamprey a doctor, sergeant," said Littlejohn on the way out. "Your prison doesn't seem to agree with his kidneys. And, by the way, take away his necktie and shoelaces; he's threatening to commit suicide..."

The sergeant smiled. He'd heard it all before.

"We followed up your idea, sir."

He showed Littlejohn some doodles and hieroglyphics on a pad to prove it. It looked like a combination of a chemical formula and a diagram illustrating nuclear fission.

"We got in touch with the tours-round-the-island people... McHarrie's... They remembered the party they picked up for Castle Rushen. They didn't remember 'em singly, of course, but the whole crowd, bar about three, came from The Eldorado Hotel... A boardin'-house, by rights. We rang up The Eldorado. They remembered the little man. He was swankin' afterwards, they said, that the Scotland Yard man on the Deemster's murder was a friend of his; often had a beer together. *Where*, he didn't mention. Well, he checked out to-day. Left by the eight 'plane. His name was Sammy Crook, of Liverpool..."

"You might get his full address from the register..."

"It's here. 34, Minshull Street. We looked it up in a directory. It's a well-known multiple-tailors' shop. We rang 'em up. Never heard of Sammy Crook..."

"You've not let the grass grow under your feet, sergeant! Well done! Did you check the 'plane schedule, too?"

The sergeant smiled contentedly...

"Yes, sir. He was on board, all right. And now, he's vanished into the blue..."

"That's right. But perhaps not for long. We'll have to see. You've excelled yourself, sergeant. Well done, again!"

The policeman blushed, his moustache bristled, and he lowered his eyes modestly and started to draw more nuclear fission diagrams on the blotting-paper.

This time, Knell drove the car fast over the T.T. road, across the mountains past Snaefell, through the thin upland air, and down into Ramsey round the Hairpin Bend.

Deemster Milrey was taking morning coffee before cases. He looked surprised to see Littlejohn.

"Could you spare me just a minute or two of your time, Your Honour...?"

In his black gown and wig the Deemster looked stern and imposing.

"Certainly..."

With his smile all formality vanished.

"You mentioned the Carrasdhoo Men when we called the other evening. Was there any significance in the name, Your Honour, and did the idea of Ullymar Glen convey any meaning to you?"

Deemster Milrey nodded two or three times.

"I've thought of it since our talk the other night. It implied smuggling, I thought, although the Carrasdhoo Men were wreckers. Quantrell had discovered, it seemed, that a Ramsey ship, the *Jonee Ghorrym* was, or had been, engaged in smuggling, and it was his theory that a previous captain, on discovering that some of his crew or his employers had been, unknown to him, carrying on the trade, had threatened to denounce them and was killed for it. He said he had a theory about who committed the crime."

"Is that all he could say, sir?"

"Yes. Except that he thought his nephew was mixed up in it and that he was worried, because he was responsible for interesting young Lamprey in the shipping business."

"He mentioned no names?"

"No. He said he'd have to see me later. He was following a certain line of inquiry. The reason he came to me was, that if young Lamprey was in any way guilty of the offences of smuggling or other illegal uses of the ship, Quantrell would have to resign his offices on the bench at once."

"You saw him after that?"

"Yes. In Douglas two days later. He said he'd see me in a day or two with the full facts of the case. He was killed the next day."

"Thank you, Your Honour..."

They drove down to the water-front again. It was mid-morning and the tide was in. The sky looked as if someone had washed it clean, and little white clouds drifted idly across it. The vast bay was peaceful and the old and new promenades were almost deserted, except for a few men airing their dogs. The quay-side was active with traffic; cars parked in front of warehouses and shops, lorries carrying produce to and from the merchants and chandlers. Two coasters were unloading coal in large buckets slung from cranes.

The Duck's Nest was deserted. Inside, you could see the tables piled up and Silas was mopping the floor of the bar. Littlejohn leaving Knell with the car, entered.

"There's nobody in and the bar's closed."

Silas didn't want to be bothered with customers.

"How long have you been here, Silas?"

"Since the place opened in 1947. Why?"

"Has Jules been here all that time?"

"Yes. Why?"

"Did he live over here before he started this place?"

"Came durin' the summer the year before. Said he was just lookin' around for a place. Bought this in the autumn and opened up for the next season. That's when I started. Why?"

"Don't keep saying, why, Silas. I can't tell you all my business. Curiosity killed the cat."

"I know. Just an 'abit of mine. Can't seem to get out of it. Won't do me no good to know why, will it?"

"You a native of the Island?"

"Why? Do I sound like one? I come from Newmarket and I wish to God I was back there. But it ain't too 'ospitable, as you might say, to the likes of me... old, sewperannyated jockeys..."

"Where is everybody?"

"Jules and Amy gone out buyin' in. They won't be long."

"Are they on good terms?"

"Meanin'?"

Silas bared his yellow, uneven teeth.

"How friendly are they?"

"As much as needs be. Though they don't show it in public. But I know all that goes on here. No use tryin' to kid me, however much they do the others. Get me?"

"But I thought there was something between Amy and Joe Alcardi."

"The Eyetalian, you mean? Naw. Not fer the Eyetalian's want o' tryin'. But Amy hadn't no eyes for anybody but Morin. Sort o' mesmerized by 'im."

"Has she been here ever since the place opened?"

"Came a coupla years since. Her and Morin fell for one another, so she stopped on. What 'e can see in 'er, I don't know. Skinny, that's wot I call 'er. Give me women with a bit of uphol-stery on 'em. Not skinny, flat-chested bags o' bones, like Amy. From the way I seen 'em carryin'-on, though, when they thought they was on their own, I'd say Amy was a bit 'otter than she looks. No accountin' for taste..."

"Quite a specialist in the arts of love, aren't you, Silas?"

"Done me share in me time, though to look at me now with me mop an' bucket, you'd doubt it. Thank you, sir..."

He spat on the half-crown and slid it in his waistcoat pocket.

"By the way, Silas. The other evening, when old Mr. Parker gave his party... Was Morin in all night?"

"Dunno. But I never see 'im after half-eight, when the cookin' was done and the stuff on the 'ot-plate ready for servin'. Left me with the drinks for a spell... Champagne cocktails! Pah! Gimme beer, a proper drink."

Littlejohn strolled to the door. No sign of Jules or Amy. There was a constable talking to Knell at the car. He held a paper in his hand. He saluted Littlejohn.

"Note from the Archdeacon, sir. We took it over the telephone. He said to let you have it immediately. Perhaps you know what it means. We don't."

Teare......Dead.

Vondy......Married at Bride. Emigrated to U.S.A.

Skillicorn......Engineer on liner. At present on high seas.

Killip......Still on *Jonee Ghorrym*, now first hand.

Fred Moore......Still lives Onchan. Now working on the roads.

Kermode......No Trace.

Philip Moore......Dead. Buried Onchan.

Costain......Now farming at Cregmanaugh Farm, Bride.

Gordon......No Trace.

Fred Moore and Costain were all who were available, and Fred had not been able to sail after falling in the quay after a bout of drinking.

Good old parson! His grapevine had worked well. Littlejohn could imagine him marshalling all his clerical colleagues, running them round in search of present and ex-parishioners, hustling them on. And, as a result, here was Costain at Cregmanaugh...

"Where's Cregmanaugh Farm, constable?"

"Have you a map, sir?"

He pointed it out, circling round and round it, like a man picking winners with a pin, and then stabbing it long after the other two had spotted it, with a large index.

"There!"

It was up near the Point of Ayre at the very north of the Island.

"Have you ever heard of the Ullymar Curragh, Constable?"

"I once did, I'm sure. It's not far from Jurby... On the Ballaugh side. If I was you, sir, I'd make for Ballaugh after you leave Bride and then ask again..."

"Thank you. Is that the Friendship Inn along the quay there?"

"Yes, sir. A seamen's house. Landlord's called Gawne and a very decent fellow he is, too... But you won't get a lunch there, sir, if that's what. . ."

"No. Just a word with Mr. Gawne..."

Just a word! It was a masterpiece of understatement, for Mr. Gawne revelled in a little chat, as he called it... another understatement. But his memory was good... Excellent.

"Fred Moore, did you say? Used to be on the *Jonee Ghorrym?* Dear me! Don't make me laugh! Fred Moore..."

Mr. Gawne was a little fat man, with a round tight face and charming kindly eyes. He had a button nose and a button mouth and his eyes were like little smiling blue buttons as well.

"Fred Moore..."

Mr. Gawne started to laugh and Littlejohn, by the volcanic convulsion which seized the landlord, began to fear the fat man would burst before he could confide his secrets or the reasons for his mirth.

"Fred Moore... Oh, dear me. A fellow comes in here and starts to be pally with Fred... Oh dear..."

Between the gusts which seized Mr. Gawne, he told his tale in instalments of three words at a time.

"Starts to pay for drinks... ow, ow, ow... till Fred's full to the brim... oh, oh, oh... Then, out they go by the front door... ow, ow, ow... Stranger turns right, Fred keeps straight on... oh, I can't stand it... funniest thing you ever saw... Straight on and into the quay... We could hear him splashin' about in the water, shoutin' he was drownin'... ow, ow, ow... Fished 'im out with a boathook..."

Mr. Gawne pushed Littlejohn in a jolly fit of mirth and the Inspector reeled and clutched the counter for support.

"Then with Fred gettin' his death o' cold, the stranger goes an' gets his berth on the *Jonee*... ow, ow, ow..."

He mopped himself, drew them both a pint of beer to cool them off and after a deep draught, spoke in a normal, sober voice, full of gravity.

"My opinion is, that the stranger got Fred tight so's he could get his job..."

"Well, well, well..."

And they both started to laugh again.

As Littlejohn made his way back to the car parked in front of *The Duck's Nest* Amy was returning loaded with a shopping basket full of vegetables. Littlejohn signalled to her in greeting and raised his hat.

"Amy!"

She halted and waited for him, a question in her eyes.

"Good morning, Amy. Where's Jules?"

She shrugged her shoulders. She was her old sallow, flat-chested, slightly bedraggled self again. She removed the cigarette from the corner of her mouth.

"Somewhere about the town... Buying-in, I think."

"Do you remember the night of old Mr. Parker's party? The night I stayed at *The Duck's Nest*. . .?"

"Yes..."

She tapped the cigarette nervously with her forefinger.

"Was Jules in all the time till he came up to bed?"

Her eyes flickered.

"Yes."

"Sure?"

"Quite sure."

"In the kitchen all the time?"

"Yes. Till the party ended."

"I'm in a hurry now, but I'll probably be back this evening. You'll both be in?"

"Why not?"

She looked Littlejohn in the eyes, turned pale, tottered, then ran indoors, staggering on her high heels and under the load in her basket.

16

THE MASTER OF CREGMANAUGH

T hey took the road to Bride, nestling from the winds in its
gentle hills. Knell grew excited.

"I was born here, sir. The loveliest village you ever saw. And it's
here I hope to end my days..."

Littlejohn could understand his enthusiasm. The sun shone on
the snug little place, with its foreign-looking church-tower, its
cosy cluster of clean houses, its large prosperous farms. To the
north stretched the flat barren land of the Ayre and between this
and the village lay Cregmanaugh. A few children playing round
the village shop, two old men basking in the sun and gossiping, a
dog lying by the roadside and stretching himself voluptuously...

Costain of Cregmanaugh was wiring a fence in the home field.
The place was beautifully situated, in full view of the Point of
Ayre and its neat lighthouse, with the sea in sight, and beyond, the
coast of Scotland, visible miles away. A large white farmhouse, a
tidy yard, solid outbuildings; long lawn and wild garden leading
to the front door. Tall palms and a monkey-puzzle sheltered the
neat porch. The land looked rich and the cattle well-fed and
strong. Costain had done well for himself. According to old
custom, the master of a farm sometimes took its name instead of

213

his own. He liked to be called Cregmanaugh instead of Costain, for Costain was a one-time ship's fireman. Cregmanaugh implied prosperity, position, security. He laid down his roll of wire and removed his leather gloves, approaching the policemen with slow easy strides.

Costain was tall and wiry, with a shock of fair hair and a shaggy moustache straggling across his top lip. His face was long and thin, with high cheek bones, hooked nose, tight-lipped mouth and secretive grey eyes. He was tanned and healthy-looking and dressed in a stained navy-blue suit and cloth cap. In his mouth, a curved pipe.

He didn't speak, but stood in their path, inquiring their business with a look.

"Mr. Costain?"

"That's me... Cregmanaugh..."

"We're from the police. Can we have a talk?"

You could see Costain pondering his recent conduct, trying to think of any misdoings that had been found out.

"Come in..."

He cleaned his large boots on the scraper at the front gate and led them down the garden path. At the front door he rubbed his boots again on a piece of sacking. Then he turned the knob and found the door locked.

He must have known the door was usually fastened, but now he seemed to resent it. He shook the handle and beat on the panels with his clenched fist.

"Open up, mistress... Do you hear?"

"All right. Can't you go round?"

"No. Open up..."

Two small children, a boy and a girl, about school age, peeped shyly round the corner of the building and withdrew looking scared.

You could hear someone drawing bolts and unfastening a chain behind and then there was a struggle to get the door open.

It mustn't have been used for some time, for the woman inside was unable to get it to budge. Costain put his shoulder to it and it flew back almost projecting him flat on his face.

"You took long enough..."

The woman was small and dark, with a healthy round face, and hair parted in the middle giving her a Madonna-like placidity. She glanced anxiously at her husband and looked surprised at his ill-temper.

"Police wanting a word with me. We'll go in the front room. You've got the gun licence and the ration cards handy? It's that you're after, isn't it?"

Littlejohn knew Costain didn't think that at all. There was something deeper and he was scared. Mrs. Costain threw open a door on the right and indicated they might enter. The place was chilly and smelled of mildew. The furniture was of modern shiny light oak and the three-piece suite was new. The usual photographs of family and friends on the walls and mantelpiece and a framed one over the fireplace of Mr. and Mrs. Costain on their wedding day. He hadn't had a moustache then and his face wore a sickly grin as though someone near the camera were making fun of him. Below the large frame stood another small picture of Costain again; this time he wore a jersey and a sailor's cap. His expression was wooden...

Mrs. Costain withdrew and closed the door quietly. There was no sound of retreating footsteps and Littlejohn imagined her listening, scared, with her ear to the panel. In spite of Costain's surly manner, they seemed tolerably happy together at Cregmanaugh with their little family. Littlejohn felt sorry for her; she had much to lose...

Costain kept on his cap. He was going to get it over quickly by the look of things. Littlejohn's eye caught sight of a telephone on the window-sill.

"Has anyone rung you from Ramsey to say we might call, Mr. Costain?"

"No..."

But you could see from Costain's amazed look that Littlejohn had hit the nail on the head.

"It's about the *Jonee Ghorrym*..."

"I can't tell you anythin' about her. It's years since I left the sea and took to farmin'. My wife didn't like me on the sea. So I came to her father's farm. He died last year..."

Littlejohn had to interrupt. Costain was trying to talk things away from the ship, ready to tell all his personal and family history to avoid it.

"Deemster Quantrell called the other week, I believe..."

Littlejohn didn't know anything about it, but so far, they had followed the Deemster's tracks. No reason for assuming he'd stopped before they led to Cregmanaugh.

"Yes. Happened to be passin'..."

"Was he a friend of yours?"

"Sort of..."

"Let's stop beating about the bush, Mr. Costain. The Deemster came to ask about the *Jonee Ghorrym* too, didn't he?"

"Yes, but I told him the same as you. It's years since..."

"I know that. But you were aboard the night Captain Teare lost his life, weren't you?"

"Yes. But I don't know anythin' consarnin' it. I was in the fo'c'sle. I told the Deemster that, too."

"Suppose you tell us all that happened that voyage..."

"There's nothin' to tell..."

"Suppose you try..."

Costain plucked off his cap and flung it on the table in rage. His hair hadn't been brushed for some time and stood on end on the crown of his head.

"What are you after? I told you... It's so long since..."

"All the same, an event like that just doesn't disappear from your mind completely. Tell me what you remember, right from the start of the trip."

He scratched his head. His pipe had gone out and he tried to light it again, striking match after match without success.

"We set out from Ramsey..."

"All the crew are now scattered except Killip, who's still with the *Jonee*, and Fred Moore, who lives at Onchan and works on the road."

"I only know that Killip's still there. I lost touch with the others."

"You left Ramsey with an extra hand to replace one who was laid-up. Gordon was the extra man's name."

"That's right. We picked up coal in South Wales and discharged it at a port on the French coast."

"Quiberon?"

"That's it."

"What happened at Quiberon?"

"Gordon didn't come back. We also took on a passenger. A French chap who came over to Ramsey."

"A sailor?"

"No. A business fellah. Came to live here. I've seen him since in Ramsey. He keeps an hotel or something."

"Morin, he's called."

"I never knew his name. He came aboard with a lot of luggage. Said he was emigrating. A trunk and two packing-cases. Some of the crew said he was smugglin'..."

"Was he?"

Costain licked his thin lips. This was evidently the part he feared.

"I never saw inside the boxes."

"But you knew what was in them."

"It had nothin' to do with me."

"That's not an answer. Did Captain Teare know what they contained?"

"They weren't opened, I tell you."

"Did the captain say anything about them? Come on, Mr.

Costain, this is going to take us all day..."

The farmer's face contorted with rage.

"What are you tryin' to get me to say? I didn't have a hand in it."

"In what? Shall I tell you what happened? Captain Teare wasn't satisfied with the cases. He was an honest mariner and wasn't going to be a party to dirty work. You might have been in the fo'c'sle all the time, but someone told you all about it. They even paid you to keep your mouth shut."

"Look here... Who's been talkin'? Is it Killip? Because if it is, I'll..."

"I'm not interested in a smuggling adventure years ago, Mr. Costain. I'm after the Deemster's murderer. If you think I'm here to run you in for running contraband while you were at sea, you're mistaken. No more dodging. What happened that night?"

Costain sat down. He was exhausted with fear and all his fight had gone.

"Killip and the captain were on watch. Philip Moore... he's dead now... relieved me in the stokehold while I went for a sleep. Moore told me after that, he came on deck for a breath of air. It was a wild night and the ship was bobbin' like a cork. She's nearly like a submarine in rough weather. Moore heard Captain Teare and the Frenchy we picked up havin' words. The captain was sayin' he'd got to see inside the cases before we docked. Frenchy talked in a low voice and Moore couldn't hear. They were in the captain's cabin. Captain Teare suddenly bursts out. Somethin' about havin' a clean record and he isn't startin' lawbreakin' now. The cases were bein' landed at Ramsey or not at all..."

"So, the Frenchman was trying to get the captain to put off the cases in one of the boats and land it somewhere quiet?"

"That's what Moore thought, too."

In the hall, someone started to sob, there were running feet, and a door closed. Mrs. Costain thought the end of her little world was just round the corner.

"What about Captain Teare?"

"After the row, the Frenchy rushed out of the cabin and slammed the door. Moore went below as the captain went on the bridge. They woke us in the fo'c'sle near on four to say the captain was missin'. We hung around till it was light, huntin'... But we never saw him again."

"And Killip, who was on watch? What had he to say?"

"Nothin'. He saw the captain go down on deck and that was the last he see of him."

"You think he might have been after the cases and their contents?"

"I think he was. Either he heaved 'em overboard and fell over as he did it, or else he opened them and the Frenchy found out and killed him. The cases weren't there next mornin'."

"And how did the Frenchy explain their absence?"

"He said he brought them on deck and they were washed overboard. Said they held books and things."

"And he paid you all... or those who knew anything, to keep quiet about the cases and his quarrel?"

"He gave us all a bonus of twenty pounds for the trouble he'd caused."

"You brought him on to Ramsey?"

"Yes."

"So, it seems that Captain Teare, suspecting contraband in the boxes, either quarrelled with the Frenchman about it and was, to put it mildly, cast overboard. Or else he opened them and the Frenchy caught him. Were they heavy?"

"It took two men to handle them after the crane dropped 'em in the hold. Nobody could have carried them to the side or even heaved 'em over without help. He must have taken them piece by piece and thrown them in the sea..."

"Did you tell the Deemster all this, Mr. Costain?"

"More or less. He got it out of me the same as you have. You'll not hold it against me, sir?"

"No. You've helped us a lot..."

Costain's face lightened and he put on his cap again as though it gave him confidence.

"Did the Deemster know the Frenchman?"

"He seemed to."

"Did you tell anybody about Deemster Quantrell's call?"

"Not particularly. But I saw Captain Kewley in Ramsey one day and passin' the time o' day, just mentioned, casual, that His Honour was interested in the history of the *Jonee* and had he been to see Kewley, yet?"

"So that's it. That's how they knew things were getting hot."

"How do you mean?"

"Nothing for you, Mr. Costain. We'll be going now. Many thanks."

"And there won't be any... any...?"

"No repercussions or prosecutions for you? No."

"Thank God! I dream about that night still..."

Costain opened the door of the room for them.

"Mother! You there? The gentlemen are goin'..."

You could hear his wife sobbing in the kitchen. Costain anxiously opened another door, and there she sat, her head in her arms, crying her eyes out.

"It's all right, mother. Nothin's wrong..."

The detectives left him stroking her hair and comforting her.

"I call that neat, if I may say so, sir..."

Knell couldn't contain himself. He was on fire to undertake a case on his own, now... In his imagination, he could see another murder being committed and no Littlejohn there. Knell with a clear field. Knell on the trail. Knell solving it, just like Littlejohn. The Governor wringing *Superintendent* Knell's hand. 'You've saved the Island from disgrace, *Superintendent*...'

"Mind where you're going, Knell. If the fellow on the bike hadn't wobbled then, you'd have been over him..."

Knell blushed and coughed and clutched the wheel in a grip of iron. No sense in getting themselves killed just as they'd solved it.

"It's not solved yet, by a long way, Knell. But we're on the way. How are we for time?"

"Half past eleven..."

"Let's try to find the Ullymar Curragh... Ballaugh way, isn't it?"

"Yes, sir. Ballaugh, and ask there."

Knell forded a stream with a mighty splash. Littlejohn expected the engine to fail and leave them to wade out. but they landed safely, reached the main road and sped on, along the T. T. track again under arches of fine old trees to the bridge at Ballaugh. Knell's first inquiry yielded nothing.

"Do you know a spot called Ullymar, sir?" he asked a grey-haired, abstracted-looking man on the bridge.

"Ullymar? *Artemisia absinthium*, eh?"

They looked blankly at one another and Knell turned to Littlejohn beside him.

"Nuts, eh?"

The elderly eccentric heard him.

"Not nuts; wormwood. Ullymar is Manx for wormwood. *Artemisia* is the Latin for it..."

"Thank you, sir. That's very useful. Good day..."

"How might it be spelled?"

The next shot got home. An old Manxman, watching passers-by with shrewd curious eyes.

Knell raised his eyebrows at Littlejohn to indicate that the ball was with him.

"I couldn't really say, sir."

"You mean Ullimer, master. Years since I heard o' that. It's a marsh now... There's an old house standin' there still, I reckon, but noborry in it. Wasteland, like..."

He told them how to get to it. Loughdhoo, where the metalled road ended, and then a track to the left.

"Terrible bad that track is. All loose little flints. Terrible bad for the tyres of a car..."

Follow the track to the end and then take the earth road to the left. The Ullimer curragh was by the ruined house.

"They did say someborry was tidyin' up the place with a view to livin' in it, on account o' the housin' shortage. They must be hard put-to for a place, to go there. Dark and damp..."

He also knew the way from the place. A mere stride or two to a good road which soon joined the main Jurby one...

Knell carefully followed the directions. They plunged into the maze of secondary roads which covers the marshland like a net, shaded on each side by high, lush hedges, with fields beyond, some green and productive, others covered in rushes and coarse grass, with willows and bog oak growing round pools and ditches. Past Loughdhoo they had to slow-down to walking pace on the loose flint tracks. Finally, the old house of Ullymar, and not so tumbledown as predicted.

The officers got out of the car and strolled round. Somebody had been rebuilding the place. The thatch had been roughly replaced by cheap asbestos tiles; the windows boarded-up, the gate newly hinged, and the front door secured by a padlock and chain.

"Perhaps a farmer storing stuff. Potatoes or seeds of some kind..."

Knell looked round as he spoke. This was the worst curragh they'd seen yet. The fields behind the croft were mossy green, with reeds and rushes sprouting from them and, as if that were not enough, the land beyond degenerated into pure bog, with its surface cracked and channelled, and with slimy pools opening here and there on the top. Littlejohn remembered Deemster Milrey's bit of poetry.

> *For the Ullymar bogs have a hideous slime,*
> *And the Ullymar bogs wear the hue of crime!*

Quite right, too. There was something funny going on here.

Deep tracks of vehicles left the front of the cottage and ran in the direction of the Jurby road. Heavy traffic had been coming and going here. Something heavier than farm carts...

Littlejohn looked round. Not a soul about. Not even a house, a farm, a fertile field. The large trees and overgrown fuchsias around screened the place from sight; nothing but barren curragh, bog and rough road, with, in the distance, the great bastion of hills, rising north of the Ramsey-Ballaugh road, straight out of the flat plain...

"Let's see what's inside, Knell..."

"It's locked. And they've seen to it that nobody can get in through the windows or the roof. Look at those boards fastened with six-inch nails."

"Let's see..."

Knell's eyes goggled as Littlejohn produced pieces of wire and a knife with a hook in it. He juggled with the large padlock for a minute or two. Then, with a grunt, he gave it a jerk and it opened.

"A little trick or two I learned from an old lag..."

Knell was flabbergasted. There was nothing about all this in the policeman's diary *or* in the constabulary vade-mecum he studied in his spare time... !

The light from the little torch like a fountain-pen which Knell religiously carried about, stabbed the dark interior. Except for a couple of spades and a few planks of wood, it was empty. The earth floor gave off a dank smell and as the light caught them, you could see bats hanging from the rough-hewn beams. They examined the place without result. Littlejohn eyed the spades. They were bright and clean. He picked one up and started to prod the floor.

"Take the other, Knell, and do the same all over the earth of the floor..."

In one corner, at length, the steel of the spade rang against some stone or brick obstruction. Littlejohn cleared the surface away and revealed a large flagstone, like a paving slab.

"Give a hand, Knell, please..."

They levered and lifted the stone with an effort and revealed a cavity below. Knell shone his torch down it...

It was like the cellar of a wineshop! Hundreds of bottles of whisky, wine, brandy, gin... A small cellar, excavated and made into a cemented cell for storing liquor.

"How far away is The Lhen shore, Knell?"

"I'd say three miles cross country..."

"The Deemster was around there, wasn't he? They must ship this stuff from the Continent on the *Jonee Ghorrym*, unload it at The Lhen at night, and then bring it here. They may have several such places round about. How do they get it to and fro, though...?"

The answer was approaching. A builder's lorry labelled PARKER, CONTRACTOR, RAMSEY, was drawing slowly along the road to the house. An easy way of deceiving the curious. Builder's lorry, ostensibly bringing materials for renovating tumbledown property, actually shifting liquor to and fro... The Lhen, the Curraghs, and then by instalments to *The Duck's Nest* and other customers as required.

"Better make a dash Knell, and get some help. Stop a car on the Jurby road... There seem to be five or six of them with the lorry... I can't take on all that lot whilst you're gone, but I can perhaps talk till you bring help... Try a farm... or..."

The lorry had stopped and out of the cab and the back tumbled the toughest lot of no-goods Littlejohn had seen for some time.

There were five of them, led by an enormous fat man, who carried a spade over his forearm like a shotgun. He was followed by another huge man, not so fat, with a broken nose, a cauliflower ear, and the stupid expression of an over-battered ex-pugilist. He was lovingly fingering a small crowbar. A completely bald, wiry fellow, with a huge Roman nose followed. His face was more sinister than those of the other two; the two fat men looked full of brute force and no brains, but Baldy combined cunning and cruelty with strength, like some Gestapo torturer who might beat victims to death... On his heels, a man who resembled a superannuated pirate; rolling gait, strong as a gorilla, a gap in his teeth and a hook where his left hand should be. He looked as if he had come off badly in a free-for-all and was seeking a dirty revenge. The rear was brought up by the driver of the vehicle, who provided the comic relief, for he was small, wizened and had only one eye. He wore a set of blue overalls a size too large for him, as though his wife had bought them with the hope that he would grow a bit. He carried a large spanner. All they needed was the Jolly Roger flying from the builder's waggon to set the tone of the party.

Fatty halted for a moment, lowered his spade, leaned on it, and gazed at Littlejohn and Knell. His little pig eyes reminded you of a mole's, deep set in his head and hardly visible for fat. Broken-Nose, Baldy, Hook and Monoculous drew-up with a jerk and glared at their quarry, as well. Baldy, true to type, carried a stiff piece of rubber piping and Hook raised his infernal steel claw which was weapon, tool, knife-and-fork, and brush-and-comb, as well as many other things to him.

Fatty spat on the ground.

"Well... well... well... Seems we've jest got 'ere in time. We wuz told to keep an eye on you two, jes' in case you wisited our little grey 'ome in the west, like. So out we comes and wot do we find? Wot do we find, chums?"

Fatty considered himself a bit of a comedian. When engaged on his cover-up job of house building and repairing, he jocularly bullied apprentices, talked a lot about the young being out of hand, and of a boy's best friend being his mother. He had been known to break down and sob when a gangster shot a policeman at the movies. But he believed in divorcing business from pleasure. He licked his lips now.

"We've come to teach you a little lesson, gents. Jest to stop yer nosin' abaht in the fewcher... Which of you shall it be first...?"

He eyed Knell and Littlejohn up and down, seemed to decide that they weren't worth using a weapon on, and dug his shovel in the earth and abandoned it.

"You first?"

He marched right up to Knell with outstretched arms, and his gang fell-in behind him.

Somehow, Fatty, with his pig-eyes, his sloppy mouth, and his indecent sense of humour, rattled Knell. In the course of a split second Knell imagined Fatty approaching Millie Teare with those huge outstretched arms, and he advanced a pace to meet him. Then, he side-stepped, buried his left in the pneumatic folds of Fatty's abdomen and, as his adversary bent with a grunt, caught the huge fat jaw a rousing blow with his right. Fatty stood upright like a ramrod for a second, squinted horribly, his legs slowly grew bowed, and he laid himself on the ground before his remaining quartet.

"Beat it for help," said Littlejohn, and Knell flew round the party as fast as his legs would go. Monoculous, in the background, tried to follow, brandished his spanner, failed to see Fatty's spade standing upright where he had left it, mixed himself with it, and fell flat on his face. The rest, momentarily nonplussed by the tactics, turned, divided and began to mill around. The two in the rear, including the staggering Monoculous, tried pursuit of Knell and then gave it up, but succeeded in preventing his taking the car. He vanished round the corner, running steadily. Littlejohn slammed the door, wedged it from behind with the two spades and waited for events.

Fatty rose, assisted by his pals, shook himself, spat and kicked at the door.

"Come out an' take wot's comin' to yer..."

Baldy was disgusted. He thrust Fatty aside and made himself dictator of the crew.

"Come on out, or we'll BURN you out," he roared in a fruity

voice, almost chuckling with sadistical anticipation. "Moe... Just bring along the can of petrol..."

Moe, the man in the boiler-suit and with a single eye, opened the latter wide. He *had* no can of petrol. Baldy put his finger to his lips to show he was simply being cunning. Baldy was the only craftsman of the party. He hid his villainy behind a respectable mask of plumbing...

Inside, Littlejohn sat on the floor behind the door and lit his pipe.

Outside, Hook was trying to tear down the door with his claw, which he also used as a jemmy when he burgled.

"Come off it, 'ector," said Fatty to Hook. "Yore on'y wastin' time. We got a crowbar, 'aven't we? And there's five of us to one, ain't there? Let's rush the door, an' if it doesn't give then, we'll crowbar it open. And then leave 'im to me, see? I got a score to settle with 'im on account o' wot his pal done to me..."

They gathered themselves together in what seemed to Littlejohn a solid mass, withdrew down the path, thundered up it again to the door, met it with a crash, shattered it, and pitched into the room where Littlejohn was braced to meet them with a shovel. Then they all halted and turned to the door. Outside there rose a shrill noise like that made by angry bees. It grew nearer and nearer and became recognizable as the concerted shout of young voices.

Fatty, inspired by the new menace to finish his job, stretched out once again his enormous arms to seize Littlejohn. Before the huge paws could close, the Inspector's right fist smote him on the left jaw. The blow made Fatty behave strangely. He rocked on his heels for a moment and then, like one in a dream, leaned forward and presented the right side, which Littlejohn obliged by punishing with a left like a cannon-ball. For the second time, Fatty's eyes rolled until only the whites were visible, his legs slowly subsided, and he sat on the ground with a bump, oblivious of what was going on around him.

17

THE BATTLE OF BALLAUGH

There is no ballad about the battle of Ballaugh, but though unsung, it was a famous victory and is still talked about, especially in parts of Bolton, Lancashire.

Knell pounded to the end of the track from the curragh of Ullymar and to the main road which joined it about half a mile from the old croft where he had left Littlejohn. Once or twice as he cantered along, Knell was tempted to return and pound the five invaders to a jelly, for, inspired by his new love for Millie Teare, he felt disposed to take on all comers. Common sense prevailed, however, and he kept straight ahead. At the highroad, he halted, panting, looked to right and to left and snorted with dismay. It was about noon and there was not a soul or a vehicle visible. The only sign of humanity in the vicinity was the lodge of an invisible mansion, standing behind wrought iron gates. The gates were closed and on a clothes-line behind the cottage hung a well-darned pair of men's underpants, two shirts, and a lot of articles of feminine underwear which Knell recognized as such in a general way, but could not accurately name, for he had lived alone for so long with his octogenarian mother, who believed in wool next the skin and was greatly addicted to red flannel. He opened the great gate, knocked at the door of the lodge and got no response, for the gatekeeper was at work on a distant farm and his wife had gone to Ramsey. Knell continued his marathon run along the drive, until it opened on a wide lawn which fronted a graceful house. The sight which met his eyes as he halted to reconnoitre caused him to give a broken-winded cheer...

It was the last day on the Island of the troupe of boy scouts from Bolton who had won the first prize for deportment at a distant jamboree and earned themselves an all-in holiday in the Isle of Man. Their treat had been overclouded by the death of their comrade, Willie Mounsey, at Castle Rushen, but instead of bringing their vacation to a close, the organizers had toned it down in keeping with the tragedy and, after Willie's body had been returned to the mainland, they tried to make the best of the few remaining days. Knell found them being entertained to a garden party by Mr. Christopher Gelling, Member of the House of Keys, Captain of the Parish. Fifteen of them were sitting at a long table, eating ham sandwiches, meat pies, soda cakes and trifles, and washing them down with tea and lemonade. At one end of the table sat Mr. Gelling urging them to tuck-in, and at the other, Mr. Buzzard, their scoutmaster, a little, wiry, earnest man, with a small sandy moustache, a sharp manner and a sharper blue eye. Knell reached Mr. Buzzard's side in a few long hops and spoke huskily to him in gasps. Mr. Buzzard rose, beat upon the table for silence and addressed the lines of eager faces with mouths full to capacity and jaws chewing rapidly.

"Boys! The police need us. They are being attacked by a crowd of hooligans responsible, we believe, for the death of Willie. They want our help..."

It was like the starting gun of a cross-country race.

Mr. Buzzard gave rapid orders, the scouts seized their ash staves from a large heap, lined up in single file, right-turned, and left the field at the double.

"Come back and finish when you've won," shouted Mr. Gelling

after them, and then ran indoors to telephone for the police at Ramsey.

Knell removed his hat and coat, carefully placed them on the table with the leavings, and joined the reinforcements in his shirt, trousers and braces. Two boys, inspired by accounts of Everest, had brought with them ropes for rock climbing, in the forlorn hope that the Manx mountains might be snowcapped. With the ropes coiled round them, they ran lopsidedly with the rest...

The Enemy at Ullymar re-acted strategically. When the solitary astonished eye of Moe fell upon the approaching mass of the rival army, he turned and called to his comrades.

"A lot of kids!"

Littlejohn was just emerging into the open from the cottage and Baldy, the crafty one, acting true to type, flung the piece of heavy rubber piping he carried full in the Inspector's face. Before Littlejohn could recover, he and Hook were upon the Inspector, bore him down and tied him by the wrists and ankles with a piece of dirty rope lying in the garden. They would have murdered him, then and there, if they'd been quite sure of not being found out. Then they turned to face the foe.

The Ullymar gang lined up and tried to defend the gateway to the house. Both armies halted momentarily and then someone on the scouts' side shouted a war-cry.

"Up the trotters!"

It was the legendary name for Boltonians, their pride, their famous football team, and the honour of the scouts of St. Oscar's. Knell, who, having lost his wind from his first run had been lagging behind, thereupon trotted into view, couldn't stop in time, ran right into the middle of the defending party, staggered and fell. This was lucky, for the spanner of the man in the overlarge overalls, whirled through the air where Knell's head had been, found no mark, carried Moe through with its energy, and he lost his balance and fell across Knell's prostrate form. Both men raised themselves, but Monoculous, only able to see what was going on on one side of him, missed the sight of Knell's raised fist, and only knew of it as it caught him full on the receding jaw and put him to sleep.

The remaining trio of hoodlums were surrounded by uniformed boys, milling round, beating about with staves, clutching their opponents and one another. High above the melée, the iron hand of Hook kept rising and glittering malignantly, only to be smitten down again and again by an ash pole. Luckily for the scouts, their massed attack prevented the toughs from using their weapons. They wriggled and toiled to get their gross bodies free, their arms back for blows, their big boots swinging for hacking kicks, but they struggled in vain.

In the doorway appeared the huge bulk of Fatty, his wits now cleared after Littlejohn's blow, shaking his head like a dog out of water. He cast his pig-eyes round and they fell upon Littlejohn. He raised his enormous hobnailed boot to kick the helpless Inspector in the ribs and then, like young David, a boy let fly with his cata-pult. A small white stone, carefully selected from the beach, smote Fatty Goliath on the nose. One leg raised for the kick, the huge man pirouetted on the other like a burlesque ballet dancer, uttered a wild cry which distant superstitious Manx people thought was that of the fabulous Tarroo Ushtey, the Water Bull, and met mother earth for the third time. Shaking himself he rose unsteadily, lowered his head, and rushed into the fray, failing by his tactics to see the rope now held taught in his path by the mountaineering section, tripped, fell on his face and was trussed up and tied before he knew where he was.

Hook and Baldy were hard pressed, but not yet vanquished. Like giants possessed they flung the clinging scouts from them, one after another, only to be again assailed by reserves who crowded round like furious bees. Finally, Hook got his great claw free and raised it like an engine of doom above the head of the scoutmaster. A loop of rope from the rock-climbers hooked itself on the damnable weapon, which hung in mid-air for a perilous second, and then jerked spasmodically down on the head of its owner. Hook thus rendered himself unconscious and was tied up like a silkworm in a cocoon of hemp...

The man with the cauliflower ears and the broken nose, had throughout the fight been behaving in punch-drunk, dimwitted fashion, sparring, weaving, shadow-boxing on the edge of the skirmish, resisting with a head like a rock, all the blows of staves which fell upon him. Finally, a small boy in large spectacles, climbing on the gate with an old bucket, fell down upon Broken Nose as he passed beneath, still sparring at nothing, and thrust the receptacle, like the casque of a knight of old, over the Ears and the Nose down to his shoulders, and swinging on the handle, bore the roaring pugilist to earth, where, with suffocating muffled cries, he was set upon by six boys.

Then they discovered that Baldy had taken to his heels across country, followed by three adhesive lads who, in the heat of the chase, ignored all danger.

"Stop! Stop, boys!" bawled Knell with the last of his wind. And in true scout fashion, the boys obeyed. Baldy did not, and discovered too late that he was in the bog. He thought he could flounder through a shallow pool, but soon found his mistake. He sank to his waist in brackish water, but it did not end there; he continued to vanish before their eyes. Roaring and clawing the air, Baldy disappeared from view. First the cruel face, then the bald head. The bog seemed to gobble-up Baldy. At length, two arms with hands convulsively opening and closing were all that remained in view. Knell, lying on his stomach, hooked a rope round the wrist of one arm before it finally sank into the hideous slime, and they slowly drew out the collapsed thug like some ghastly monster from underground. It was difficult practicing artificial respiration on Baldy in his casing of evil-smelling mud, but they restored him to consciousness after half an hour's toil. Only to find he had completely lost his wits. That night, Baldy died of fright...

The police van arrived when the battle was over. They

bundled the toughs inside and it was only then that the scout-master got angry and rebuked the boys for turning what could have been an easy victory into a rabble by their eagerness. Some-body had untied Littlejohn and he took their part. He thanked them all, the boys formed fours, marched back to Mr. Gelling's mansion, where their hacked shins, broken heads, barked knuckles and black eyes were attended to, and they were then regaled on more sandwiches, pies and mineral waters, which they disposed of to the last crumb and drop. Then, the ice-cream arrived...

Littlejohn and Knell were sorry they couldn't stay to celebrate the victory.

"It's half past one Knell... I want to get back to Douglas in time for the arrival of the boat. Can we make it?"

"Easy."

With the cheers of the scouts to help them along, the two detectives, having promised autographs and a farewell celebration the following day, drove off to Douglas.

Littlejohn and Knell turned in at the police-station in Ramsey. The motley gang from Ullymar were already in the cells, having their wounds attended to. Fatty had a plaster in the form of a St. Andrew's cross over almost half his ugly mug and a pad of lint over one eye. Hook had recovered consciousness and had a lump the size of a pigeon's egg where his steel claw had smitten him to sleep. Moe, the monoculous one, had somehow got himself a broken collar-bone. Broken Nose alone seemed unhurt and every now and then, at times which might have corresponded with the ringing of the starting-gong at a professional fight, kept leaping to his feet in his cell, prancing on his toes, and boxing with an adver-sary nobody could see.

"That's 'im," roared Fatty as Littlejohn entered his cell. "That's 'im. Book 'im for trespass. Broke into a private resindents, he did, and was a-burglin' of it. When we arrived about our buildin' busi-ness, wot did 'e do? Set on us as if he'd like to kill us. Set on us maglinantly. Look at us. That's wot 'e done. It's trespass an' assault and battery..."

"Charge the lot with smuggling and assaulting the police," said Littlejohn and left Fatty, glaring over his St. Andrew's cross and roaring abuse.

Littlejohn spoke to the sergeant in charge.

"There's quite a little job for you, as well as looking after that motley crew. I want you to keep an eye on a number of people and see that none of them leaves Ramsey... Here's a list."

- Jules Morin.
- Amy Green.
- The Parkers, father and son.
- Dr. Harborne-Smith.
- Tremouille, the advocate.

The sergeant whistled.

"Quite a lot! What have they all been up to, sir? Not all smugglin' with that riff-raff in the cells?"

"Worse," said the Inspector. "Get your men to call and see them all and tell each one except Amy, that there's a meeting of the *Jonee Ghorrym* Company at Parker's office at five o'clock to-day and they'd better all be there. Then, when your men have seen them all personally, they're not to let them out of sight. If any one of them tries to bolt, he's to be arrested on suspicion of smuggling, and held. Follow?"

"Yes, sir. This little lot's likely to cause an unholy to-do in Ramsey. It isn't often we get anything like this."

"I'm sure it isn't. By the way, the *Jonee* isn't in yet, is she?"

"No, sir. She's due, though. Captain Kewley wirelessed he's on the way back from Dublin and should dock around five. Do you want him held, too?"

"I guess not. He'll stick to his ship and she won't turn round and get away very lively, will she?"

"We'll see she doesn't, sir..."

"Thanks. And now for Douglas."

They took the T.T. road over Snaefell again.

"Are there any special features in the *Manx Clarion*, Knell, which might call for a reporter disguising himself?"

Knell turned astonished eyes on Littlejohn. He'd grown used to unorthodox ways, but this was a new one.

"Why, sir? I can't think of any."

"I've just got an idea, that's all. The funny little man in the overcoat that's a bit too big for him. The man they said was in the fish-and-chip shop where Irons' supper came from and who, as likely as not, dropped the poison in his coffee. I think it might be Colquitt, the reporter from the *Clarion*..."

"But surely, sir..."

"In fact, I'm nearly sure it is, Knell. That's why I want to be there when the boat arrives..."

They had reached the summit and were now descending the fine road down to the town. To the right the mountains and to the left, the wide bay and stretch of blue sunny sea, with Douglas Head sheltering the port like a great arm. On the skyline a whisp of smoke and then, almost too small to see, a ship riding on the horizon.

"There she comes," said Knell. "That's the *Mona* on her way in. We've plenty of time... But what's this about disguises, sir?"

"I believe Colquitt's quite a dab hand at disguises and makeup. Some connection with the theatre, they said. Now, I've met the funny little man twice. Once coming over on the boat and again at Castletown with a party of sightseers. You can disguise anything almost, except a pair of ears. And, as you know, a good policeman always looks at ears when it's a case of identity. In fact, I always notice them, just as a matter of habit. Don't you? I'm sure you do."

"Oh, yes. I always notice ears, sir..."

Knell had his doubts about recognizing the same ears again, but he didn't say so. In fact, he brooded, he couldn't recognize

Millie Teare by her ears if she were disguised. He made a mental note about this great rule of expert investigation.

"I wondered where I'd seen Colquitt's ears before when I first met him. It was on the little man. That's why I wondered..."

Knell smote the wheel a blow with his hand, made the car wobble, and righted it.

"You're right, sir. Charlie Wagg! !"

It was Littlejohn's turn to look surprised.

"Charlie Wagg?"

"Yes, sir. All summer the *Clarion's* been running a sort of competition. They have a reporter moving among the holiday crowds, on the beach, in motor-coaches, at the pictures... Wherever there's a crowd. It's known he's in town every day and the competition is to find him. He talks to people and then prints things they've said and done, in the next edition. The idea is to recognize him, say 'Are you Charlie Wagg?' and if it's him, you get a five pound note..."

"That's it! On the boat crossing, at the Castle that day... He was there about his business. Was he ever spotted?"

"Not once. In fact, there were letters to the paper saying it was a swindle and there wasn't any Charlie Wagg. But they soon put it right, because the reporter spoke to the very man who wrote the letter to the *Clarion*, and printed some of the things the man had said and done."

"Then Charlie Wagg poisons Irons' coffee. Very silly of him. Or perhaps it wasn't. We'll have to see. We traced Charlie to his boarding house and found he'd left by the first 'plane this morning. Which means that, having discovered Irons was murdered by a man like Charlie, Colquitt had to make Charlie leave the Island and never come back. I wonder if Colquitt's gone for good..."

"I don't think so, sir. You see, *nobody* knows what Charlie Wagg looks like, not even his own editor. Everybody has to guess. Colquitt, or whoever Wagg is, doesn't dress up at the office. He does it in private. So, nobody knows him. That's up to the vigilant public. You're right. Charlie has left the Island. He won't come back. But Colquitt will, and on the next boat. That's clever of you, sir."

"No. Just routine, Knell. Let's call at Douglas police-station first..."

As they ran down Prospect Hill, the siren of the incoming boat echoed over the town.

"We'll have to look sharp, sir. She's near the Head."

The constable who'd brought in Irons' supper was on duty and very fed-up, too. He hadn't slept properly since the dealer's death. He held himself responsible for it.

"I don't know what I was doing, letting somebody dope the drink like I did. It wasn't as if..."

"You can't blame yourself, Constable. How were you to know...?"

"You think so, Inspector? It's good of you to say so. I can't get it off my mind..."

"You can help me, perhaps..."

"Anything, sir. Anything..."

The bobby had a cheerful open face of the Manx variety, but there were bags under his eyes from worry and sleeplessness. He smiled sadly at Littlejohn and looked ready to cry.

"What happened to make you go out for all Irons' meals?"

"It was his partner who upset him. He came after Irons was brought here and..."

"Excuse me... How long after?"

The constable scratched his chin.

"As far as I remember, about an hour or so... He came and Irons was having a cup of tea, which we'd made for him."

"Very decent of you."

"We always try to make them comfortable and treat 'em humane, like. After all, they're innocent till they're proved guilty."

Having delivered himself of this masterly piece of judicial

wisdom, the bobby paused and pondered on the majesty of the Law.

"I didn't know Irons had a partner."

"Neither did I, but it seems he had, and this one said could he speak to Irons about carrying on the business while Irons was detained. One of our men was there at the interview. All the visitor seemed to do was to upset Irons about his food. I wasn't with them, but after his pal had gone, Irons said the prison food wasn't good enough for him and wanted some sending for to the cook-shop round the corner. It's a fish-and-chip shop and Irons seemed to know the bill of fare. He said he wanted steak puddings for his tea and at supper they'd better get him fish and chips and some coffee instead of police tea, which I think's very nice, but which Irons said was like washin'-up water..."

"So it looked as if his partner told Irons where to send for food and what he could get?"

"That's right... Why... You mean to say it was all planned beforehand and his partner upset him about the food and persuaded him to have it sent for so that he could hang round and poison it as soon as he got a chance...?" Then the bobby paused for breath!

"It looks very much like it. Irons knew too much and they had to get him out of the way before he grew dangerous. His partner, as he called himself, must have come to find out if Irons had told the police anything and, discovering he hadn't said anything up to the time, he felt he couldn't trust Irons, or else Irons grew threatening, so he fixed a plan to poison him. He obviously couldn't murder Irons in front of the police. Who was the constable at the interview?"

"Constable Shimmin, sir. He's off duty, but he won't be in bed. You'll like as not, find him at his mother-in-law's in Walpole Avenue. His wife's in the maternity home having her second, and he's living at her parents' place till she comes home..."

"I know it," said Knell, the omniscient where island affairs went.

They made for the pier, stopping at Walpole Avenue nearby, on the way.

P.C. Shimmin was in his shirt sleeves reading the daily paper. He was bashful in the presence of C.I.D. men and hastened to clothe himself properly by putting on an old police tunic without buttons, which gave him a derelict look. He, too, was large, red and round, and he, too, had pouches under his eyes from watching and worrying about his wife's condition.

"Yes, sir. It's a boy. A fine bouncin' one, by all accounts. She had an easy time, too, they say..."

He sounded as if it were he who had gone through it all and that his missus had somehow avoided her dues.

"Yes, I remember the man who called. Foreign, I think. Hungarian, by the sound of him. Medium built, carried an overcoat, although it wasn't what you'd call overcoat weather. But these foreigners have rum ways, haven't they?"

"Had he a scar on his face?"

"Yes, sir. A long cut right down his left cheek. Might have been done with a sword or something. Carried on shocking about the police food, though I've always said we do them too well in jail. But he upset Irons and nothing would do but that we should send out for his vittles. Steak puddings and fish and chips! Ours was sausage and mash. What more could he want? Just pure cussedness! If I wasn't on the side of the law, I'd say, sir, it served him right getting poisoned."

"Excuse me... Is the paper in here?"

A heavy man with a huge moustache and in his shirt sleeves and carpet slippers, shuffled in, took it all in with a nosey-parker look, fiddled with the papers, and then, as the conversation had ceased, took himself off.

"Wish the missus was back," groaned Shimmin. "That's my

father-in-law. They're in everythin'. Can't mind their own business. What were we sayin', sir?"

There was a sound of many feet descending the stairs. Voices raised, quarrelling among themselves as to where they should go between then and teatime. Boarders on the move...

"I want to hear the minstrels on the Head, mummy... Why can't we hear the minstrels...?"

"We can't be everywhere at the same time. Yer dad wants to go for a walk on the prom and a drink. Now, stop it, or I'll give yer a good hidin'..."

P.C. Shimmin raised his baggy eyes to heaven.

"I wish we were 'ome again..."

"I think that's all, Shimmin, thanks. We'd better be off. We want to see the boat in. By the way, what made you think the visitor was Hungarian?"

"He said the police food was like 'ogwash... Isn't 'ogwash an Hungarian food or drink, or something made from milk, sir?"

Knell tittered.

"Hogwash, Jimmie?" He chuckled. It was the first time Littlejohn had heard him do it! "*Hog Wash*, see? Pig food... Right?"

"O.K. Sorry..."

Outside, it was still going on.

"I want to go to the minstrels on the Head..." With howls, now!

They left P.C. Shimmin to his troubles. Knell began to brood on the thought that he might suffer similar paternity himself one day and his mirth left him.

18

THE LAST OF CHARLIE WAGG

They parked the car and hurried towards the pier. The *Mona* was just entering the harbour and the signal gun went off at Fort Anne to greet her, sending echoes round the bay.

Knots of people had gathered to meet incoming friends and porters lined the quayside as the ship slowly drew alongside and gently came to rest. The captain rang down 'Finished with Engines', the gangways came out, the porters scuttered aboard to claim their clients.

Passengers began to shuffle down the gangways, there was shouting and greeting, and those who had merely strolled along the quay to watch the boat dock, began to melt away.

Colquitt was one of the last to leave the *Mona*. He seemed to be enjoying himself, talking with the officers, hailing friends and acquaintances, like a man on a day's outing and intent on having a good time.

"Had a good crossing?"

People kept asking the newcomers the same thing, though the answer was obvious. It had been perfect. The last off was a party of ambulance men with a stretcher on which an old man was lying. He had fallen and cut his eye on the way. They were taking him to hospital for a check-up. Gulls wheeled round and cried for food and a chef in a white coat flung scraps through an open porthole. The ship's cat ran daintily down the gangway and went for a walk along the pavement of the pier... Strangers pointed her out as she frisked along, for she was pure Manx and had no tail.

"Are you Charlie Wagg?"

Colquitt had spotted the two detectives as he came down the gangway. As Littlejohn addressed him, he halted, smiled a sickly smile, and then tried to bluff it off. It was too late.

"Hello, Inspector. Meeting somebody?"

Littlejohn repeated his greeting without a smile.

"Charlie Wagg? We want five pounds, please."

"Look here, Inspector, is this a joke, because I don't get you. . .?"

"Yes, you do, Mr. Colquitt. We want you to come quietly with us to the police-station..."

Colquitt was scared now. He started to perspire.

"You left by the early 'plane and were in nice time for the morning boat, sir. You left Charlie Wagg on the other side out of harm's way, did you?"

"Don't make a scene here, Inspector. I'm sure I don't know what you're talking about. People are watching us."

He was right. The idlers on the pier all knew Littlejohn and Knell by now, and knew what they were investigating. They drew nearer in eager curiosity.

"Come to the car, then, and we'll drive to the police-station."

"What's all this about? I want my lawyer, if you're starting to be awkward..."

"Tremouille? I'm afraid he won't be free to help you. We're holding him at Ramsey. You see the whole game's up, Colquitt. Better come along quietly."

All the bounce went out of Colquitt. He walked in a daze between the two officers and climbed in the car without another word.

"I don't understand what you're getting at," he said on the way. "But you'd better be careful. The press here is powerful. I can make it hot for you if you don't play fair by me."

"No fear of that. We just want to ask you a few questions. If you can satisfy us, then it will be all right, I promise you."

"But I haven't done anything wrong..."

They took him into one of the rooms at the police-station and he sat down and started to mop his face and head with a handkerchief.

"You can't mix me up in the Deemster's murder, Inspector. I've got an alibi..."

"Yes. You were on the *Mona* with me, weren't you, when I crossed? You could hardly have murdered Deemster Quantrell then. But where were you at the time Irons was poisoned? They say a man answering to the description of your Charlie Wagg role was in the restaurant when Iron's jug of coffee was poisoned and he was near enough to put in the arsenic..."

"I was in Ramsey. You remember. I was with you at *The Duck's Nest.*"

"No, you weren't. You'd left me long before Irons was killed. You could easily have got to Douglas in the time. You'd better think fast and explain if you don't want charging with murder..."

"You can't do that. I warn you..."

Littlejohn lit his pipe.

"Well? What scared you so much that you ran away to make Charlie Wagg disappear for ever? You were afraid Charlie would be accused of murder, weren't you?"

"I didn't do it. You can't pin it on me."

"That's what Morin tried to do, isn't it? He borrowed your Charlie Wagg disguise. Why didn't you come to the police and say you'd lent it and that Morin had killed Irons at the time *he* was Charlie Wagg instead of you? That would have put us right on the track. Instead of which, you bolt and give us endless trouble."

"How was I to know he'd done it? You'd have said it was me."

"You were afraid of Morin. Why? Was it that you'd an idea he was at the bottom of the murders and you hadn't told the police? Were you afraid you'd be charged as an accessory? Or were you in the smuggling racket and scared of it coming out?"

Colquitt was as white as chalk. He looked ready to faint.

"Can I have a drink. I'm not so well..."

They gave him some water.

"Well?"

"Morin said he wanted to borrow my outfit."

"How did he know you were Charlie Wagg? I thought nobody knew. Not even your own editor."

"I went to Ramsey one day. He spotted me. Said he could tell me by my ears..."

Knell and Littlejohn exchanged glances.

"It's right. Morin was in the French underground in the war. He knew all the dodges. If I say any more, you'll have to promise me police protection. Morin's a killer. He won't stop at murder. It comes easy to him. He accounted for no end of Germans in the war. He just doesn't care..."

Colquitt was desperate and whining now. He sank in a chair and flung his arms out in despair.

"We'll look after you. In fact, we're going to keep you here in jail till we've rounded up the lot of the *Duck's Nest* gang. What about Morin and Charlie Wagg?"

"When he heard Irons had been arrested he went to see him in jail. You'd moved Irons to Douglas, but Morin followed and saw him some way. What went on, I don't know, but Morin turned up at *The Duck's Nest*, where I was hanging round covering Parker's party, and said he wanted my Wagg clothes. I asked him why, and he said I'd better ask no questions. He was a killer. I lent them to him."

"How did you know he was a killer?"

"He used to talk about how he did in the war. He'd stop at nothing. The lot of us were a bit scared of him. He just used to go berserk and there was no doing any good with him. I had an idea that he was involved in the Castletown murders, though I'd no proof. When he asked for my clothes, I lent them to him. I drove him to Douglas and got them from my rooms. Then I went to the office for a bit and he brought them back later. They were too big for me and they fitted him. He'd even stuck on my moustache..."

"*Fitted* is a mis-statement. They hung on him like they did on you. He looked like you. Did anybody see you at the office at the time Morin was in the restaurant poisoning Irons' coffee?"

Colquitt milled eagerly around, waving his arms, laughing with relief.

"Yes, yes. Old Joe, the watchman, was there. He'll tell you. I brought in some bottled beers and we drank them together. Thank God for old Joe! He'll bear me out. He'll give me an alibi. Good old Joe..."

"Don't get excited. Then, when you heard about Irons' death, you thought it was Morin and tumbled to the idea that he might have done it whilst impersonating you in your Charlie Wagg get-up. Is that it?"

"Yes. I knew you'd be on that. I thought it better to get rid of Charlie and all about him. I hoped nobody would know. I went to Liverpool, after checking out of the hotel I'd been staying at getting copy and playing my Charlie part. Remember, I saw you and Mr. Knell in Castletown that day? That was me. I flew over to the mainland, changed in a lavatory, threw the bundle of clothes in the Mersey, and returned here on the boat as myself. Now I've told you everything and it's up to you to play fair by me..."

"We'll play fair. You must have suspected a lot of what was going on. You were always in Ramsey hanging around the *Jonee Ghorrym* and *The Duck's Nest*. Did you never suspect there was jiggery-pokery and even murder going on?"

"I guessed things weren't right, but I'd no proof. You've got to believe me. After all, I'm a reporter, not a policeman."

"But you can help the police, and you could have done then.

However, you'll be detained here till we've settled matters at Ramsey. You're far too talkative, Mr. Colquitt, for us to let you loose to go chattering at *The Duck's Nest* again. You'd better settle down till it's safe to turn you out."

"That's all right by me, provided you *do* get Morin."

"And whilst you're here, think things out and write out an account of your own connection with *The Duck's Nest* lot."

"It won't be much, I'll tell you."

"It had better be the truth and all of it, Mr. Colquitt."

"I haven't done anything wrong. I was only following my profession as a journalist, and surely I can't be convicted for getting news..."

Littlejohn turned back and faced Colquitt.

"News, did you say? What news did you hope to find in sneaking round the crowd that congregated at *The Duck's Nest?* Anything they told you wasn't of public interest and anything you discovered of their activities... illegal ones, I mean... couldn't find its way to print, because your editor wouldn't have printed it before he'd handed it over to the police..."

Colquitt blinked. He took a cigarette from a battered packet and lit it with trembling fingers. Already the tin-lid which served as an ash tray was filling up with spent matches, fag ends and ash.

"Have you any cigarettes on you, Inspector? Or could somebody get me another packet? This is my last..."

Littlejohn passed over his own case.

"Take the lot. I'll get some more..."

He sat down and faced Colquitt.

"Are you sure you haven't something you want to tell me? Something you found out. . .? Something vital in this case? Why were you always hanging round *The Duck's Nest?* It wasn't for news. In fact, by spending so much time there you were neglecting your duties. Were you on the payroll there?"

"I told you, the set-up interested me... The queer types... The gang of characters... I'm going to write a book one day and they provided good copy..."

"Who was the hidden contact-man between the Ramsey gang and their hirelings in Douglas... Irons, Fannin, Lamprey? Was it you?"

"No... No... I didn't..."

Littlejohn drew his chair nearer. Colquitt's wild eyes and his twitching fingers told the truth better than his gasping answers.

"Who followed the Deemster round on his investigations into the *Jonee Ghorrym?* Who passed on the orders that Lamprey must get the keys to the Deemster's room and desk? Who trailed poor scared Alcardi about and set the thugs on him who killed him? Was it you, Colquitt, or Charlie Wagg? And who gave you the orders...?"

"I don't know what you're talking about. It's fantastic..."

Another cigarette from the battered packet and another in the tin-lid. He wasn't troubling to smoke them to the end now, and the ash-tray was filling up with half-finished cigarettes.

"Was it Amy?"

Colquitt sprang to his feet, his face twitching, his jaws clenched. He was white with fury. Knell took a step forward fearing Colquitt was going to attack Littlejohn.

"Don't you dare bring her into this! She's nothing to do with it. She's a decent girl trying to earn an honest living..."

"How? As mistress to Alcardi...?"

Colquitt waved his arms.

"Who told you that? She was never..."

"I know she wasn't, but she told me so. She said she was Alcardi's girl and he couldn't marry her because he had a wife somewhere."

"It wasn't true! She was trying to stop you bullying her... Why can't you lay off her...?"

"You're in love with Amy? Is that why you're always hanging round there? Is that why she twisted you round her little finger

247

and got you to do all she asked... Spying on the Deemster, spying on Alcardi, acting as an errand-boy for her orders to Irons and Co. Orders given to her to pass on by Morin, the man you'd like to kill or else betray to the police but daren't... Why daren't you?"

"It's all lies. Amy and I were going away together when all this was cleared up..."

"So, to keep her out of trouble, you shielded Morin?"

"She told me that if things blew up, she'd go to jail. That gang had her in their clutches. If I'd help, they'd clear it all up, sell out and get away..."

"So you followed the Deemster around, found out how closely he was on the track of the smugglers and the murderer of Captain Teare, told them all you'd discovered, and then they killed the Deemster, the boy scout, Irons..."

"Captain Teare? He was drowned; he wasn't murdered."

Another cigarette and one more to the collection of fag-ends smouldering in the metal cap.

"He was murdered... by the *Duck's Nest* gang... However, we're wasting time here. We're due in Ramsey at five. On second thoughts, you can go free. If you were mere news-hunting, there's no reason for locking you up till we really need you. Only don't try to leave Douglas..."

"I don't want to stay in Douglas. I want to stay here. It's not safe for me if Morin's not arrested. He'll think I blew the gaff on him dressing up as Charlie Wagg, and he won't rest till he's had his revenge on me, like he did... like he did. . ."

"Like he did to Irons?"

"Let me stay in jail till you come back..."

Colquitt was whining now.

"Very well, but you were the 'shadow' who followed the Deemster and Alcardi, were you?"

"Yes..."

You could hardly hear him say it.

"What happened the night Alcardi died?"

"For some reason, as soon as he heard that Scotland Yard were here, he got fright. He was on the run..."

"Who started him on the run...?"

"Amy asked me to do it..."

Amy! The girl with the large mysterious eyes and nothing else. The thin, dreamy, flat-chested, sinuous girl, who, now and then painted her lips, rouged her cheeks, washed and waved her hair, put on a false bust, and looked attractive, after all.

Amy, who pretended to fall for Colquitt, the man who had no success with women, whose wife ran out on him, who was the hanger-on of the *Duck's Nest* mob. He suddenly finds Amy making eyes at him, offering herself to him, just to get him to do as she wanted, to help her and Morin...

"*What* did she ask you to do?"

"I rang up Alcardi and told him you were on the case. You'd found out about Alcardi making the keys for the Deemster's room and were on his track on suspicion of murdering the Deemster."

"Yes..."

"He bolted as I said he ought to. But he didn't quite do as was expected. They thought he'd make for the *Jonee Ghorrym* right away; instead, he started hunting for you to try to explain. I think he must have gone mad..."

"Or had an alibi?"

"Alibi? How could he? He killed the Deemster. He was guilty... But it seemed folly to come to you with that on his crop."

"Not at all. He wasn't the murderer..."

Colquitt gasped.

"Not Alcardi? Who was it then?"

"Not for publication. Go on with your tale."

"Instead of bolting for the *Jonee* and getting a passage to the mainland, he started hunting for you. Luckily, you were out, otherwise I guess he would have told all about the smuggling and Morin and the rest. They had to stop him. Fannin and me did the work in turns. Fannin got drunk and nearly messed it up. Alcardi made for Grenaby vicarage. I knew you were staying there. It had got round you were coming to Parson Kinrade's before you even arrived..."

"When he found me not there, what then?"

"He took the Round Table road. I knew if I stayed near the vicarage, he'd probably come back."

"Why didn't he go to the police?"

"I telephoned Amy from Colby and she arranged for Morin and Kewley to keep an eye on Douglas and Ramsey police-stations and for one of Parker's men to watch Castletown..."

"One of our toughs, Knell, I'll bet..."

Knell rubbed his hands at the recollection of the Battle of Ballaugh. Colquitt was so immersed in his tale, he didn't even notice the interjections, and he'd stopped smoking.

"...Amy said they were only going to find him and take him off to the *Jonee* and get him away..."

"Indeed! And what happened next?"

"He seemed mad with panic. As I came from the 'phone box at Colby, Alcardi passed on the way to Douglas. He went to the pictures. Fannin lost him, but I was there. He seemed to be hiding till he could be quite sure he'd find you home. When we came out, there was somebody else on Alcardi's heels. Must have been one of the police, I think..."

"Me!" said Knell proudly. Colquitt went on as if nobody had spoken.

"Alcardi took the coast road, the other car followed, and I followed them both, but I didn't want the police to see me on their tail, so I took other cuts. If you know the road to Ramsey, you can do that. You can even follow the main road by parallel older roads and see the headlights on one from the other. Onchan, Lonan, Ballarach... It was easy, popping on and off the main road..."

He waved his arms and lit another cigarette.

"When we got to Ramsey, Alcardi tried to get in *The Duck's Nest* but Morin wouldn't let him in. There were people there. He told him to come back. Alcardi tried the *Jonee*, too, but the man on watch didn't know him and pushed him off. Then the Italian took to his heels again. This time Jules came out and followed him and the police car. I went back to *The Duck's Nest* and stayed the night..."

"Was Amy there?"

"What are you getting at?"

"Nothing. Was she there?"

"Of course she was. There'd been a party and she was clearing up..."

"That was after you left Alcardi to Jules after you chased him from the pictures?"

"Yes. Why?"

"Go on..."

Knell's pencil flew across the paper of his book. It was almost full and he hoped they were near the end.

"She stayed with you?"

"Look here, it wasn't as you think. I sat in the kitchen with her till two o'clock, when she'd finished, and we made some tea and had a chat... Then we both went to bed, in our own rooms."

"No doubt. And when, the following day, you heard Alcardi had been murdered, too, what did you do?"

"I tackled Jules. He said there'd been trouble. The Italian went to Grenaby again, in spite of the hour, and Fannin was there and later, a bobby arrived and they had to out him..."

"Me!" said Knell.

Colquitt ignored him and crushed out another cigarette.

"They got hold of Alcardi and tried to take him off quietly, but he pulled a gun and fired at them. They hit him and it seems he fell and cracked his head on the stone floor... He was dead..."

"Very good! Full of virtue, weren't they? They *had* to lay Knell out, and Alcardi killed himself by the way he fell... Well, well..."

"What do you mean?"

"Never mind. You can stay here till I give you the all-clear.

Better spend the time writing it all out. I'll tell the sergeant in charge to find you pen and paper, or else a man to take it down."

Knell's mouth moved and he pointed to his black book, but Littlejohn was on his way to the car, so the sergeant followed.

"We've time to get to Grenaby, I hope, and pick up the Archdeacon, Knell. He deserves to be in at the *finale* and we seem to be working up to it in Ramsey," said the Inspector, as they drove away.

19

GENERAL MEETING

It was always like entering another, calmer world when you left the main highroad and turned to Grenaby, and once the circle of trees which marked the boundary of the hamlet was passed, you felt the peace of the place take hold of you like a drug and lull you into inactivity and quietness.

The car ran down the hill and past Joe Henn's house. Joe was in the garden with two walkers he had waylaid and was, with excited gestures, showing them his summer-house, his 'ut, and reciting, like a ballad, the account of how murder was committed and how his precious retreat was violated by somebody parking a car in it whilst the deed was done... He paused in his story to wave as the police drove past and pointed after the car, obviously telling his audience who was in it and why they were there...

Across the stone bridge and up to the vicarage. An angler, tall, gaunt, concentrated, was holding a line over the parapet, outrageously trying with a worm to hook a trout. Women in sunbonnets came to their doors to see who was passing, and the postman emptied the pillar-box...

The Archdeacon was standing at the door as they turned up the "street" leading to the vicarage. The housekeeper was feeding

253

the hens behind a fence of wire-netting, scattering handfuls of corn over them like a baptism. She raised her head, gave the police a look of alarm, and went indoors.

"We're on our way to Ramsey, sir. Care to come?"

The vicar seemed to scent tragedy and looked grave. Without a word he turned indoors and re-appeared with his hat and a shawl for his shoulders.

"Is it the end?"

"Yes, sir..."

They drove all the way in silence, the parson lost in thought, Littlejohn turning over the points of the forthcoming interview, and Knell pretending to be intent on the road and his driving. They drove over the moor to South Barrule Plantation, struck the main road through Foxdale and St. John's, past Michael and the Bishop's Palace, Ballaugh and Lezayre. But they did not notice the calm of the sunny day, now drawing to evening, or the mild sea as they ran into Ramsey. It was as if every mile brought them nearer the dreadful end of the story and the men waiting for retribution. They pulled-up at the police-station. Two grim men, a sergeant and a constable, joined them in another car.

"Is it all fixed, sergeant?"

"Yes, sir. We told them the meeting would be at Mr. Parker's office. Two of our men have gone for Morin and the girl."

"Any trouble?"

"Not much. Old Mr. Parker seemed to expect something or other. His son, Mr. Lawrence, daren't refuse to come if his dad says he must. Dr. Smith tried to laugh it off. I told him if he didn't come, I'd send men to fetch him. Mr. Tremouille was wild. You bet I'll be there, he said. Something about it bein' an outrage and somebody was goin' to be made to suffer. He didn't say who..."

"You kept an eye on *The Duck's Nest*?"

"Yes, sir. The *Jonee* docked half an hour since. I put a man aboard and told the captain he was wanted at the meetin'. He said he'd come if he felt like it. I said he'd come whether or not, and if not under his own steam, then we'd provide some for 'im. He'll be there."

"What about Morin and Amy?"

"They're there, all right, just as if nothing was happenin'. But I guess they're a bit suspicious by now with none of the usual party arriving. As a matter of fact, they're so cool about things, I wonder if they've got somethin' up their sleeves. When they get to Parker's and put a sight on the crowd there, I reckon we'll have to be watching them..."

"Right. Let's go, sergeant."

They ran up Ballure to the large builder's-yard and turned in at the gate. It was striking a quarter to five and none of the party had arrived. Old Parker, however, was in his room, sitting at his desk, his hat on his head, as usual, watching all that was going on from the large window. They parked the cars by the side of a large limepit with a treacherous dirty white scum covering it.

"I'd better go in myself... Just the Vicar and I, if you don't mind. I'll let you know when I need you, sergeant. I want a word with old man Parker first..."

Miss Caley, the office typist, met them at the door. She was obviously scared by the invasion. She barred the way with her body until she'd had her say.

"Mr. Parker, senior, expects you. I'm to take you to him. He's a sick man and must not be excited. I hope you'll bear that in mind. Follow me..."

She led Littlejohn and the Archdeacon into the old man's room. He greeted them with a nod. Somebody had brought in a lot of chairs as if in readiness for a large gathering.

"Sit down, both of you. What do *you* want, vicar?"

"He's with me, sir."

"Hmph..."

They drew up chairs to the desk.

Humphrey Parker's cheeks were flushed a dangerous pink. Otherwise, he looked steady enough. His thin silver hair flowed from under his old-fashioned black billycock. His eyes were bright, his thin lips tight. His pale bony hands rested on the desk as he slumped in his chair. One hand trembled with the palsy; the right hand was still. Through the knee-hole in the desk you could see his paralysed legs dangling from the armchair in which he sat.

"What is all this about?"

Parker's voice was audible, but he slurred his words like a half-drunken man. Except that the voice was sharp, with none of the comic jollity of the classical tipsy fool. He did not wait for an answer; his eyes instead fixed themselves on the group of men entering the yard. Lawrence Parker, Harborne-Smith and Tremouille. They arrived aggressively; there was something almost jaunty in Harborne-Smith's manner. Tremouille eyed the cars and approached the police officers. His lips moved and the police seemed to be replying diffidently. Littlejohn waved to Knell to bring them all in.

"Miss Caley will stay... Take all that goes on down in short-hand... Don't miss a word, my girl..."

"Certainly, Mr. Parker... No, Mr. Parker..."

The typist began to fuss about after a pad and pencils, laying them all out on a desk at the side of the room. In her excitement, she knocked over a box of pen-nibs and went down on her knees, picking them up one by one, like some bird feeding on seeds. Old Parker eyed her balefully.

"Sit down and control yourself..."

"Yes, Mr. Parker. Certainly, Mr. Parker..."

Shuffling feet, and the party entered. Tremouille made straight for Littlejohn. His nose was pinched and white at the tip with anger. He was dressed formally in black coat and grey trousers, with a monocle dangling from a cord round his neck.

"I don't know what all this is about, Inspector. It's an outrage and will need a lot of explaining away. I'm here in my capacity as lawyer of the company, and I warn you that..."

"Shut up, Tremouille, and sit down quietly. Your turn'll come..."

The old man's sliding voice broke in suddenly and Tremouille halted in the middle of a sentence. He looked dumbfounded. He'd been expecting the old terror to side with him.

"Well, what're you all waiting for? Sit down. Let's hear what the police want. Find chairs and sit on 'em..."

Lawrence Parker gave his father a scared look, drew up a chair and sat down. The rest sheepishly followed, including the police. Knell sat by the door guarding it, and the other two local men by the window, as if expecting somebody to jump through it. The evening sun shone in and made a patch of light on the wall behind old Parker. Miss Caley sat intent, pencil poised, tautly eager to carry out instructions to the letter.

"Well? Who's going to speak first? Waiting for the parson to open with a word of prayer?"

Humphrey Parker looked malevolently around.

The Archdeacon fixed him with flashing blue eyes.

"Don't be vulgar, my friend. There's a time for everything, and there'll be plenty of it for prayer and the need for prayer when this meeting's ended..."

Miss Caley was taking it all down. Old Parker rounded on her.

"No need to take all *that* down. Stick to business..."

"Yes, Mr. Parker. Certainly, sir..."

Lawrence Parker sat licking his lips.

"What are we waiting for?"

Littlejohn sat with his pipe between his teeth, his legs crossed in front of him, apparently comfortable and content to wait all night if necessary.

"We're waiting for Jules and Amy..."

"Hah!"

Old Parker saw the relevancy at once, but the rest took it otherwise.

Tremouille was on his feet.

"This is supposed to be a private meeting. I protest. We can't have all the town in here..."

"Shut up, Tremouille... You can put that down, Miss Caley..."

The typist firmly wrote two symbols in her book.

"Damn' well shut up... Put that down, too..."

Old Parker was enjoying himself.

Two policemen arrived in the yard with Morin, Amy and Captain Kewley. Jules was talking and gesticulating, Amy followed despondently, her shoulders drooping, and Kewley made up the rear. They crossed by the limepit and entered the office.

"Sit down, you lot, and be quiet... Now we can start... Anybody going to read the minutes...? No?"

The excitement was affecting old Parker. His lips began to tremble and his half-paralysed left hand beat a tattoo on the desk which he tried to stop by placing his right hand on top of it. Both hands then started to dance, as though the top one were patting the one beneath.

Morin was truculent.

"What's all this tommy-rot, eh?" he said in his overdone idiom. "Why am I brought here? You can't arrest me or keep me. I'll come and go as I feel fit. You can't stop me..."

"You'll be quiet and sit down. I can't sit listening to your gabble all night. What are you laughing at Smith?"

Harborne-Smith seemed to be enjoying a private joke. He looked up.

"Harborne-Smith..."

"It's SMITH, and Smith I'll call you, you miserable little half-baked dud of a doctor..."

Flecks of foam appeared at the corners of Humphrey Parker's mouth.

"Be careful, Mr. Parker..."

He turned to the typist, slowly, like a machine.

"I don't need your advice... Give me a cigarette..."

"The doctor said..."

"I don't care what he said. GIVE ME ONE..."

She fitted a cigarette in an amber mouthpiece and stuck it

between the old man's lips, where it hung trembling as she lit it with unsteady hands. He smoked it with short noisy puffs.

"Now. Get on with it, Inspector..."

Old Parker slumped down in the chair, motionless. Only his eyes moved from one to the other of the assembled men. Then he spoke again.

"Where are my workmen?"

"In jail, sir. We arrested them for handling smuggled goods and they resisted arrest..."

"Where?"

"At Ullymar..."

The eyes moved balefully to his son. Lawrence Parker turned his head away.

"More of your folly, you fool! Go on, Littlejohn..."

There was no sound from the rest; they sat there expectant, wondering what was to come next. Littlejohn turned to Lawrence Parker.

"Tell us, please, Mr. Lawrence, what happened on the *Jonee Ghorrym* on the night of March 24th, 1945 and the rest of the trip."

Young Parker's eyes opened wide and he licked his dry lips again. He looked round as though seeking relief of some way out.

"It's so long since. I don't remember..."

"Tell him. Tell him that, after what happened, I always treated you as a fool clerk who couldn't be trusted with my affairs. Tell him, and no more stuttering and stammering. Go on..."

The old man didn't move; only his lips and mouth spat out the slurred command.

"I went to the mainland with the *Jonee*. We picked up coal and took it to Brittany."

"Quiberon?"

"Yes..."

Jules's breath came in a hiss.

"Well?"

259

Lawrence Parker raised his eyes to Littlejohn's face in a pleading look as though he'd rather speak in private.

"You went to Brittany to arrange some smuggling. Wines, whisky, tobacco, perhaps drugs..."

"No! Not drugs..."

"That's as may be. You found a contact-man who proved too enterprising... You signed-on Jules Morin, alias Charles Cosans."

Morin was on his feet, but the constable pulled him down again. "You sit quiet..."

"On that trip, you made all arrangements for the smuggling enterprises. Then, on April 26th of the same year, the *Jonee Ghorrym* sailed from Ramsey with Captain Teare as master for the last time. When she reached Quiberon, Morin shipped as a passenger. Morin had a box of smuggled goods which Captain Teare suspected and tried to search. I believe that for his conscientious curiosity, Captain Teare was murdered..."

Morin was on his feet again.

"It's a damn' lie you're telling. You can't put the frame on me..."

Humphrey Parker roused himself. He even tried to stand and fell back with a groan.

"Why do you think I never trusted my son again? Why did I always treat him, after that trip, as a half-wit? I'll tell you... I'm sick of all this hiding and subterfuge. Let's get it in the open before there are more murders. They brought back the body of Ebeneezer Teare. He'd been knocked on the head. Morin hid it till they docked and then fetched my son. I caught them at it. They put the body in the lime-pit... ! Didn't you? Tell 'em, you little yellow-livered spawn... Tell 'em..."

"Mr. Parker... Please be careful... The doctor..."

He brushed her aside.

"Yes... That's it... I didn't kill him. I was scared... Morin said it was me who told him to do it if Captain Teare turned awkward... I didn't kill him and I didn't. . ."

Morin rose with a roar and leapt half way across the room to get at Lawrence Parker. The constables had him by the wrists and dragged him back.

"I never killed him. He fell against the rails... It was a mistake..."

"Be quiet, all of you..."

Littlejohn's voice was like a lash. Amy was sobbing, the tears making grooves in the powder on her cheeks. She looked like a bedraggled waif. Her eyes kept turning beseechingly to Morin, full of solicitude and support for him. He ignored her.

Littlejohn was speaking.

"You dropped him in the lime-pit, did you? And then the good work went on. You signed-on a good-for-nothing skipper and he didn't mind what went on on the *Jonee Ghorrym*..."

Captain Kewley started to shout.

"You'd better be careful. You can't prove anything. I've got a clean ticket..."

"Tell it to the marines!"

Old Parker said it almost jocularly. He had calmed down and was listening with one ear turned to the Inspector.

"You're getting all this down, I hope, Miss Caley... We shall need the typescript when I take up the case in court..."

Tremouille said it officiously and started nervously to polish his monocle which he then put back in his pocket.

"When we want your help, we'll ask you, Tremouille. You'll be lucky if you see court again outside the dock..."

"Really, Mr. Parker. I thought..."

"Shut up... Go on Littlejohn."

"The smuggling then continued very profitably. Until one of the few shareholders wanted to dispose of his holding. Deemster Quantrell knew nothing about the shady trade going on in the *Jonee*. He drew his regular dividend whilst you got his nominee in your clutches and used him to keep things dark. When the Deemster started to get ready to retire, he changed his investments and was surprised to find how much he got for his shares. Five times what he paid for them! And why? Because the directors, eager to get full control of the *Jonee*, started to fall-out and outbid one another for the Deemster's holding..."

Harborne-Smith suddenly started to cackle. His neck swelled with his vicious mirth.

"Wrong, Inspector, like all the rest of this rambling story. You're making it all up. The directors will all tell you that's not true..."

Humphrey Parker cut him short.

"Keep out of this, *Smith*. He's almost right. It was Morin trying to buy the shares drove them up. The rest of you wanted to keep him out, and a pretty penny you paid to do it. Just stop this child's play and don't interrupt. I've made up my mind we'll end all this murder and violence once and for all, if it's the last thing I do. My disreputable son has brought all this on me... I was content with my business here and the normal commerce of the *Jonee Ghorrym* till he started to be clever. Well, we'll end it now. Do you know what brought me to this helpless, drooling pass? Eh? Tell 'em, Lawrence. Tell 'em what you did to do it..."

Like a boy ordered by his master, Parker junior spoke.

"He had a stroke when he caught us putting the body in the lime..."

"And though I'm nearly helpless, I'm not so paralysed I can't make you suffer for it. Every hour of every day, you've prayed I might drop down dead, and every hour I've seen to it that I turned the screw a bit harder... Go on, Littlejohn..."

Littlejohn took his pipe from his mouth. There was a look of patient tolerance on his face. If the gang wanted to talk all day among themselves and incriminate one another, he could wait. *Traa-dy-Liooar*... Time enough for everything...

"Deemster Quantrell was of a logical, inquiring mind. He was also by way of being an amateur detective. He intended writing a book on detection and its relations to the judiciary after he retired. The price his *Jonee Ghorrym* shares realized made him smell a rat. He set out to find what was going on..."

Tremouille raised his face and looked keenly at Littlejohn. His expression had changed. From being arrogant and defiant, he now took on a look of intense interest, felt in his pockets, pulled out a diary, and started to write in it with a fountain pen, jotting down points as Littlejohn made them.

"...The Deemster's first line of inquiry was through his nephew, Lamprey, who was his nominee in the shareholding, because the judge had to keep free of financial entanglements on account of his office. Lamprey was an impecunious, shiftless spendthrift, and soon up to the neck in the seamy side of the affair. He also betrayed his uncle's moves to the opposite camp, rightly named by my colleague Knell, the *Duck's Nest Lot*..."

Knell blushed and let fall his hat in his confusion.

Littlejohn looked round at the faces of the party. Amy was stock still, deathly pale, the fatal eyes which seemed to attract men, large and fixed first on the Inspector, then on Morin.

The Frenchman smiled faintly and shrugged his shoulders.

"I can't help it if men choose to meet at my place. I hold no responsibility for what they talk about when they're there. Do I? O. K?"

He put a cigarette in his mouth, asked one of the policemen sitting beside him for a match, and lit it.

"The Deemster also had another case running side by side with the *Jonee Ghorrym* one. It concerned counterfeit banknotes made by an Italian, Alcardi. Mr. Quantrell must have questioned Lamprey about both matters and Lamprey passed on the account to his shady associates, who thereupon tried to confuse the issue by mixing up both cases and trying to make it seem Alcardi was both a counterfeiter and a murderer..."

Tremouille was writing furiously in his diary and Miss Caley was breathlessly splashing shorthand symbols in her notebook. The lawyer looked up keenly at the latest piece of news but remained silent. It was Harborne-Smith who spoke.

"What's all this rubbish? I know nothing about it. Murder!

Counterfeiting! What have we been brought here for? To hear a sort of whodunit solved... or what?"

Old Parker didn't even look up. He stared straight ahead, the fingers of his left hand twitching on the table, his right resting in his lap. He spoke slowly.

"You keep out of this, *Smith*. It's too deep and involved for your dim wits..."

Littlejohn's voice broke in as if corroborating Humphrey Parker's words.

"A doctor who'd become a remittance-man and lived above his means and spent his money on young girls..."

"Look here, I'll..."

"Lawrence Parker, who, in an effort to show his father what a big man he was, arranged a smuggling business with the *Jonee Ghorrym*, got involved with an unscrupulous French black-marketeer, who wouldn't stop at killing if it suited him. He'd had plenty of experience in the underground during the war..."

"You can't pin the frame-up on me," sneered Morin in his usual idiom. He rose to put out his cigarette in the ash-tray on old Parker's desk and the flanking policemen rose with him. He turned, smiled at them, and discomfited them.

Littlejohn's voice came slowly.

"You needn't worry, Morin. The French police are waiting for you when we've finished with you. You left Quiberon in a hurry and they wondered where you'd got to. Actually, you were here in Ramsey and so safe and comfortable that you were ready to kill again if your comfort was threatened. However, to go on with Deemster Quantrell's investigation. He set about finding out what went on aboard the *Jonee*. He inquired about events, found out about the death of Captain Teare, saw a man who was a member of the crew on the night Teare died, and generally surmised that there had not only been smuggling, but murder going on. In the course of his case, he stumbled across the *Duck's Nest* set-up. He was also seen around the Curraghs and The Lhen. In other words, he was hot on the trail of the landings of contraband at The Llen shore and the storage of it at Ullymar. The *Duck's Nest* gang were informed of this by one of their contact men... either Lamprey or the journalist Colquitt, who's now in jail, by the way, in a little matter of the murder of Irons..."

Knell's lips curled in a smile and, somehow, Morin looked more content.

"Colquitt? That little toady! What's he got to do with things?" said Harborne-Smith. "A little damn' spy, huntin' for a scoop for his blasted paper..."

"Colquitt was in love with Amy there..."

All eyes turned on the girl whose rouged cheeks went even redder at the idea of being the centre of the stage. She smiled faintly and shook her head, as though she hadn't known anything about Colquitt's secret passion, but was flattered all the same.

"She's in love with Morin and does everything he bids her. She was prepared to go to any lengths to protect her lover. I saw her enter his room the night I was there. Oh, no, Amy. You didn't bluff me that night..."

"It's a lie! I never..."

The first bit of vehemence any of them had heard from Amy. They all looked surprised.

"Amy persuaded Colquitt to keep an eye on the Deemster, I'm sure. At any rate, they found out and didn't know what to do about it. It meant prison for the lot of them. Tremouille, there, is a lawyer with an inborn respect for the bench, even if he doesn't act like it. Another extravagant and penniless man, trying to keep his accounts balanced with the help of the illicit profits of the *Jonee*..."

Tremouille blushed.

"Go on, Inspector. These people will all be witnesses... I'll deal with all your statements in my own good time. I shall require a copy of your transcribed notes, Miss Caley, if you please..."

"Certainly, Mr. Tremouille... By all means..."

Old Parker looked up and uttered a single obscene word which

Miss Caley didn't understand but which made the attendant bobbies, at least, jump and look awkward.

"...There was only one man with any initiative. He'd become leader of the gang long ago. He was a practised criminal, an unconvicted murderer, one determined that nobody should stand in the way of his plans, which, I guess, included a comfortable life here away from the French police, and an increasing and profitable connection in smuggled goods both here and on the mainland. Yes, you Morin..."

Morin grinned again.

"You can't prove it. The night I came to live here, Captain Teare was killed by cracking his head in a storm. Since when, I've only sold at my restaurant stuff I've bought from Mr. Parker, junior, at proper prices..."

Lawrence Parker jumped to his feet.

"Why, you dirty swine..."

"A little spirit at last, Lawrence. Well, well. It's too late now. You're dished, my boy. Go on, Littlejohn..."

The old man shook his head, fished in a drawer in front of him, took out a tablet and swallowed it, leaving the drawer open as Miss Caley, the faithful, rushed to give him a drink of water.

"Morin decided to act. He tampered with the Deemster's car in the hope of causing a serious accident. He was too eager and overdid it. The Deemster found it in time. Then, Morin threw bricks down from a building being demolished, but his aim was a bit too erratic..."

"No proof..."

"All right, Morin. But that brought me in. You had the idea that because this is a small, leisurely place, the police weren't capable of solving a well-planned murder. Let me tell you, that had I not been here, they'd have had you. They are quite up to mainland standards and are modest enough to call in expert help if necessary... After two failures, you decided on something more desperate. You couldn't quietly knife Deemster Quantrell. Such a murder would immediately attract attention to you... Knifing in the back isn't a Manx or an English method. Nor could you shoot him. He was always surrounded by people who'd immediately come to see what was going on, and you daren't risk the scuffle of strangling him. You'd doubtless heard of the Deemster's noted cough-mixture..."

"Cough mixture? I never... That's a good one..."

Morin laughed harshly without mirth. His eyes were shifty and the thin cheeks looked more like a rat's than ever.

Littlejohn turned to the police sergeant.

"By the way, sergeant, were the boy scouts ever entertained in Ramsey. If so, where?"

The sergeant coughed importantly. He looked surprised at the sudden burst of irrelevancy. Boy scouts! What next?"

"Yes, sir. They were took over one of the *Ben* boats and then given a good feed at *The Duck's Nest*. Mr. Tremouille there knows of it. He was one of them who arranged it...

Tremouille nodded. He was a bit puzzled by the diversion.

"Good! That explains it. Morin found out the habits of the Deemster when on court work, probably from Colquitt, who was often there on press duty. During the sitting of the court, he sneaked in the castle, went by the private staircase to the Deemster's chambers, and poisoned the cough mixture. He let himself in with a key obtained by Irons, one of his contact men, who'd got Alcardi to make it from copies supplied by Lamprey. He also had a similar key to His Honour's desk at home, which he rifled for any notes the Deemster might have made... As he came down the private staircase, however, he heard footsteps approaching and hid in the old coach in the passage. Little Mounsey, a sharp lad, must have seen Morin inside. Perhaps he didn't recognize him, but he mentioned to the custodian of the castle that he'd seen someone, and got laughed at for a tale. Poor Willie turned back to make sure, opened the door, and there he found sitting the intriguing man who, in white cap and apron, had paraded before him and his mates at *The Duck's Nest*..."

Tremouille and Miss Caley were writing excitedly like a couple of competitors in a shorthand contest.

"It wouldn't have done for Morin to be recognized, even by a boy scout... So..."

Morin lit another cigarette. He truculently used his own lighter this time.

"All you want is proof to frame it on me. But you ain't got it. So what?"

"I admit I have no proof. It's all circumstantial... Not enough to arrest you on."

"Then we're wasting our time. Let's go."

Morin rose to his feet.

"Wait! Sit down. I've not finished, Morin. There are other dead men in this case, you know. Irons, for example. First, Charles Cosans, then Jules Morin, and finally, and ridiculously, Charlie Wagg!"

They all looked at Littlejohn as if he'd gone mad.

THE PARTING SHOT

There was a sudden silence. The two scribblers ceased their writing and Miss Caley eagerly turned over a page. It looked like an anti-climax. Littlejohn filled and lit his pipe slowly. Knell took out his own notebook and consulted it soberly, after taking a pair of horn-rimmed spectacles from a case and putting them on. Until Littlejohn's arrival, Knell had worn his glasses only in secret for close reading. Now, having several times seen Littlejohn wearing his own, he felt reassured and slipped them on to look more official and scholarly.

"...But first, there's Alcardi, who kept an art shop on Douglas promenade. Alcardi was a small-time sneak-thief, a good engraver, who thought he'd make a pound or two forging banknotes. This got him in the clutches of Irons, who was able to make use of him as a handyman in the *Duck's Nest* work. Useful with his hands, Alcardi also made the keys for Morin. Having killed the Deemster and Willie Mounsey, Morin, with his usual guile set about putting the blame on Alcardi. Through Irons and Lamprey, he roused our suspicions of Alcardi, then through Irons, and Colquitt, told Alcardi we were after him, presumably in connection with the counterfeit notes, the keys and, through them the murders. He even took the trouble to leave traces of prussic acid in Alcardi's shop to confirm our suspicions. He hoped to get Alcardi to leave the Island on the *Jonee Ghorrym* and thus turn suspicion from himself—that is, Morin—to the Italian on the run. But Alcardi didn't act as expected. Instead, he tried to get hold of me and tell the extent of his crime. Better to get a stretch for counterfeiting than hang for murder. Morin was lucky. When Alcardi called to see me at Grenaby, I wasn't there. After that, Morin saw to it that he was kept away from me until he could deal with him, one way or another."

You could have heard a pin drop. Tremouille had stopped writing in his diary and had put it away. Miss Caley alone was active; doing her shorthand like grim death because her boss had told her to do it. When Littlejohn paused, you could hear her pencil moving as she got down the last words. Amy clutched her throat, her eyes wide. Now and then, when the fumes of tobacco died down, you could smell her strong, cheap scent on the stuffy air of the office.

Morin seemed the coolest of the lot.

"Go on... Most interesting tale... You can't prove a word and we might just as well all be wasting our time..."

"Morin set Fannin and Colquitt, as well as some of Mr. Parker's roughneck labourers, to keep an eye on Alcardi and stop him going to the police-stations. The idea seems to have been to shanghai him off on the *Jonee Ghorrym*, then, they could do as they liked with him. They'd got to give the police the impression that Alcardi was on the run for murder, for there was another act in this drama ready to start. Amy was all primed for her part as Alcardi's mistress. In apparent secrecy, she was to get hold of me and tell me Alcardi's so-called confession of his murder of the Deemster. It was a complicated tale, and she implicated all the gang except Morin. I half believed it though, until I saw her all dressed up on the night of Mr. Parker's party at *The Duck's Nest*. She had become a *femme fatale*, the death of her so-called lover,

Alcardi, meant nothing to her; she was obviously all got-up and agog to please someone else... Morin. The whole trumped-up story about Alcardi was to lead us away from Morin, for, having joined himself in the desperate effort to keep Alcardi as our suspect, he came up with him, haunting the vicarage, in the small hours, intent on telling me his tale. And when Morin and Alcardi met, Alcardi drew a gun and shot at Morin, who thereupon killed him..."

"No proof..."

Morin lit another cigarette. He was pretending to enjoy himself, but his long black hair was lank and damp with a sweat of fear. He was beginning to look like a cornered animal. Amy's eyes were fixed on him in apprehension and with dog-like devotion. She looked ready to die for him...

"The next thing was to get Irons and Fannin away to keep them quiet. Fannin was just a stupid youth gone wrong, but Irons knew most of the story. When we arrested Irons, Morin was desperate. He began to lose his grip. He didn't know what Irons would say. So he went to see Irons in jail, pretending to be his business partner wanting to consult him. What Irons said in jail to Morin, we may never know, but it settled Irons' fate. He may have blackmailed or threatened. Morin took a great risk. Helped by Amy, with whom the rather forlorn Colquitt had fallen in love, he hung round the jail, desperately intent on poisoning the food he'd persuaded Irons to send out for during his first visit. Colquitt had been dressing-up as a character called Charlie Wagg, whom visitors were supposed to hunt down for reward. A man in a moustache and an overcoat too large for him. The Douglas police heard such a character had been hanging round the restaurant where a constable went for Irons' supper..."

Morin was now sitting up and taking alarmed notice. He hadn't thought the police would get so far. He shouted to Tremouille.

"Are you listening, lawyer? If they try to frame this over me, you're my lawyer, ain't you? Are you taking it all down?"

Tremouille didn't even answer.

"News reached Colquitt that someone like Charlie Wagg was involved in the death of Irons. He got fright, bolted to the mainland as Charlie Wagg, and came back as himself. Charlie Wagg had left the Island never to be seen again. Colquitt was arrested this morning and he's now in jail..."

Morin threw out his arms.

"There you are! Colquitt. Didn't I tell you? He did it."

"Colquitt had a perfectly cast-iron alibi at the time of the crime. After lending you his makeup, he went back to the office and had some beer and talked for an hour with a decent old nightwatchman, who confirms Colquitt's statement... I haven't much more to say..."

All eyes were on Littlejohn. If he *hadn't* much more, it was vital to them all.

"You, Harborne-Smith, Lawrence Parker, Tremouille and Captain Kewley, will be charged with smuggling, to start with. So far as I know, you're not implicated in the murders, though how much you suspected is another matter. Parker will also have to answer for the incident of putting Captain Teare's remains in the lime-pit. Amy Green will be held pending serious charges of complicity in murder, and as for you, Jules Morin, I arrest you for the murder of Alexander Irons and..."

He got no farther.

Morin was on his feet, his back to the wall. In his hand an ugly revolver.

"Put up your hands everybody... Anyone not putting up hands, I'll shoot at once. I've shot plenty together before. This is nothing to me..."

Slowly, like voting at a meeting, hands were raised, all eyes glued on Morin's pistol.

"Littlejohn and the police... Quick..."

Littlejohn put up his hands and spoke.

"Now, lads," he said to the constables. "Do as he says. We want no heroics and no widows. This man isn't going to get away and, if he leaves this place, we shall get him..."

Morin sneered.

"I ought to plug you, Littlejohn. You caused all this. Maybe I will... But let me tell you, before I do, I'm going from here and nobody's gonna stop me... nobody interfere... see? I've got a motor-boat in the harbour and you're going to stop just here for half an hour till I get on my way. And in case anybody wants to follow, Amy's goin' to see they don't... Aren't you, Amy?"

Amy gave him a puzzled, questioning look.

"Yes. Amy's just as good with a gun as me. She can shoot straight as me. Her father was a gunsmith..."

"My father was a banker, but I've no money..."

Harborne-Smith couldn't resist the effort to be clever.

"Shut up, *Smith*."

Morin grinned at him and wagged his gun.

"Now... All turn your backs to me..."

Hands in the air, they started to turn. All except old Parker, who couldn't move and whose hands wouldn't go above his head. He sat there, his immovable eyes on Morin, one hand trembling on the table, the other on his lap.

Then, before anybody quite realized what was going on, Humphrey Parker's right hand appeared above the desk. In it was a large old-fashioned revolver. His finger jerked on the trigger and kept jerking. A stream of bullets hit Morin one after another. At each shot, the Frenchman's body quivered with the impact. His gun slithered from his hands and, as Amy tried to get it, a bullet struck her on the breast in the V of her blouse. The pair of them fell together, their bodies intertwined...

Old Parker's finger kept on pulling the trigger long after the magazine was empty. Click, click, click...

Everybody seemed to move at once. The police stood at the

doors, Knell knelt down by the two bodies, touched them, and shook his head. Littlejohn looked at Humphrey Parker. He was sitting like a dummy, his eyes fixed on the gun, now lying on the desk before him. In the confusion, Morin must have spasmodically fired one shot. There was a hole through the crown of Parker's old-fashioned hat...

Miss Caley was concerned only with the old man. She must have cherished for him all the compassionate love she'd never been able to lavish elsewhere. She held his head and gave him brandy from a little bottle.

"Are you all right, Mr. Parker? You shouldn't excite yourself... Remember what the doctor said... There, there, Mr. Parker. He's going to be a good, quiet Mr. Parker now. Isn't he...?"

Her arm was round his neck and the old man laid his head on it.

"Yes..."

They were all on their feet and two constables had gone for something to cover the bodies. The sergeant was telephoning for the ambulance to take them away.

"Yes... Yes... You know Parker's builder's yard on Ballure... It's there. Get crackin'. It's urgent..."

The rest of the *Duck's Nest* gang stood around waiting for the next move.

Tremouille was on his feet, nervously polishing his monocle. He put up his hand.

"Quiet, please. I've something to say..."

All eyes turned to him in surprise.

"I am amazed at the turn of events..."

His feet firmly planted, one hand playing with the cord of his eyeglass, he looked like an advocate in court.

"...I admit I was a shareholder in the steamship company. I also admit I wasn't careful concerning where the profits came from..."

Harborne-Smith flushed an ugly purple.

"You bet you weren't. What we're getting's coming to you, too, Tremouille. You needn't try to be pious now..."

"I admit this is ruin for me. But neither I, nor you Harborne-Smith, nor Parker, I venture to say, knew that murder was involved... We knew of the crimes but did not associate them with our affairs... *Let me speak...*"

The rest were getting restless.

"All I wish to say is this. Throughout this meeting, if I may call it such, Mr. Humphrey Parker has assumed the part of chairman, supposedly on the side of the law..."

Old Parker raised himself from the supporting arms of Miss Caley and cast a malevolent glance at Tremouille. Both his hands were trembling, beating a tattoo on the desk before him.

"...Such a pose is intolerable. Who provided the money for the *Jonee Ghorrym* when we acquired her? None of *us*. We had no money. He lent it to us and we were his nominees, the guinea-pigs who held the shares on his behalf. I myself drew up the trust deeds for the holdings. He still actually controls the ship. Who found capital for the smuggling venture. . .? The same man. Who arranged the scheme for carrying and hiding the contraband in his vehicles posing as contractors lorries, and in his old property on the Curragh? Whose workmen were really the handymen of the smuggling business?"

Tremouille pointed an accusing finger at the old man.

"Humphrey Parker had been the brains of this business since its inception. He didn't murder Captain Teare, I admit, but he sent for Kewley... Didn't he, Kewley? You knew Mr. Parker from other days, didn't you?"

"Yes... And he told me what he wanted and he paid me my bonuses..."

Humphrey Parker just sat and blinked, his eyes more ghastly with hatred than if he'd spoken the words of evil.

Tremouille was still pointing at him.

"He renovated *The Duck's Nest*, he had us all in his grip because he could ruin us if he wanted. He was old and with one foot in the grave and wouldn't suffer if he blew the whole racket wide open... We..."

With a gesture Tremouille made it all clear.

"He is an accessory of all that has been done. His money has financed it, his brain—quite alert in spite of his useless body—has organized it all, and he has known all that has been going on and said no word of condemnation. It is strange that now that the police have shown-up the whole scheme and those guilty of the many crimes, he should pretend to be the patron of law and order... He has done that because he feared he himself might be murdered by the ambitious Morin. Already half-dead, he still feared death."

Tremouille hung his head. The rest followed in a whisper.

"I am a member of the bar. The law is sacred to me. I have betrayed my trust. I will take what is coming to me. But now that matters have reached their culmination, I will see to it that justice is done to all and this evil thing shall be cleared up once and for all..."

He sat down trembling. There was something pathetic and even dignified in his final ruin.

Old Parker rose to his feet and with a great effort pointed a shaking finger at Tremouille.

"Liar... Liar... You pettifogging little lawyer... I'll..."

And he fell face forward across the desk. Miss Caley screamed.

"Mr. Parker... Dear Mr. Parker... What have they done...?"

Humphrey Parker had had a final stroke. They carried him away completely helpless and he died on the way home.

Kewley, Harborne-Smith and Lawrence Parker were condemned to long terms of imprisonment. Tremouille was past harming. He hanged himself with his braces in his cell on the night of his arrest.

It was quite dark when Littlejohn, the Archdeacon and Knell reached Grenaby parsonage. The old man was upset by the day's events and could hardly speak for emotion, until they once more ran through the ring of trees round the hamlet and heard the river driving its way under the bridge. The very atmosphere seemed to change. "It'll get you... You'll see," Colquitt had said, and it was true. This seemed a new and peaceful world.

Knell left them at the door.

"I'll see you to-morrow, Knell. And thanks for all your help. Without you, I'd never have managed it, and I shall see you are commended to the proper quarter."

Knell's heavy breathing could be heard in the dark. He was a proud man and was itching to get off to St. Mark's and celebrate it and give a full account of it all to Millie Teare.

"Good night, sir. Good night, Mr. Kinrade..."

His feet crunched down the path and they could hear them for a long time, until he reached the car at the gate, started it up, and whined off in the distance, noisily changing gears as he took the hill.

The night was clear, with stars. Out at sea the siren of a steamer sounded and the owls in the trees began to hoot. They went indoors where Mrs. Keggin was laying the table.

"It's all over, Maggie... Kenneth won't come to much harm now..."

She burst into tears, threw her apron over her head, and groped her way to the kitchen.

On the table under the window lay a fishing-rod and a shot-gun, just where the Archdeacon had left them when they'd called for him earlier in the day. He touched them gently.

"I suppose you'll want to be getting home, now. All this will have made you weary of this place..."

Littlejohn could hardly hear what he said.

"On the contrary, sir. It's all the better for what we've done. Now I can really enjoy it. To-morrow the holiday begins... We'll both be afoot as soon as you're ready. And heaven help the rabbits and the little fishes."

They sat down together in the lamplight before the homely meal, the parson said grace, and they fell to, like the old comrades they were.

It was then that Littlejohn realized that he hadn't eaten since breakfast...

ABOUT THE AUTHOR

George Bellairs is the pseudonym under which Harold Blundell (1902–1982) wrote police procedural thrillers in rural British settings. He was born in Lancashire, England, and worked as a bank manager in Manchester. After retiring, Bellairs moved to the Isle of Man, where several of his novels are set, to be with friends and family.

In 1941 Bellairs wrote his first mystery, *Littlejohn on Leave*, during spare moments at his air raid warden's post. The title introduced Thomas Littlejohn, the detective who appears in fifty-seven of his novels. Bellairs was also a regular contributor to the *Manchester Guardian* and worked as a freelance writer for newspapers both local and national.

THE INSPECTOR LITTLEJOHN MYSTERIES

FROM OPEN ROAD MEDIA

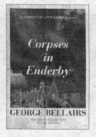

OPEN ROAD

INTEGRATED MEDIA

Find a full list of our authors and
titles at www.openroadmedia.com

FOLLOW US
@OpenRoadMedia